HELL'S HALF ACRE

HELL'S HALF ACRE

William W. Johnstone
with J. A. Johnstone

PINNACLE BOOKS
Kensington Publishing Corp.
www.kensingtonbooks.com

ISBN-13: 978-0-7860-3944-9
ISBN-10: 0-7860-3594-3944-2

First printing: March 2015
Fourth printing: February 2017

12 11 10 9 8 7 6 5 4

Printed in the United States of America

First electronic edition: February 2017

ISBN-13: 978-0-7860-3594-6
ISBN-10: 0-7860-3594-3

CHAPTER ONE

Just to set the record straight, no matter what you might have been told in recent years, Jess Casey was not a named draw fighter. Sure, during his cowboying days he'd used a Colt a time or two but only to string wire and hammer tenpenny nails. In other words, he was eminently unqualified to be the sheriff of Fort Worth, the brawling, bawdy and dangerous Gomorrah of Tarrant County, Texas, a city where the West began and a place where many a gallant young buck met his demise by the gun, knife, garrote, sap, billy club, or bad whiskey and badder women.

But let's not tar the entire city with the same brush.

As Jess would soon learn the hard way, the trouble was confined to the Third Ward, an infamous, rambunctious area known as Hell's Half Acre, a suppurating pit of perdition that was the first thing drovers saw as they approached the town from the south on the old Chisholm Trail. One- and two-story saloons, bawdy houses, dance halls, opium dens and a scattering of honest businesses beckoned the traveler, though only those seeking excitement or hunting trouble ever ventured into the Acre. As the importance of Fort Worth as a major crossroads and cow town grew, so did Hell's Half Acre. Originally confined to the bottom end of Rusk Street, it spread like a malignant cancer into the city's main north-south thoroughfares, Main, Rusk, Calhoun and Jones. The Acre's lower boundary ended at the Union Station train depot and the northern edge by a vacant lot. In between, the gunmen, highway robbers, card sharks, whores and con artists prospered mightily.

To sum up, one local newspaper thundered on its front page, "It is a slow night which does not pan out a cutting or shooting scrape among the Acre's male denizens or a fatal morphine experiment by one of its frisky females."

Into this inferno of violence and vice would very soon head Jess Casey, two hard decades of cow nursing behind him and as about as stove-up, used up and stiffened up as a puncher could be.

It was Long Tom Muldoon who—after watching Jess take his usual five minutes to struggle out of his bunk—turned him on to the Fort Worth job.

"Jess," he said, "you're too old and too beat-up for cowboying any longer. Leastways, that's how it seems to me."

"Hell, I'm but thirty-four," Jess said. "Went up the trail for the first time when I was just a younker."

"Thirty-four, hell, even twenty-four is old for a

puncher," Long Tom said. "You've broke jest about every bone in your body and you get the rheumatisms in winter. I know you have, so don't try to tell me different."

"Maybe that's so, but I reckon I'll stick," Jess said.

"Well, that's a sore disappointment to me since I hear there's a cozy berth going over to Fort Worth way. They're looking for a lawman, a deputy, like."

"I ain't nobody's idea of a deputy," Jess said.

"Hell, folks say Fort Worth is a quiet burg," Long Tom said. "All you'd be expected to do is sit on the hotel porch, drink beer and catch a chicken thief now and then. You think about it, Jess. Staying away from cows, now that's the berries as I see it."

"That could be so, but being a lawman is not for me," Jess said. "You recollect that time in Dodge when Ed Masterson busted me over the head with a pistol barrel for being drunk?"

"And for pissing on the mayor's prize pumpkin patch, taking pots at the moon and then telling Ed you aimed to clean his plow directly," Long Tom said.

"Yeah, well, I was talking through rum punch so he'd no call to buffalo me. It's skewed my thinking about lawmen ever since."

Long Tom said, "Jess, I'd think it over."

"My answer would still be that I'm not interested."

"Don't be too hasty, Jess. Tossing your rope without buildin' a loop don't catch the calf."

"It's time I went to the cookhouse and rustled up a cup of coffee," Jess said.

Long Tom sighed deeply. "Go see the boss first. He sent me to fetch you."

"What does he want?"

"I reckon he'll tell you when you get there," Long Tom said.

"So you see how it is with me, Jess," Nathan Swift said. "The way beef prices are right now, I got to lay off three, four hands."

Jess Casey felt like he'd been punched in the gut.

"But the gather . . ."

"I plan to hire a couple of seasonal hands," Swift said. "It won't be much of a roundup, Jess. There's no market for my cattle."

"After six years riding for the brand I'm taking this hard, Mr. Swift," Jess said.

"An' I don't blame you," the rancher said. "You were a good hand, Jess, but all you've done recent is polish the seat of your pants on the saddle leather. A man's got to know when it's time to quit and walk away." Swift, lean as a nail and tough as rawhide, managed a smile under his great sweeping mustache. "I never regretted hiring you, Jess. Believe me on that."

Jess nodded and said, "A pat on the back don't cure saddle galls, Mr. Swift."

But the rancher's talking was done. "Go see Mrs. Swift and draw a month's wages. And good luck to you, Jess."

Swift settled a pair of pince-nez reading glasses on his nose then dropped his head to the ledger on the desk in front of him. Jess's spurs chimed as he walked to the office door and stepped outside.

Long Tom was waiting for him. "Got canned, huh?"

"Yup. Turn down the lamps, the party's over."

"There's still that lawman's job in Fort Worth," Long Tom said. He stood a foot shorter than Jess, hence his nickname. "The sheriff's name is Hank Henley. Tell him Tom Muldoon sent you and he'll see you all right."

Jess said, "I'll study on it."

"But not too long, Jess," Long Tom said. "Hard times are coming down fast and good situations like that ain't easy to find."

CHAPTER TWO

Hard times had come down, but Jess Casey wasn't in a woebegone frame of mind. He had a good saddle and a hundred-dollar paint pony under it and he had forty-two dollars and eighteen cents in his pocket. He had a Colt's gun and a Henry rifle, both in .44-40 caliber, two clean shirts, a razor, shaving brush and a prized bar of Pears soap that he'd been assured was the personal favorite of Lillie Langtry.

After all was said and done, Jess considered himself a prosperous, good-looking cowboy. And he'd decided to take the Fort Worth job, if it was offered, so his prospects were bright and could only get brighter.

Above him little white clouds drifted across the blue sky like lilies on a pond and the flats smelled of sage, shy wildflowers and the ever-present musky scent of the nearby piney woods.

So moved was Jess by the wonders of the natural world around him he launched into song, much to the distress of his horse and all the wildlife within earshot.

"I'm going to leave old Texas now,
They got no use for the longhorn cow."

Jess saw a rider in the distance emerge from the rippling heat haze and head in his direction. He adjusted the lie of his gun belt, but kept on singing.

"They've plowed and fenced my cattle range,
And the people here all seem so strange."

The horseman drew closer and Jess thought it mighty peculiar that he rode bent over in the saddle, like a man with a bellyache.

"I'll take my hoss and I'll take my rope,
And hit the trail . . . upon . . . a . . . lope . . ."

Jess's song faltered and died as he watched the rider roll slowly off the back of his mount and hit the ground with a thud. Drunk, Jess decided. But his paint tossed his head, whinnied and took a few dancing steps backward. There was something about the fallen rider that troubled him.

One of the first lessons a young puncher learns is: When in doubt, trust your horse.

And Jess Casey now followed that advice. He

swung out of the saddle, slid the Henry from the boot and stepped toward the fallen man. A red-tailed hawk flew overhead and its shadow fell sharp on the ground, as though it had been cut from black paper by a razor. Crows quarreled in the nearby pines and Jess thought they might be arguing about the hawk.

When he was close enough to the rider he was about to say, "On your feet, cowboy," but then he saw the blood and what looked like a face, but one battered beyond recognition.

Jess laid aside his rifle and took a knee beside the injured man.

"How are you, old fellow?" he said, aware of what a silly question that was. The man was obviously close to death. His breath rattled in his chest and there was blood in his mouth. But Jess could see no sign of bullet or knife wounds. Whoever he was, the young man had been savagely beaten to within an inch of his life with fists and boots. Judging by his head of thick, chestnut hair Jess pegged him as being in his midtwenties, no older. It was only when he turned the fellow over on his back that he saw the star pinned to his shirt.

It's difficult to have a conversation with a man who's barely conscious and hurting, but Jess gave it a try. "What happened to you?" he said, another of those banal questions with an obvious answer people pose only to the sick and children.

The man's swollen eyes fluttered open into red-rimmed slits. He stared into Jess's face for long moments, as though trying to place him. Then he spoke, each word forced, as though it had gone through a meat grinder before reaching his mouth.

"Stay . . . out . . . of . . ."

Jess stepped into the silence that followed. "Stay out of where?"

"Fort . . . Fort . . . Worth."

Pink blood and mucus frothed in the man's mouth. Jess had seen the like just one time before, up Amarillo way when a cheating gambler's kicked-in ribs penetrated his lungs. Some angry tin-pan miners had done that, gone in with the boots, and the gambler had died pretty quick thereafter.

Jess was not of a religious frame of mind, but he tried to comfort the dying man. "Best you make your peace with God, mister," he said. "Your time is mighty short."

"My . . . name . . . is . . ."

"I'd say you're Hank Henley," Jess said. "I'm a friend of Long Tom Muldoon."

"He's . . . a . . . snake," Henley said.

"He told me you had a deputy's job going," Jess said. "I rode here to apply."

"Then you're . . . an . . . idiot."

The sound of approaching horses made Jess look up. Four riders drew closer, the man in the lead astride a beautiful palomino. He drew rein, stared at Jess and said, "Is it Henley?"

The tone of the man's voice was arrogant and demanding and his hard blue eyes revealed little but contempt, as though he despised the whole human race.

Jess disliked him on sight. "Seems like," he said. "He's in bad shape, like to die."

The man swung out of the saddle and crossed to where Jess still kneeled. He was in early middle age and enormous. About four inches over six feet with a prizefighter's body, he looked like an unstoppable force of nature, as though he could stand on the tracks and stop a deadheading locomotive with his bare hands.

The big man loomed over Jess as he glanced at the wounded man in his arms. "Yeah, it's Henley all right," he said to the others. His grin was cruel. "Looks like he's got himself a nursemaid."

The sound of the man's voice registered with Henley and a look of stark terror froze his battered face into a grotesque mask. He made a sound in his throat that might have been a scream.

"Is he dead yet?" one of the riders said.

"Close," the big man said.

"You want I should finish him, boss?" the rider said. He had a broken nose, scars around his eyes and looked like a skull-and-fist scrapper.

The big man laughed, his teeth as white as new ivory. "No need, Clem. I reckon he's about to die of fright," he said.

Jess Casey was a man slow to anger, but the way the man spoke and the arrogant tilt of his handsome blond head irritated him and he was suddenly on the prod. He gently let go of the dying man and rose to his feet.

"Anybody wants to harm this man will have to

walk through me," he said. "And I ain't standing here whistling Dixie."

"Salty, ain't you, cowboy?" the big man said. "You a friend of his?"

"Never seen the man before in my life. Just came across him on the trail," Jess said. "Now let's quit jawing and get him to a doctor."

"Too late for that," the big man said. "He's already dead."

Jess looked at the fallen lawman. He was indeed dead, his eyes wide, his broken face still bearing his final expression of horror and fear.

"Best you light out of here, cowboy," the blond man said. "Unless you got money burning a hole in your pocket and you're headed for Fort Worth to see the sights."

"I was," Jess said, "but not now, I reckon. I was planning to apply for a deputy's job, but now the sheriff's dead, I've changed my thinking."

"You done peacekeeping before?" the man said.

Jess shook his head. "Went up the trail for the first time when I was fourteen and I've been a puncher since." He nodded in the direction of the dead man. "Who did that to him?"

"Not us," the big man said. This brought a laugh from the men with him. "Fact is we suspected something like this might happen."

"How come?" Jess said. He looked sharp at the man, unwilling to believe him.

"His name was—"

"I know his name," Jess said.

"He was mixed up with the wholesale opium

sellers, took a twenty percent skim off the gross profits. And he ran a protection racket, coming down hard on the local merchants and the saloons and dance hall owners if they didn't ante up. Even the whores paid Henley his twenty percent." The man's ice-blue eyes locked on Jess's brown ones. "Henley walked in the shadows, cowboy, and that's not a good place for a lawman to be."

"He was a damned crook and low-down," a rider said and this drew another laugh.

"Name's Kurt Koenig," the big man said, shoving out his hand. "I have business interests in Fort Worth.

Jess reluctantly shook hands, and Koenig said, "I like the cut of your jib, young man. You ever hear that expression?"

"Can't say as I have," Jess said.

"Well, it's a nautical saying and I learned it in the old days when I sailed on the hell ships out of the Barbary Coast. First mate I was in those days, and I laid out many a lively lad and sent him to Davy Jones's locker when he took a set against getting shanghaied."

Clem, the man with the broken nose, said, "You were a rum one in them days, Kurt. An' no mistake."

"I ran a tight ship," Koenig said. "Even in them wild northern seas where the great toothed whales spouted, I kept an iron discipline." He looked at Jess. "Now you probably wonder why the hell I'm telling you all this, huh?"

Jess had a mental picture of Koenig on a sea-swept quarterdeck, big, brutal, a knotted rope in one hand, a cutlass in the other, a snarl on his face and a dead crewman at his feet.

He blinked and said, "Well, I guess I am."

"Because Fort Worth has to be run like a tight ship, understand?" Koenig said. "What the town needs is a firm hand and strict discipline and I think you are the man to do it. There's no back-up in you, lad, lay to that, and I'm willing to stake you two hundred and fifty dollars a month in salary to prove what I say is true." He turned to his men and spread his hands. "Can I say fairer than that, boys?"

Amid grins and sniggers the consensus of the other three riders was that the offer was fair indeed.

But Jess Casey was not so sure.

"That's a handsome stipend," he said. "But I'm not Wild Bill Hickok. I ain't one of them Texas draw fighters that everybody talks about, either."

Koenig's grin stretched. His white teeth looked like a piano keyboard.

"Hell, the whole town will back you if you run into trouble," he said. "In Fort Worth we don't much care for draw fighters and pistoleros, or hard cases of any stamp, do we, boys?" After a chorus of "Sure don't" and "That's fer certain," Koenig said, "And we know what to do with hucksters, three-card monte artists, thieves, thugs, fakirs, bunco steerers and dance hall loungers. Don't we boys?"

Again Koenig got unanimous agreement and

some tough talk about tar and feathers, and then he said, "Well, cowboy, is it a go?"

Jess Casey ran it through in his mind.

On the upside, the salary was good and if these four men were representative of the citizens of Fort Worth then they'd support him all the way. And the fact was that he badly needed a job. Right then, Koenig grinning at him all friendly-like, he couldn't see a downside, not in his present situation.

"I'll take the job," he said. "It seems like it will suit me down to the ground."

"Good man," Koenig said. "True-blue." His slap on the back felt like a blow from a sledgehammer. "Mount up and we'll seal our bargain with a drink."

"What about him?" Jess said, pointing to Henley's body.

"Aw, we'll send the undertaker out for him, bury him at the city's expense," Koenig said. "Clem, take his hoss and traps."

The big man beamed at Jess. "Hiring you was a good afternoon's work," he said. "I can feel it in my bones."

"You haven't even asked me my name," Jess said.

"May the devil roast my hide, no, I haven't," Koenig said. "But I take you fer an Archibald." He grinned at his men. "Ain't he an Archibald, boys?"

"Sheriff Archibald sounds crackerjack," the man called Clem said, failing to hide a grin. "But, you know, he looks a bit like ol' General Custer."

"The name's Jess Casey and I'm no kin to Custer."

"Yeah, sure, that's your name," Koenig said. "Now let's get out of here, Archibald. It's been a long day and I've got some pretty urgent business in town."

Suddenly Jess felt that there could be a downside to this job after all.

CHAPTER THREE

In all his born days Jess Casey had never seen the like.

Main Street, Fort Worth, bisected an area of the city that Kurt Koenig told him was named Hell's Half Acre, a bustling, noisy, smelly bedlam of rickety timber buildings, some of them three stories high, featuring prominent fronts that advertised saloons, dance halls and bawdy houses. But to his surprise, Jess passed several thriving churches, grocery, jewelry, saddle, and candy stores as well as Chinese laundries and cotton and lumber yards.

The throngs of people he saw in the street seemed respectable enough, prim matrons with their broadcloth-clad spouses and pretty young girls in gaggles of three or four, each wearing the latest Eastern fashions: tiny hats, enormous bustles and high-heeled ankle boots. Vendors shouted their wares from the boardwalks; horse-drawn drays with massive steel-rimmed wheels made their way through the crowds, their drivers cursing one

another for rogues; bakers with tin trays of bread
and pastries on their heads rubbed shoulders with
butchers wearing bloodstained aprons. The din was
unbelievable and Jess heard a dozen different
tongues, men, women and children all babbling in
languages he didn't understand.

Jess saw no hint of thuggery or violence. In fact
the ringing church bells made the loudest noise,
those and the preachers who stood at the street corners and yelled about the evils of fancy women and
strong drink.

Kurt Koenig leaned from the saddle and shouted
into Jess's ear, "There's a hanging today, so there
are more folks about than usual."

"Should I get involved?" Jess said. "I mean, being
as how I'm now sheriff."

"Well, bless you for a swab," Koenig said. "No, the
hanging is the business of the Vigilance Committee, Archibald. And since I'm the committee chair-
man I have to attend." He stared at Jess, then shook
his head. "A sorry business, Archibald."

"It's Jess."

"Yeah, that's right, so it is."

"What did the feller do to get hung?" Jess said.

"He cut up a young lady," Koenig said. "By coin-
cidence she worked for me."

"He kill her?"

"No, just cut up her face real bad. She quit my
employ, said she was going into a nunnery where
she could hide her face behind a veil. Pity, she was
real pretty for a fat gal."

Koenig touched his hat to a passing matron, who

scowled at him and quickly looked away. The big man seemed not to have noticed.

"Her name was Dallas Delamonte," he said.

"Who?"

"The gal who got cut up. Feller who did it is a no-account loafer who goes by the name Andy Smith. We'll watch him dangle then go get a drink."

Koenig's features were set and hard, a face without mercy.

The gallows was set up off the main drag, on a vacant lot behind the St. John's Hotel on 13th Street, a sandy, bottle-strewn acre of ground rumored to be the last resting place of a Comanche war chief, but that had never been proven.

Jess Casey arrived late to the party and a large crowd in a picnic mood had already gathered. To the left of the gallows a dozen whores in revealing dresses had come to see justice done. They passed around bottles of Old Crow and jeered and tossed rocks at the condemned man.

Koenig turned in the saddle and pinned the dead lawman's star to Jess's shirt. "Now it's official, you can join me on the platform, Sheriff. Let's get it done."

Jess dismounted and followed Koenig to the gallows. The crowd parted to let the big man pass, most of the males going out of their way to make sure Koenig saw them tip their hats to him.

Jess thought Koenig looked like a king striding through a mob of peasants.

Once on the platform, Koenig shook hands with the mayor, a couple of other dignitaries, the parson and finally the hangman, who was half drunk. He didn't bother to introduce Jess, though the mayor smiled and pumped his hand and said, "Name's Henry Stout, Sheriff. Known to the folks all around as Honest Harry. Welcome to our fair city on the Trinity and welcome to the hanging."

The condemned man stood on the drop, his feet and hands tied.

Andy Smith was small, almost tiny, a frightened little rabbit of a man wearing a collarless white shirt and black pants held up with a knotted string. His feet were bare with long toenails. He was fairly drunk and had already pissed himself, which amused some of the crowd, including the whores, and repelled others.

Koenig stepped close to the little man, a Goliath in broadcloth, who made Smith look even punier.

"You remember what you promised, Andy?" he said.

The condemned man nodded.

"The womenfolk like it, understand. Makes them feel good about things."

"You already tole me that," Smith said. "But I fergit what I have to say."

"I'll be close and give you the words," Koenig said. "And say 'em like you mean 'em."

"Mr. Koenig, everybody, I didn't mean to cut up that gal," Smith wailed. "She just got me mad, told me I was poor white trash, and I suddenly felt the knife in my hand. I don't even remember what happened next and I'm so sorry. I beg you, just cut me down and let me go home."

This brought a chorus of boos from the whores and a respectable matron cried, "For shame! Take your medicine like a man."

Jess Casey swallowed hard. He felt as though he were the one standing on the trapdoor, feeling the rasp of the hemp noose on his neck, the feral hostility of the crowd. Would he have pissed himself? He didn't know.

The mayor stepped forward, a jolly man sporting a massive gold watch chain across his great belly. Reading the mood of the crowd he grinned and shouted, "I declare, folks! It's mighty easy to say you're sorry after the dreadful deed has been done."

The parson stared down at his Bible and his thin, bloodless lips moved in prayer and a rousing cheer followed the mayor's speech. One of the whores, who seemed to know him well, yelled, "You tell him, Horny Harry!"

Laughter rippled through the crowd and the mayor scowled and tried to hide his flushed face from view.

Koenig looked at his watch, snapped it shut and let his irritation show.

"Let's get on with this," he said. "I've got things to do. Andy, say your piece and we'll move on." Smith glanced at Koenig, a confused look on his pinched, frightened face. "I fergit the words, Mr. Koenig."

Koenig shook his head, annoyed, then said in a

whisper, "Strong drink and loose women brought me to this pass . . ."

Smith, his voice strangled, hesitant, repeated what Koenig had said.

The big man continued, "And I richly deserve my fate . . ."

"And . . . I richly deserve . . . deserve . . ."

"My fate, damn it," Koenig whispered.

"My fate, damn it," Smith said.

"You're an idiot, Andy. Now say, 'But I had a good mother,'" Koenig whispered.

"But . . . but I had a good mother."

That last pleased the ladies and even the whores were moved, a few dabbing tiny lace handkerchiefs to their black-smeared eyes. There was much discussion among the female respectable element about male drunkenness and whoring and how only a good mother had saved many a wayward son from perdition . . . the likes of Andy Smith being the exceptions, of course.

Koenig was also pleased. He'd paid Smith a jug of whiskey for the speech and the little weasel had kept his part of the bargain, though he could have been louder. Koenig smiled at the hangman, the local blacksmith, and said, "Drop him."

"Nooo!" Smith screamed. "I didn't mean—"

The trapdoor slammed open and Smith's voice was cut off in midsentence. For a full minute the rope quivered like a fiddle string then was still, creaking in the breeze.

The sound of the falling trapdoor had hushed the crowd that had grown to several hundred. Then the whores, most of them well drunk, led the cheering and the rest joined in with huzzahs and applause.

"Well done, Ben," Koenig said to the hangman. "I'm sure his damned neck snapped like a twig."

The man called Ben nodded and accepted the compliment without comment.

Koenig's boots thudded as he walked across the platform and said to Jess, "I'll have one of my boys show you to your office, Sheriff. Then maybe later you'll join me for a drink at my saloon on D Street."

Jess, who'd never seen a hanging before, took a while before he found his tongue. "I can sure use a drink," he said.

Koenig grinned. "You look a little green around the gills, Archibald, like the first time you killed a man."

"I've never killed anybody," Jess said.

Koenig slapped his back and again it felt like a blow from a sledgehammer. "Well, good for you," he said. "But I always say that it's all right to kill a man rather than let his score go unpaid. Andy Smith knew that and it's the reason why he obliged me by dying so well."

But in that Kurt Koenig was mistaken.

A tall, austere-looking man ducked from under the red, white and blue bunting that surrounded the gallows. He looked up at the hangman and said, "He's not dead."

Koenig overheard and stepped to the edge of the platform. "What do you mean, he isn't dead, Doc?"

"I mean he's breathing and his heart is beating,"

the doctor said. "My physician's training tells me that this means the man is not dead."

The crowd had drifted away and only a few stragglers remained. A whore who'd drunk too much whiskey was being carried away by three of her friends and a staggering rooster followed, shooting his festive revolver into the air.

"Hell, now I have to hang him all over again," the blacksmith said. He looked surly and dejected. I hate to hang a man twice—makes me look real bad."

"A sorry business, Kurt," Mayor Stout said. "The folks won't like it if we string him up again. They'll say we're careless."

"Then I'll take care of it," Koenig said.

When it came to official hangings, the city fathers of Fort Worth were stalwart traditionalists and they'd made damn sure that thirteen steps led up to the gallows platform. Koenig descended them two at a time and grabbed the doctor by the lapels of his frock coat.

"You sure the little rat is alive?" he said.

"See for yourself," the physician said.

Koenig ducked under the platform and Jess, figuring this was surely the business of the law, followed. Andy Smith's face was purple and his tongue lolled out of his mouth, but his eyes were not lifeless and opaque. They were bright with terror. And something else. The little man was pleading for his life.

The doctor kneeled beside Koenig and the big man said, "What the hell happened?"

"The drop was too short. It didn't break his neck."

"Can't you do something, Doc? Put him out of his misery?"

The physician shook his head, his face stiff. "Koenig," he said, "I'll bandage your thugs when they get shot or knifed and I'll treat your poxed whores, but I won't do your killing for you."

Two things bothered Jess Casey about that speech. One was that Koenig, who'd presented himself as a pillar of the community, was mixed up with thugs and whores. The second was more immediate: that Koenig would surely pound the outspoken physician into the ground.

But to his surprise that didn't happen.

Koenig merely shrugged and said, "All right, Doc, I'll do it myself."

"Then I'm leaving," the doctor said. "I don't wish to see this."

"No, stay right here," Koenig said. "You need to sign the death certificate, make it look good for the county sheriff."

If Andy Smith could have screamed, he would have done so. But the noose constricted his throat so tightly he managed only a few, frightened little squeals, more like a fussy baby than a man.

"Take your medicine, Andy," Koenig said. He pushed the twin muzzles of the derringer he'd taken from his coat pocket between the little man's frantic eyes—and pulled the trigger.

The blast still ringing in Jess's ears, he heard the big man say, "He's sure as hell dead now, Doc."

The doctor went through the motions of sounding

Smith's chest with his stethoscope, then, nodding, pronounced, "He's dead."

Koenig grinned. "Hell, have you ever seen a man shot between the eyes who wasn't?"

"I'll sign the certificate, Koenig," the doctor said. "You can pick it up at my office."

"And the cause of death?" Koenig said. His face looked as though it had been chipped from granite.

"I'll play your game this far," the physician said. "Death by whiskey and legal hanging."

"Thank God for the medical profession," Koenig said.

After the doctor left, Koenig nodded in the direction of the dead man and said, "Look at the little runt. Where did he find the cojones to cut up a three-hundred-pound whore?"

"I don't know," Jess said. He felt sick.

Koenig shook his head. "Yeah, you're right, it's a mystery. Come on, Archibald, I'll buy you that drink I promised."

CHAPTER FOUR

Jess Casey avoided having to drink with Kurt Koenig by pleading tiredness and a desire to see the sheriff's office. For his part, Koenig didn't seem in the least disappointed, dismissing Jess with, "Well, maybe some other time, Archie."

There was plenty about the big man that troubled Jess—his involvement with hard cases and prostitutes and the cold-blooded killing of Andy Smith. The little man would have died anyway when they hung him again, so it was hardly murder.

Then what was it?

Jess had no answer for that other than it was a casual killing by a man he suspected had killed many times before. Koenig said that he'd gotten his start on the hell ships that sailed out of the Barbary Coast with sadistic, murderous captains and shanghaied crews who lived a life of "hell afloat and purgatory ashore."

The big man admitted that he'd sent many a poor sailorman to Davy Jones's locker, so he was no stranger to shipboard murder where men were killed with marlinespikes, belaying pins or the bare hands of the captain and his equally brutal officers.

And he told Jess that Fort Worth must be run the same way as the hell ships, with brute force and iron discipline.

Even as he stepped into the sheriff's office, Jess began to doubt that he was the right man for the job.

The office was like any other on the frontier, a desk, a couple of rickety wooden chairs and an empty safe with its door hanging open. A door to the rear led to two cells, one furnished with only a single iron cot. The adjoining cell was fixed up like a bedroom. It had a brass bed with a mattress but no sheets or pillows, a dresser, and a bookshelf that held three volumes, *The Rudiments of Texas Law*, Edward Gibbon's *The History of the Decline and Fall of the Roman Empire* and *The Life and Adventures of Martin Chuzzlewit* by Charles Dickens.

Jess made a mental note to read the law book when he had the time and inclination—if he stayed in town that long.

Despite his misgivings he tried the chair behind the desk for size, sitting slowly as though there were tacks on the seat. A tall, rawboned man who was as lean as a lariat, the chair still creaked under Jess's weight and he figured it was probably older than the town itself.

He built a cigarette, flamed it into smoke and then bent over in the chair to check the contents of the desk drawers. That move saved his life.

A rifle bullet crashed through the office window and thudded into the wall behind the desk. If Jess hadn't leaned down when he did his head would have stopped the shot and exploded like a ripe watermelon.

He didn't take time to feel afraid.

Jess dived to his right and both he and the chair hit the floor at the same time. He kicked his tangled legs free, jumped to his feet and drew his Colt. His anger flaring, knowing that he was making himself a target, he ran for the door, threw it wide and stepped onto the boardwalk.

Darkness was crowding close but the street lamps hadn't yet been lit along Main Street. Jess stepped into shadow, away from the light of the office, and his eyes searched the opposite walk.

Bam! Bam!

A muzzle flared in an alley between a couple of stores and bullets probed the gloom close to where Jess stood, slashing through the air mere inches from his head.

Instinctively Jess fired twice into the smoke drifting like a gray ghost in the entrance to the alley. His first shot drew a yelp of pain. The second was followed by the heavy fall of a body and the clank of empty bottles.

Feet pounded on the boardwalk and Jess turned, his gun coming up fast. It was Kurt Koenig and a couple of hard cases.

"I heard the shooting," the big man said. "You all right, Archie?"

"Somebody tried to kill me," Jess said. "He was in the alley over yonder and I think I may have winged him."

"You sure?" Koenig said, drawing a Colt from his waistband. "That's a fair piece." He turned to his men. "Go see if there's anything in the alley." Koenig shot Jess a hard, calculating glance. "It's all of sixty feet."

"I never shot at something that far before," Jess said. "Not even a coyote."

"Maybe you got lucky," Koenig said. "Stranger things have happened."

"Yeah, maybe I did."

"Hey, boss!" a man yelled from the alley. "There's a dead 'un here."

"Who the hell is it?" Koenig said.

"I dunno. Wait till we drag him into the light." Then, a few moments later, "It's Porry McTurk. Shot twice in the brisket."

"You sure he's dead?" Koenig said.

"As he's ever gonna be."

Koenig was suspicious. "Anybody else shoot at Porry?" he said.

Jess said, "No. Just me."

"Mighty good shooting for a puncher," Koenig said.

"As you said, I got lucky."

"Maybe so, maybe not," Koenig said. "You ever work as a lawman before?"

"Nope. Never did. Went up the trail when I was fourteen and I've been cowboying ever since."

It was that twilight hour in the Acre when the respectable element had left the street and the sporting crowd was only now beginning to stir in their beds. Gunshots were common enough that they wouldn't have attracted a crowd anyway.

But a scrawny old-timer in greasy buckskins, a brand-new, pearl gray John B. on his tangled mane, had watched the proceedings with growing interest. Now he said, "Here, Kurt, didn't ol' Porry work for you?"

Koenig glanced quickly at Jess, then back at the old man. "He did, until I fired him for thievery." He reached into his pocket then spun a silver dollar, which the old-timer caught deftly. "Go buy yourself a drink, Jed."

The old man's toothless mouth stretched in a grin. He held up the dollars and said, "Thankee, Kurt, an' I'll be sure to drink to your good health."

Without a word, Jess left Koenig and walked across the street, his head spinning with conflicting thoughts. He'd killed a man, taken a human life, but it was in self-defense, there was no question about that. But he never wanted to kill another.

Porry McTurk's body was sprawled on the street. The man's eyes were wide open, staring at the last, tattered banners of the red and jade sky. Koenig's men stood staring at Jess. No strangers to violence and death, they grinned and slapped him on the back.

"Good shootin', Sheriff," one of them said. "Two shots right where he lived."

"He isn't living now," Jess said.

"Nope, he's as dead as a rotten stump," the man said. "Just as well, I reckon. Porry never amounted to much."

Jess said, "Why would he want to kill me?"

"Because you're the new sheriff. That's pretty plain. Porry wrote his name on the wall of your cell more times than I can remember."

"He was a drunk," the second man said. He was tall and angular. "Had a wife once and four young 'uns but about a year ago she took the kids and left him."

This man carried what looked like a brand-new Winchester.

"Was that his?" Jess asked.

"Sure was. But it's mine now."

Jess said, "Let me see it."

Reluctantly the man handed over the Winchester and Jess examined it. "This is an expensive rifle," he said. "How did a penniless drunk afford a Winchester like this?"

"Maybe he stole it," the tall man said.

Jess said, "I'd say that ain't likely."

He took a knee beside the dead man and searched through his pants pockets. He was rewarded with the chink of gold, two double eagles.

"Damn," the tall man said. "I wish I'd known he had money."

Jess rose to his feet. "It's evidence. And so is the rifle."

An hour before, the tall man would have argued the point. But two shots fired into a man's chest at twenty paces spoke loud . . . and for the first time in his life Jess Casey knew what it was like to be considered a dangerous shootist.

He knew he'd been lucky, it seemed, but nobody else did.

Emboldened, he said, "Will one of you boys get the undertaker?"

"Clem, go get Big Sal." This from Kurt Koenig, who had stepped silently behind Jess, startling him.

After the man called Clem left, Jess said, "Koenig, have you seen this rifle before?"

The big man glanced at the Winchester. "I don't know. I've seen a hundred just like it."

"But not this one?"

"One Winchester pretty much looks like another."

Jess showed the double eagles. "I found these in the dead man's pocket."

Koenig smiled. "Seems like somebody thinks your life is worth forty dollars, Archibald."

"The name is Jess. I'd be obliged if you'd use it."

Koenig sensed that Jess Casey had grown a backbone and he began to wonder if making him sheriff had been a mistake. But he covered his doubt with a grin. "Sure, Jess, sure. I was only funning."

"Who would want me dead, Koenig?" Jess said. "You've got your finger on the pulse of this town."

The gas lamps were being lit along Main Street, spreading their strange blue light, and shadows hollowed Porry McTurk's dead face.

"If I was a betting man my money would be on

Luke Short. He owns the White Elephant saloon up on Exchange Avenue. Luke has no liking for lawmen."

"I'll talk to him," Jess said.

"Then talk real low and don't say too much," Koenig said. "A former Fort Worth city marshal, feller by the name of Long-Haired Jim Court-right, said some harsh words to Luke and Luke killed him."

"Seems as though a man like that would do his own killing. Why send a drunk?"

Koenig shrugged. "Hard to fathom what Luke's thinking. He's a close one and no mistake." He turned. "Ah, here's Big Sal, as prompt as ever."

"Another one of yours, Koenig?" Big Sal said.

"His," Koenig said, nodding in Jess's direction.

"You payin', cowboy?" the woman said.

Big Sal stood well over six feet and Jess figured she must tip the scale at four hundred pounds. Her hair was cut short and she wore a man's broadcloth suit and collarless shirt. She was somewhere in her early forties.

"Well?" she said. "Who's paying the tariff?"

"I'll pay for his funeral," Jess said.

Big Sal looked Jess up and down from the crown of his battered hat to the run-down heels of his boots. "I guess you'll want the Ten Dollar Ordi-nary," she said. "Pine box and no refreshments served afterward."

"Dead men come expensive in Fort Worth," Jess said.

"It's a case of supply and demand, sonny," Big Sal

said. "Do you want the Ordinary or should I let the city throw the dear departed in a hole and use him for coyote bait?"

"Bury him decent," Jess said. He reached into a pocket, thumbed out a ten from his thin supply of folding money and passed it to the woman.

Big Sal took the ten, stepped past Jess and glanced at the dead man. "Hell, it's Porry McTurk. I knew he'd come to a bad end some day."

She picked up the body and effortlessly tucked it under her left arm. McTurk's arms and legs flopping fore and aft, she stood in front of Koenig and snapped the fingers of her free hand.

The big man reached inside his coat and produced a silver cigar case. He let the woman choose a cigar then said, "You ever think of smoking your own, Sal?"

"I can't afford these, Koenig," Big Sal said, allowing the man to light her cigar. Then, "Some of us are forced to make an *honest* living."

Koenig grinned. "Better take Porry home with you, Sal. Don't drop him on the way."

"I've carried them two at a time and never dropped one yet," the woman said. She turned her attention to Jess and the dead man's head bobbed, his hair hanging. "Come over and have a drink with me sometime, cowboy," she said. "I'll show you a good time."

As befitted a Texas gentleman of the time, Jess

touched his hat and said, "I'll keep that in mind, ma'am."

After the woman left, Koenig said, "She'll break your back."

"I think I'm fully aware of that," Jess said. "Now if you'll excuse me, I'm going to have a little talk with that Luke Short feller."

Koenig's smile was slight and without humor. "Don't take this job too seriously . . . Jess. Hank Henley did and look what happened to him."

"When a man tries to kill me, I take it seriously," Jess said.

CHAPTER FIVE

The White Elephant was a block north of Hell's Half Acre and Jess Casey decided to walk and see the sights. He unpinned the star from his shirt, thought better of it and put it back again.

He was the law in Fort Worth and folks should know it. Or was he? Koenig told him that Jim Courtright had been the city marshal but Hank Henley had been a sheriff. Did that mean Jess had a boss somewhere and that his own jurisdiction began and ended with the few city blocks that comprised the Acre? Or had the title of city marshal died with Courtright?

Jess figured he needed those questions answered, and pretty quick. He'd ask Harry Stout, the mayor, first chance he got.

It was still early evening but the saloons and dance halls along Main Street were coming to life as the sporting fraternity trickled inside. Tin-panny pianos played in the smaller establishments but some of the larger saloons with dance floors boasted five- and six-piece orchestras. No one took any notice of Jess as he made his way along the boardwalk, passing punchers in big hats, sallow gamblers, shifty-eyed men on the make, a few prosperous businessmen in broadcloth and the usual flotsam and jetsam of the frontier, hollow-eyed men who did not fit into any category. Girls in candy cane dresses stood on balconies above the saloons and dance halls and urged the passersby to come inside for a hell of a good time. Those whores past their prime, their naked shoulders scarred from bite wounds, steered clear of the big establishments and did their business transactions in the street. A dull roar of a thousand voices filled the Acre from dusk until dawn. It was a bustling, hustling annex of hell, bursting at the seams, a place where sin came easy but never cheap.

Jess's attention was drawn to the Light Fantastic dance hall across the street. Inside a lively crowd yelled, cheered and jeered but there was no music playing and no sign of female dance partners. Puzzled, he crossed the busy, jostling street and stepped inside and was immediately hit by a wall of cigar smoke, the smell of male sweat and the faint but unmistakable odor of piss and stale vomit.

A boxing ring had been set up in the middle of the floor. A tall, muscular black man stood in one corner, and opposite him glared a white man with a thick neck, sloping, hairy shoulders and a chest like a beer keg.

"Sheriff!"

Jess looked around and spotted Kurt Koenig

beckoning to him behind the smoke fug. Jess made his way through the jam-packed crowd and Koenig grinned at him and slapped his back. "Surprised to see you here, Jess, but you're just in time to see the fight," he said. "Put your money on Dave 'Killer' Kick there. He's the best damned street fighter in Fort Worth. In his time he's killed more than his share with his bare hands, ol' Dave has, and he was a shipmate o' mine on the old SS *Spindrift*, Captain Zack Irons commanding, when we sailed out of the Barbary Coast."

"Which one is Kick?" Jess said.

"The white man, of course."

"Is the black man a sailor?" Jess said.

"Nah. Of course I've seen many a big buck wearing sea boots in my time, but never sailed with one."

A man in a plug hat and sporting a pencil mustache held up a wad of notes and yelled, "Kurt! I'm giving ten-to-one on the black."

"Not a chance," Koenig said, grinning. "My thousand stays on Kick."

That last occasioned a roar of approval from the other patrons.

"I'll take that bet," Jess said. He pulled out his last crumpled twenty, elbowed through the crowd and passed the money to the bookmaker.

"Ten-to-one on Zeus for the man wearing the star," the man said. "He sure knows a good bet when he sees one."

This drew more laughter and some jeers. Lawmen of any stripe were unpopular in the Acre, especially one who was so stupid he'd bet against Killer Kick.

Jess didn't blame them. His only reason for betting on the black man was to spite Kurt Koenig . . . and now his little fit of pique would cost him almost all he had. Jess glanced up at the elevated ring and saw the black man staring at him, a bemused light in his eyes.

And then Jess saw something else that gave him a sudden chill—the black man's right arm was tied behind his back.

"Koenig, I'm going to stop this fight," Jess said.

The big man's eyebrows lifted and there was disbelief in his voice. "You're going to do what?"

"They've tied the black man's right arm behind his back."

Koenig grinned, as did others in the crowd close to him. "But that's the whole point," he said. "See that little bald feller talking to Zeus?"

"I see him," Jess said.

"Well, that's Nate Levy, Zeus's manager. He said his boy would fight anyone in town with one arm tied behind his back for a five-hundred-dollar purse, winner take all. Well, Mayor Stout put up the prize money and Dave Kick took up the challenge. And that's why you'll lose your twenty-dollar bet."

Jess was lost for words. He could kiss good-bye to his money, and all because he hadn't noticed the rope. It was a lawman's job to observe things like that, even one new to the job, and he'd failed miserably.

With considerable difficulty Mayor Stout clambered under the rope, held up his hands for silence and then intoned in a gloriously commanding voice, "My lords, ladies and gentlemen . . ."

This drew a cheer and a woman yelled, "Good for you, Horny Harry."

"This will be an Irish Stand Down contest between, in the corner to my left, the Black Bull of Boston, the Sable Sultan of Slaughter, the Prince of Darkness himself, the one and the only . . . *Zeus!*"

Cheers. Jeers. And another "Good for you, Horny Harry!"

The man called Zeus raised his muscular left arm and was awarded a scattering of mild applause.

"And in the corner to my right," Stout proclaimed, "that Mauling Master of Mayhem, that Bullying Baron of Brutality, that Savage Son of the Seven Seas. I give you Fort Worth's very own . . . *Dave . . . Killer . . . Kick!*"

The crowd exploded into wild cheers and Kick bounced up and down and threw mighty punches at the air, his broken-nosed face contorted in an expression of the most alarming ferocity.

"Toe the line, gentlemen," Stout yelled. "The time for talking is done."

Kick came up to scratch roaring, grinning, his arms pumping. The onlookers went hysterical as they cheered their hirsute champion and odds-on favorite. That meant that their nickel and dime bets would earn them little but they didn't seem to care. And Dave was a white man, there was always that.

Zeus remained stoical and stood like an ebony statue, a mahogany-skinned Greek god, his black hair cropped close to his head.

"Irish Stand Down rules apply," Stout said. "The first pugilist to step back from scratch or hit the ground loses." He stood between the fighters. "Gentlemen, do I make myself clear?"

"Clear enough," Kick said. "Let's get on with the fight." He glared at Zeus. "I'm gonna pound you into a red jelly." That bold statement drew frenzied cheers and Kick lightly punched Zeus on the chin and said, "Now are you ready to take your lickin', boy?"

Stout withdrew a white handkerchief from his pocket and let it flutter between the fighters.

"The battle is on!" he yelled.

Kick had been waiting for that moment.

He landed a right uppercut to Zeus's chin that rocked the black man to his heels. Kick followed up fast, a roundhouse left that landed high on Zeus's right cheek and split the tight skin of his cheekbone, spraying blood. The black staggered back a step and the crowd cheered, but he got back to scratch and the two men lowered their heads and stood toe-to-toe and battered each other with driving fists, Zeus effectively looping punches with his left. A cut opened up above Kick's right eye. He was a bleeder and instantly the man's face was a crimson mask of gore. But Kick shook his head, blood spraying from him, and bored in, landing heavy punches to the black man's body. Zeus, his teeth bared, countered with a hard left to the side of Kick's head, and then another. His hard knuckles split open Kick's right ear and the white man immediately broke loose, feinted, then clubbed a left to

Zeus's face that cut him over the eye. Kick came close and his and Zeus's sweat mingled as he again went for the body, pounding the black man's ribs until Zeus's mouth was forced wide open as he fought to catch a breath.

Zeus pushed Kick away with his left hand. The white man lurched back, but quickly came back to scratch. Zeus met him with a straight left to the face that smashed into Kick's already-broken nose. Lightning in his left fist, Zeus slammed a punch into Kick's ribs. Hurt, Kick cried out in pain and then clinched.

For a moment the two men clung to each other, their gaping mouths gasping for breath. But then Zeus drew back his arm and smashed an elbow into Kick's face. The man dropped, rolled and lay on his back, his face a mask of blood. The crowd roared at him to get back to scratch. Hurt bad, Kick was still in the fight. He staggered to the line and he and Zeus exchanged a flurry of punches. But the crowd could see that Kick's blows were losing power. He was blinded by the blood that streamed from cuts above both his eyes where the skin of his heavy brow ridge was stretched thin and every time he tried to brush the blood away, Zeus landed his punishing left.

The crowd bayed at Kick to end it.

His punches had lost much of their power and Kick tried a new tack. His hands came up fast and his massive, thick-nailed thumbs, filed into points, stabbed for Zeus's eyes. The black man saw the danger. He swept downward with his left and forced

Kick to drop his arms. Zeus stepped in quickly and head-butted the bridge of Kick's destroyed nose. Kick staggered back and hit the canvas hard. He struggled onto his hands and knees and stared up at Zeus.

The black man spoke for the first time. "You're done," he said. "Stay down."

Through split lips Kick said, "The hell I am."

He crawled to scratch and started to rise to his feet. Zeus met him coming up with a magnificent uppercut that caught Kick perfectly on the point of the chin. The punch sent the white man sprawling, but he rolled over and made a dive for Zeus's feet. The black man stepped back as all the fight suddenly left Kick and he slowly sank onto the canvas.

Now he was done.

At first the crowd was silent, but then as the mindless rage of the mob possessed them they roared their anger. All of them had lost money, and the sight of an uppity black man standing victorious in the ring as his Jewish manager accepted a fat roll of notes from the mayor, drove them insane. Lynching is the creature of the moment, and that moment had come.

Jess Casey saw the danger. Just a day before he would have considered it no business of his and walked away. But the star on his shirt made it his business and however reluctantly he accepted its dictate.

He quickly scrambled into the ring, drew his gun and stood near Zeus and his manager. Around him the angry crowd was a many-headed beast baying for blood. Jess caught a glimpse of Kurt Koenig. The big man was staring at him, a slightly concerned look on his face, but he made no move to calm the people around him.

Mayor Stout walked into the middle of the ring and held up his arms for silence. "Listen!" he yelled. "Listen to me! Please leave the premises in an orderly fashion."

But he beat a hasty retreat when he was bombarded with bottles and glasses. He turned a brief, frightened glance on Jess and said, "It's all yours, Sheriff."

A few drunk roosters tried to climb into the ring and Jess booted them away, but there were more right behind them. He saw Nate Levy push Zeus into a corner and try to shield him from flying missiles.

Jess, his heart hammering in his chest, decided that this was a hell of a time to play lawman.

He drew his gun, fired a shot into the air, then yelled, "I'll kill any man who sets foot in this ring." Jess knew he sounded like a two-bit version of Ed Masterson or one of those gunslinging town tamers, but right then a show of force was all he had.

Maybe it was the star on his chest or perhaps the crowd figured the tall, loose-geared man with the big hat and spurs meant business, but Jess's warning worked. The crowd hushed a little and men drew back from the ring out of the way of the field of fire. Then Kurt Koenig put the clincher on things.

With a laugh in his voice he said, "All right, boys, let's git over to the Silver Garter and we'll drown our sorrows. The first drink is on me."

Koenig owned the Silver Garter, one of the Acre's more luxurious saloons, and his suggestion went over well with the crowd. People drifted away but Koenig remained for a few moments, his eyes on Jess.

"I'm obliged to you," Jess said.

The big man nodded then said, "You're trying too hard, cowboy. That could be dangerous."

He turned and stepped away and Jess watched him go and wondered what he'd meant by those words. It was a warning certainly. Was his stopping a sure lynching trying too hard?

Nate Levy, small and stooped, with a crafty face and the luminous dark eyes of a poet, stepped beside Jess and said, "Thank you, Sheriff."

Jess nodded. "Better get Zeus out of here. A lot of people lost money tonight because of him."

"He's good, isn't he?" Levy said. "I've helped train some of the best, Paddy Ryan and John L. Sullivan among them, but Zeus will make his mark as the greatest prizefighter the world has ever seen."

"If you keep tying an arm behind his back, he'll make his mark in the graveyard," Jess said.

Levy threw up his hands in horror. "No more of this bare-knuckle stuff for my boy. From now on it's Marquess of Queensberry rules all the way."

"Glad to hear it," Jess said. He bent under the rope and accepted a wad of notes from the book-maker. "Is it all here?" he said.

"Two hundred and twenty dollars, cash on the barrelhead, Sheriff. They don't call me Honest John Jennings for nothing."

"Made a killing tonight, huh?" Jess said.

"A few bucks, Sheriff. When a man's got as many hungry mouths to feed as I do he has to scrape. Make do or do without, that's the motto of the Jennings family."

The little bookmaker turned and walked away, the diamond rings on his fingers glittering. Zeus and his manager were gone and Jess was alone in the ring.

"Hey, Sheriff," a burly man said, looking up at him. "We got to take this ring down and get set up for dancing, so move your ass."

Jess smiled. "Would you say that to Ed Masterson?"

"Huh?" the man said.

Jess shook his head. "Never mind. I'll get out of your way."

CHAPTER SIX

Jess Casey lingered and watched the boxing ring dismantled and then as white, slippery stuff was scattered onto the wood floor. One by one the musicians stepped inside carrying their instruments and the bartenders had cleaned up for the dancers. The men began to arrive first, then the girls. Unlike saloon girls the dance partners dressed as demurely as schoolmarms, but their calculating eyes made it clear they were chasing the same thing . . . the mark and his buck.

Jess stepped out of the hall and into a street still thronged with people. Here and there visitors from outside the Acre, mostly couples, made stately promenades along the boardwalks, taking in the sights.

Jess was tired, used up, the killing of Porry McTurk and the close call in the dance hall weighing on him. All in all, his first day as sheriff of Fort Worth had been almighty busy.

Hank Henley would have told Jess that he'd just

experienced what was a routine day in Hell's Acre and that much worse was waiting in the wings. But Henley was dead and Jess Casey had no way of knowing what was to come.

Jess stood to the side of the dance hall door and built and lit a cigarette. Men, most of them half drunk, streamed inside, and one belligerent ranny decided to take exception to Jess's lawman's star.

"Why don't you take the gun off and we'll see how tough you are, law dog," the man said, putting up his dukes. He was a dapper, aggressive little banty rooster who obviously had something to prove.

"Git away from me," Jess said. "Go inside, get a drink and cool off."

"Scared, huh?" the runt said.

"Yeah, that's right. You scare me," Jess said. "Now go away and leave me the hell alone."

A few people had gathered to watch the fun and this emboldened the little man, who giggled, unbuttoned and proceeded to piss all over Jess's boots. Now by nature Jess Casey was an easygoing man, but even he had his limits. As soon as the little man's amber stream drummed on Jess's boots it drew a laugh—and the sheriff's Colt.

Jess reached out, removed the man's plug hat, then whacked him on the side of the head with the big revolver. Before the glassy-eyed little man dropped, Jess had time to replace his hat and then he watched him fall.

"Here, that won't do," one of the onlookers said, outraged. "That man has friends here."

"And he was drunk," another man said. "You shouldn't buffalo a drunk."

"He'd been notified," Jess said.

Then he remembered. Ed Masterson had said those same words as he dragged Jess, semiconscious and bleeding, to the hoosegow. All at once Ed grew in Jess's estimation. He hadn't pissed on Masterson's boots, but he'd watered the mayor's pumpkins and in Dodge that was as heinous an offense as the other.

Jess holstered his gun and said, "If you boys are his friends, take him inside until he recovers."

"Mister, you've made a bad enemy," a serious-looking man with an English accent said. "Do you know who you just clocked?"

"No," Jess said. "And I don't much care. He pissed on my boots."

"My dear fellow, that's Luke Short," the serious man said. "The next time you see him he'll have a gun in his hand."

Short was sitting now, rubbing the side of his head. He seemed groggy and unfocused. Jess saw no sign of a gun, but that didn't mean he wasn't carrying one. This was the man Jess suspected of ordering him killed, and he wanted to take no chances with him. By all accounts Luke Short was a deadly gunman and a killer.

The serious Englishman and another helped the reeling little man to his feet and Jess spotted a sagging weight in the back pocket of Short's pants. He told the men to hold up and took a short-barreled Colt from the leather-lined pocket. "Tell him he can come collect this at the sheriff's office when he sobers up," Jess said.

The Colt was beautifully engraved and had ivory grips, the kind of weapon a man would not want to lose.

"A real hardnose, ain't you, copper?" This from the Englishman's companion, another belligerent runt, though well turned out and prosperous.

Jess's honest reply would have been, "No, I'm not. I'm just a stove-up cowboy and one way or the other I've been scared since I rode into town."

Instead he said, "Just don't try my patience and find out just how hard-nosed I can be, mister."

The prosperous man's smile was nasty. "No, I'll leave that to Mr. Short. He'll find out when he comes for you."

After the trio disappeared into the dance hall, where the orchestra was playing "Polly Wolly Doodle" and the girls were laughing, Jess shoved Short's Colt into his waistband and decided to call it a night. He was dog-tired and even the mean bed in the sheriff's office all at once seemed inviting.

But often when a man makes a decision, fate immediately conspires to prevent it. And so it was with Jess Casey.

Walking with the horseman's short-gaited stride, lanky Jess Casey made his way along the jostling boardwalk. Noting the star on Jess's shirt, a young man and woman hurried their pace toward him.

The couple was of the more respectable sort.

The man looked like a clerk of some kind and the girl was pretty and wore a dress of rustling silver silk with a huge bustle. A small heart-shaped hat was perched on top of her swept-up amber hair and when she drew closer Jess noticed a diamond brooch above her breast that spelled out in emeralds around the glittering stone, *Toi et Nul Autre.*

Seeing the dazzlingly pretty girl was the only pleasant thing that had happened to Jess all day and he touched his hat and greeted her with a smile. But it soon slipped as she said, "Sheriff! They're killing a man in the alley." She pointed behind her. "Down there!"

"I'll go take a look," Jess said. He touched his hat to the girl, pulled his gun and stepped toward the alley entrance. A white moth fluttered briefly around an oil lamp outside the apothecary that formed one wall of the alley and then fell scorched and dead at Jess's feet. He was too concerned about what lay ahead of him to take it as an ill omen.

His heart hammering again, an occurrence that was becoming all too familiar to Jess Casey, he held his Colt high and quickly ducked his head around the corner of the apothecary building. Somewhere close a woman yelled, "Here, what goes on?"

Jess ignored her, his attention riveted on the sprawled form of Nate Levy on the ground. Ahead of him in the gloom he heard punches slam home into a human body, like the thudding of an ax on the trunk of an oak. Jess had still not been seen and he bent over in the darkness and felt the little manager's chest. Levy was still breathing but was in a bad way.

The sound of vicious blows landing went on, the groans of a man in pain providing a cruel counterpoint. His mouth dry, Jess advanced slowly into the alley. He still hadn't been seen. Now as his eyes became accustomed to the gloom he saw two men holding another against the wall of the building to his left. The third, a big man with bulging arm muscles, pounded punches into the pinioned man's ribs and belly.

"You! Get the hell away from him!" Jess yelled. He sounded more confident than he felt.

Suddenly the muscular man moved. Something gleamed in the darkness then a gun flared. Jess felt a bullet cut across the meat of his right shoulder, searing like a branding iron. He thumbed off two shots fast and then heard a shriek followed by the fall of a heavy body.

The two men, vague shadows in the darkness who'd been holding the beaten man's arms, let go and beat a hasty retreat into the waste ground behind the alley. Then orange lantern light bobbed along the walls on either side of Jess and he heard a woman's voice say, "Are you all right, Sheriff?"

Jess turned and saw the girl in the silk dress. Her companion held the lantern and behind him several men were silhouettes in the gloom.

"Just fine," Jess said. He felt sick to his stomach.

He grabbed the lantern and stepped to the rear of the alley.

Zeus sat with his back against the wall. His face was swollen and bruised, both his eyes battered shut and blood streamed from his nose. Jess reckoned he had other injuries he couldn't see.

Through broken lips, Zeus said, "Who were they?"

Jess said, "I don't know. Sore losers, I guess."

The man he'd shot was dead with two bullet wounds in his chest, so close together Jess could have covered them with a playing card.

It seemed to Jess that he had a natural talent for revolver shooting, a skill he didn't know he possessed. A few men, probably not more than two or three in a thousand, are born with fast hands and the ability to use a firearm well under duress, the reason that though many men carried guns in the West very few became skilled shootists.

Jess Casey was one of them and he'd discovered the skill by accident.

"Nate tried to save me," Zeus said. "But he didn't stand a chance. Is he . . ."

Jess said, "He's badly beaten, old fellow, but he's still alive."

"Help me to my feet," Zeus said. "I have to go to him."

"I don't think you can stand," Jess said.

Zeus said, "I can stand."

A couple of stray dogs tangled with a coyote in the darkness beyond the alley. The coyote screamed and ran and the dogs took off in growling pursuit. Somewhere close a piano played "Lardy Dah."

Zeus kneeled beside Nate Levy and held the little man's head in his arm. "Nate, can you hear me?" he said. There was no answer and the big fighter said, "I'll take him to Dr. Sun. His house is close by."

"Hey, Sheriff," a man said. He held a lantern high as he stared down at the muscular man's body. "This here is Max Major."

Jess nodded. He felt weary. "That's his name, huh?"

"You don't know?" the man said. He had a florid face framed by great muttonchop whiskers.

"Not until you told me," Jess said.

Muttonchop said, "He was one of the Panther City Boys, Kurt Koenig's hard crowd."

The girl placed her hand on Jess's arm, shock in her voice. "Oh, I'm so sorry," she said. She saw blood on her hand and said, "And you're wounded."

"The lady has a right to be sorry, Sheriff," Muttonchop said. "You better leave town when you still can. Them Panther City Boys are nothing to mess with."

Zeus carried Levy in his arms and stopped beside Jess. "You better come with us," he said. "Don't let Koenig's boys find you here. There are a whole lot of them."

The girl looked distressed. "Do that, please," she said. "Dr. Sun will see to your wound."

Lantern light guttering around him, Jess said, "What's your name?"

"Lillian. Lillian Burke. My father owns the Black Horse brewery in town."

"Then I'll see you again, Lillian," Jess said.

"Yes, perhaps. Now go."

Jess said, "I look forward to it."

Then Zeus motioned with his head. "That way, Sheriff. You don't want to die in an alley."

CHAPTER SEVEN

Dr. Sun's home and surgery was located on Main Street, a converted general store that still boasted a false front with the faded name GEO. GRANT & SON still readable. A brass nameplate on the door said only DOCTOR SUN, and the window above it was boarded.

Jess knocked on the door and after a while it opened, wafting incense from inside. A slender young girl stood in the doorway. She wore a blue silk dress embroidered with flowers and her face was in shadow.

"Come inside," she said. "Dr. Sun is expecting you."

Jess Casey had no time to wonder at that because of the shock of seeing the girl's face in the hallway lamplight. Her long hair framed horrific features that were scarred almost beyond recognition, as though she'd been burned in a raging fire. Yet her shoulders and beautiful arms were untouched, as smooth as silk.

Jess knew he'd gaped and was instantly embarrassed. But the girl, no doubt used to this kind of reaction from strangers, seemed not to notice.

"This way," she said.

Jess followed, Zeus carrying the unconscious Levy behind him. In her tight dress the girl had a figure a man would dream about at night, a tiny waist and swelling, shapely hips. But her ravaged features destroyed her beauty completely. Like a rock thrown through the face of a Gainsborough portrait her disfigurement made a slum of her body.

The girl opened a door and bade Jess and the others enter.

The room was small, smoky with incense, lit by lanterns that threw a crimson light. In the middle of the floor, bowing, stood a small Chinese man, much wrinkled, wearing a gorgeous black robe embroidered with silver dragons. On his shaven head was a small round hat with a tassel and there was a faint, elusive smile on his lips.

"I am Dr. Sun. Welcome to my humble abode," he said. Then to Zeus, "Put the wounded man on the table over there by the wall, my gigantic friend."

Zeus gently laid the groaning Levy on the leather examination table. But Dr. Sun took time to look at Jess's shoulder. "Ah, a bullet wound," he said. "But slight. Would the honorable gentleman mind waiting until I see to his friend, who is hurt more seriously?"

"You go right ahead, Doc," Jess said.

The little man bowed. "You are most gracious." He kowtowed to Zeus in turn. "And you, too, must pause for my administrations, I'm afraid."

"See to Nate, Doctor," Zeus said. "I think he's hurt real bad."

The little man nodded. "We shall see."

Jess watched Dr. Sun as he examined Nate Levy. His hands were as small and delicate as a woman's yet they looked strong, especially his right, the hand and forearm banded with muscles like steel cables.

After a few minutes, the little man said, "Your friend will live. He has three broken ribs from powerful blows, but I will bind him tight and that will help. I can give him something for pain and to help him sleep. Does he live close by?"

"At the National Hotel," Zeus said. "I'll take him there."

"Then you must do so," Dr. Sun said. "He will stay in bed for several days to let his body recover. He is a Child of the Book?"

"Yes, he is," Zeus said.

"Good. Then his will is strong."

Dr. Sun declared that Jess's wound was little more than a bullet burn and he applied a salve that was purple in color and smelled of wood smoke. It removed the pain almost instantly.

"Doc, who is the girl who met us at the door?" Jess said.

"Ah, her name is Mei-Xing. In Chinese that means Beautiful Star. I have made her my ward."

"Her face . . . I mean . . ."

"In China, Mei-Xing was once the concubine of a powerful warlord who lived in a fortress tower in Guangdong," Dr. Sun said. "The warlord was old and very fond of Mei-Xing and this made his wife jealous. Zhuo, for that was her name, had one of the fortress guards shove a flaming torch into Mei-Xing's face so that her husband would never again be enthralled by her rival's beauty. Zhuo then had Mei-Xing sold into prostitution and by various and devious means she arrived on American shores. But what man would wish to pay for a whore with a scarred face? Mei-Xing's descent into despair and degradation ended here, in Hell's Half Acre. I found her living on the streets and took her in and made her my ward. When I die, all I have, she will have."

"I hope . . . what's the wife's name?"

"Zhuo."

"Yeah, her. In the end I hope she got what she deserved."

"No, to this day Zhuo thrives as a great warlord's number one wife and her beauty and riches grow." Dr. Sun smiled. "Do not think that all evil is punished, young man. Here in Hell's Acre it walks among us daily and prospers."

Jess would have liked to talk more about the city

and its evils, but the little physician turned away to concentrate on Zeus's battered face.

Jess rose from his chair and said it was time he sought his cot at the sheriff's office. "How much do I owe you, Dr. Sun?" he said.

The little man smiled, his face forming a network of wrinkles. "I'll send you my bill, Sheriff," he said.

"It's a long time since I've had one of those," Jess said.

CHAPTER EIGHT

"You've had a busy day, Sheriff," the girl said. "I spoke to Big Sal and she says she's got two dead men lying on slabs in her morgue with your bullets in them."

"You'd better come in," Jess Casey said. The girl's knock on the door had wakened him from sleep and he wore only his hat and long johns.

"Do you often greet female callers in your underwear?" the girl said.

Jess beat a hasty retreat behind his desk and sat. "I didn't expect a female . . . I mean a woman . . . I mean . . ."

"I'm catching your drift, Sheriff. I didn't know that grown men could blush."

The girl laid the bundle she'd been carrying on the desk. She smelled like flowers.

"Pillows, clean sheets and a blanket," she said. "Compliments of Kurt Koenig. He likes the way you handle yourself and means to keep you cozy."

"Thank him for me," Jess said. "Now, if you'll excuse me, I have to get back to bed."

The girl ignored that and pulled up a chair and sat opposite Jess. "I could use a drink," she said. "After I talk with Big Sal I can always use a drink. She says both men you shot were dead when they hit the ground. The whiskey is in the bottom drawer right."

"I know where it is," Jess said. In his underwear and bare feet he felt vulnerable and ill at ease.

"Well?" the girl said.

Jess produced the Old Crow and glasses and poured for both of them.

"Cheers," the girl said. She sampled the whiskey, then said, "Name's Destiny Durand, by the way." She was pretty in a blond and blue-eyed way and her clinging red silk dress left little to the imagination.

"Pleased to meet you, Miss Durand," Jess said. "Now if you will drink up I must be getting back to my bunk. Thank you again for the bedding."

"Hold on, cowboy," Destiny said. "I have something for you from Kurt."

"You work for him?" Jess said.

"You could say that."

The girl reached between her breasts and produced an envelope. "Open it," she said. "It's a love token."

Jess opened the envelope and let its contents drop to the desk. It was ten twenty-dollar bills.

"In addition to your salary you'll get that amount every week to keep your nose out of Kurt's business," Destiny said. "He'll tell you who to arrest, who to shoot and who to ignore." The girl looked intently into Jess's eyes. "You catching my drift?"

"And if I don't?"

"Then the same thing that happened to Sheriff Hank Henley will happen to you, only a sight more sudden."

The bribe, for that's what he reckoned it was, had come as a shock and Jess hadn't had even a moment to collect his thoughts. Playing for time he said, "What will the city marshal think of this?"

Destiny smiled, her scarlet lips slightly moist. "Why bless you for a pilgrim," she said. "Kurt Koenig is the city marshal."

"I don't want this money," Jess said. "I plan to ride out of Fort Worth come morning."

"And then do what?" Destiny said. "Go back to nursing cows for thirty a month? You fool, stick with Kurt for a few years and you can buy your own spread. Then find yourself a sweet little gal who says her prayers at night and who will cook and sew for you and be content to live happily ever after like happens in the picture books."

Jess stared at the two hundred dollars on his desk and said nothing. But his mind was racing. The money was either the down payment on the future J-C Ranch or a vile payoff to be ignored.

Destiny rose from her chair, her dress rustling. "You've had long enough, cowboy. I tell you what, you saddle up tomorrow, ride the grub line and then die like a dog from bad whiskey in some dunghill town west of nowhere." She smiled. "It's a pity because you're a right handsome young feller. You look like General Custer. Anybody ever tell you that?"

Jess shook his head.

"And you got about as much sense as him, too," Destiny said.

She reached for the money, but Jess said, "Leave it."

"Money talks, huh?"

"The J-C Ranch talks."

Destiny said, "Yeah, for Jess Casey. It's a good brand. So I can tell Kurt you'll stick and you swear that you'll do no more revolver work unless he gives you the say-so."

"Yes, tell him that. Tell him anything the hell you want."

"Don't take it hard, cowboy. A lot of people draw wages from Kurt Koenig. You'll find that he's a generous man."

Destiny stepped to the door and her pretty face hardened. "Just think of cows with the J-C brand on their rumps and do as you're told. Learn to live with it, cowboy. Like me, you're now officially bought and paid for."

After Destiny Durand left, the memory of her perfume lingered but there was now only empty space where a beautiful woman had been.

Jess sighed and got to his feet. He left the money where it lay on the table and made up his bed with the clean sheets and pillows. The mattress was still lumpy and hard, but it was an improvement.

To his surprise Jess slept well and didn't wake until a gray dawn light filtered through the office windows. The dressing on his shoulder had worked loose in the night, uncovering an angry red scar that hurt to the touch. He rose quickly, stripped to the skin, then put on his hat and slicker to cover his nakedness. A bar of lye soap lay next to a scrap of towel in the office and he grabbed both and took the back door to the outside. As Jess expected, there was a water pump that dripped into a full horse trough. He stripped off the slicker and washed himself thoroughly. It was still early and there was no one about, though a small calico cat with amber eyes sat and watched his every move, wondering at this latest evidence of human weirdness.

Jess dried himself as best he could and stepped back into the office, where he shaved, combed his wet hair and dressed again. He buckled on his gun belt and left in search of coffee.

Along the boardwalk a ways a hanging wooden sign said:

MA'S KITCHEN
HOME COOKING
AT ITS FINEST

And indeed the place emitted odors of coffee, frying steak and grilling bacon and Jess, his stomach growling, made a beeline. After the events of last night he had some thinking to do, but a man can't study on things with an empty stomach.

Jess stepped inside and found himself a table in the corner near the kitchen. A pretty young waitress took his order for coffee, steak and eggs and when it arrived, the food was good and the coffee better.

After eating, Jess burped his satisfaction and concentrated on building a cigarette, his first of the morning.

"Remember me?"

Jess glanced up and beheld the small, dapper form of Luke Short. Unfortunately the fat bandage wrapped around his head and the precarious perch of his plug hat thereon somewhat spoiled his sartorial splendor. In addition, Short's face was sour.

"Sure, I remember you," Jess said. "You tried to pick a fight with me and then pissed on my boots."

"I did that?" Short said.

"Sure did. That's why I put that bump on your head."

A scholarly-looking man sitting within earshot turned in his chair and said, "A gent should never touch another gent's hat or piss on his boots. Now, that's a natural fact."

Short glared at the man but then turned his attention back to Jess.

"You got something that belongs to me," he said.

Jess said, "It's back at the sheriff's office. If you care to accompany me I'll give it back to you." He rose to his feet, towering head and shoulders over the diminutive gunman. But Jess wasn't fooled. Sometimes big trouble comes in mighty small packages.

"After you, Mr. Short," he said, motioning to the door.

"Don't trust me, do you?" Short said.

"Should I?"

"No. You shouldn't," Luke Short said.

Jess took Short's Colt from the desk drawer and passed the revolver to the little man. Short immediately checked the piece and scowled his annoyance.

Jess smiled and said, "You didn't think I was going to give you a loaded gun, did you?"

Short shoved the Colt into his waistband and said, "I heard your name is Jess Casey and that you killed two men last night."

"You heard right. I will never boast of it."

"And why should you? Taking the life of another human being is not something to be proud of." Short turned to go, but stopped and said, "I don't like you, Jess Casey. I'm letting last night go because I pissed on your boots. Another time I will not be as contrite."

"Obey the law, Mr. Short, and there won't be another time."

The little man's smile seemed genuine. "There is no law in Fort Worth. That's why I'm here."

"And that's why I'm here," Jess said.

"How do I take that?"

"Take it that I'll uphold the law."

"You mean Kurt Koenig's law, don't you?"

Jess had no ready answer for that and Short said, "I thought so. He's already got you in his pocket." He shook his head and then regretted it, wincing slightly. "A word of advice, Sheriff—stay the hell away from me and the White Elephant. Understand?"

"I'll do my job, Mr. Short."

Luke Short smiled. "Anybody ever tell you that you look like George Armstrong Custer?"

"The resemblance has been noted before."

"Well, remember what happened to him when he took on more than he could handle and maybe you'll keep your hair."

Then Short did something that shocked Jess Casey to the core.

The little gunman drew his Colt from his waistband, thumbed back the hammer and aimed the revolver right at Jess's head. He pulled the trigger and the hammer snapped on an empty chamber.

"Bang," Short said. "You're dead."

CHAPTER NINE

Big Kurt Koenig looked at Jess Casey and then at the desktop in front of him. "You haven't picked up the two hundred dollars I paid you," he said. "What's the matter, Sheriff? You don't like money?"

"Sure, I like what money can buy," Jess said.

"There's a lot more where that came from," Koenig said. "Stick with me and I'll put you on easy street." Then, slowly, his great muscular bulk looming large in the small office, "Pick . . . up . . . the . . . money."

"I need to think this through, Mr. Koenig," Jess said.

"Call me Kurt. Destiny told me you want to buy your own ranch someday. Is that right?"

"It's been a dream of mine since I was a younker, I guess."

"And I'm a man who makes dreams come true— the bigger the dream, the harder I work to make it a reality. Savvy?"

"I guess," Jess said.

"Don't guess. I hate a guessing man. You got two choices: take the money or ride out of here a pauper. Will you be a rancher or a rat catcher? It's a simple question and guessing don't enter into it."

Jess said nothing and Koenig slammed the table. "Man, we got this town in the palms of our hands and all we have to do is squeeze it dry, wring it out like we'd use a whore and then, when it's all used up, we walk away from it and don't look back."

Looking at him, Jess decided Kurt Koenig was a ruthless man who always got what he wanted. He seemed unstoppable, not human but a force of nature. To stand in his way would be like a man trying to stop the progress of a tornado.

Jess picked up the money. He would hitch his wagon to Koenig's dark star but only for so long . . . only until he had enough money saved. That was it . . . the way it would be.

Koenig gave a little smile of triumph. "All right, Sheriff, saddle up. We got riding to do," he said. It was only then that Jess saw the city marshal's shield pinned to Koenig's vest.

"Ride to where?" Jess said, getting to his feet. Koenig said, "Not far, only to Mary's Creek just west of town."

"Who's Mary?" Jess said. "Is she a farmer's wife?"

Koenig smiled. "Bless you for a swab. The creek is named for Mary LeBone, an Indian woman who drowned there a few years back. It's open grass country and good graze for cattle. The Comanche and Apache hunted buffalo out that way, but the Indians and the buffs are all gone now."

"Out of my jurisdiction, isn't it?" Jess said.

"I'll tell you what your jurisdiction is," Koenig said. "We're going to stop a crime before it happens. Now get your horse and rifle and we'll ride."

Two men were with Koenig, both of them with the broken-nosed look of street-fighting toughs. They introduced themselves to Jess as members of the Panther City Boys and let it go at that. Koenig, his eyes on the trail ahead, heard but said nothing.

As the noon hour approached horses and riders cast shadows that pooled on the grass. The day was sultry, holding the promise of a summer rain, and the sun burned the sky like a red-hot coin.

Koenig drew rein and turned his head to Jess. "You'll soon make the acquaintance of Jeddah Burns and his sons Caleb and Jethro. They are breeds and not nice people."

One of the toughs sniggered as Jess said, "What crime are they about to commit?"

"The murder of one Kurt Koenig, late of Fort Worth in the great state of Texas. At least, that's the plan."

"How do you know?"

"Because Jeddah sent me a message by a passing rider." He reached into his coat pocket and produced a crumpled piece of paper. "Read it and weep," he said.

Jess smoothed out the note and read:

KONEG YOU DONE FER MY DOTTER
LITTLE AMY AND ME AND MY BOYS
IS COMIN INTO FORT WORTH TO
DO FER YOU. THIS IS A RECKONING.

It was signed, *Jeddah Burns.*

"Seems like he's on the prod, all right," Jess said. "What did you do to little Amy?"

"I didn't knock her up, if that's what you're thinking," Koenig said. "Amy Burns worked for me at the Silver Garter strictly as a singer and dancer. But then she met a gambler who promised her marriage and a new life and then left her." Koenig shook his head. "She cut her wrists and even Doc Sun couldn't save her. She was eighteen years old."

"And Jeddah Burns blames you."

"You read the note."

"You've met him before?" Jess said.

"Oh yeah. About a year ago he came to the Silver Garter and tried to take his little girl home to the family cabin by force. He shot one of my boys and would have plugged another if Johnny Dash here"—Koenig jerked a thumb over his shoulder—"hadn't put a bullet into him. Jeddah hightailed it out of town, leaking blood, and this is the first I've heard from him since."

The man called Dash, about as tall as Jess but twice as big, said, "Amy told me later that her pa and her brothers wanted to keep her as a slave and for other stuff I can't mention in polite company. Damn, but she was a right purty little gal."

Koenig grinned. "Johnny, I'm impressed by your sensitivity," he said.

Dash said, "Huh?"

"I heard there's a whole Burns clan up Cooke County way on the south bank of the Red—white, Mex and black all mixed up," Koenig said. "Seems they're an inbred bunch on account of how the daughters can never outrun their brothers. If Amy hadn't met that gambling man she'd have done all right. She was well rid of her pa."

Koenig sat straighter in the saddle, his square chin jutting and determined. "All right, let's go kill some breeds."

"Kurt," Jess said, using the man's given name for the first time, "we can arrest them and take them back to Fort Worth."

"Arrest them for what? Sending a threatening note? This is not an arresting time, Jess, it's a killing time. So we ride and get it done."

CHAPTER TEN

The messenger who delivered the threat from Jeddah Burns said the three men had camped by Mary's Creek in a ruined cabin that had been burned by Comanches in times past. The smell of smoke in the breeze led Jess and the others directly to it.

A skilled draw fighter, Koenig dismounted and told Jess Casey to do the same. A horse's back was not a good place for a fast draw and shoot. His two men remained mounted, rifles across their saddle horns.

Jess and Koenig walked their horses across sun-dried grass and stopped when they were within a long rifle shot of the cabin.

"Jess, start earning your money," Koenig said. "Go tell Jeddah he has a choice—come out of the cabin and fight in the open like a man or stay inside and force us to come in after him."

"Hell, he'll gun me for sure," Jess said.

"No, he won't. Men like Burns are born to the

feud and respect the parley. He'll let you deliver your message and walk back here."

"I wish I had your confidence," Jess said, his belly tight.

"Get it done, Sheriff. It's clouding up to rain and I don't want to get wet."

Jess handed off the reins to Koenig and stepped toward the cabin. The dry grass crunched under his boots and the roofless cabin's two burned-out windows seemed to stare at him with coal black eyes.

When he was within hailing distance, Jess shouted, "Jeddah Burns! Step outside and hear my words." He knew he sounded a tad melodramatic, but then this was an intense moment. The possibility of a bullet between the eyes concentrates a man's thoughts wonderfully.

"What the hell do you want?" This from the cabin. "Speak up, now."

"I have a message from Kurt Koenig," Jess said.

"I see him there," the man yelled. "Dirty yellow coward is scared to come close. State your business and be damned to ye for looking like that dog George Custer. He done for some of my kinfolk."

Jess, stung by the Custer remark, stepped a few yards closer and said, "Mr. Koenig says he's calling you out. He says for you to come face him and fight like a man, instead of hiding in the cabin like a frightened old woman."

"This is Caleb Burns," another, younger voice said. "Is that what he said to my pa?"

"Well, there was a lot more, about how your pa is

a fraidycat and how he's gutless and low-down, but I don't want to say it. Mr. Koenig told me that your pa is so mean he stole a widow woman's only milk cow and then pissed on her kindling, but I don't want to tell you that, either."

Jeddah Burns roared, "Damn it, we're coming out, and tell Koenig to be ready to get his work in because I aim to see that he's skinned an' his hide hung out to dry."

Jess backed away, wondering just how much old Jeddah set store by the parley. But he reached Koenig and the others without drawing a bullet.

"I caught the gist of it," the big man said. "Jeddah was loud enough."

Jess said, "You heard him say he's coming out?"

"I heard him," Koenig said. "Now we'll see."

Only two walls of the rock cabin still stood, the front and left side. It was enough to hide the Burns boys from view and it made their surprise attack all the more unexpected.

Digging spurs into their horses, they came around the cabin and headed straight for Jess and the others. Jeddah was in the lead. He fired and worked a Winchester from his shoulder and the passing breeze flattened his long gray beard against his chest.

Behind him Jess heard the mallet *thud!* of a bullet hitting flesh and one of Koenig's men screamed and hit the ground hard. Its stirrups flying, the man's panicked horse galloped away.

Without conscious thought, Jess found his Colt in his hand. He and Koenig fired at the same time.

Jeddah shrieked and threw up his arms, his rifle cartwheeling away from him. One of his sons—Jess later identified him as Jethro—let out a strangled cry of grief and fury and rode hard at Koenig, his reins trailing, a bucking revolver in each hand in the old hell-for-leather charge that Captain Quantrill had made so famous.

Koenig stood and worked his Colt, his face set and his legs spread wide. Bullets tugged at his coat but he fired steadily, refusing to give ground. Jethro jerked in the saddle as he was hit in the chest and his left arm suddenly flopped to his side and his revolver dropped to the ground. He tried to bring up his right arm but the momentum of his horse carried him past Koenig and he failed to get off a shot. The surviving rifleman behind Koenig jerked his mount to one side and fired into Jethro's belly as the young man thundered past him.

Jethro was done. His horse ran for about fifty yards, stopped dead and the man flew over its head and crashed onto the ground. Even at distance there was a distinct *snap!* as the man's neck broke.

Meantime Jess had his hands full with Caleb.

Not trusting to the charge like his brother, he drew rein, slid his rifle from the boot and slammed a shot at Jess. The bullet was close enough that it clipped a shallow arc from the top of Jess's left ear. Alarmed, he returned fire instinctively, a reaction to danger that had served him so well the night before. His bullet slammed into the receiver of Caleb's Winchester then ranged downward into the man's shoulder. Hit hard by the mangled round, his right shoulder a mess of blood and splintered bone, Caleb there and then decided to quit the fight.

"I'm out of it!" he yelled. He dropped his rifle and raised his good arm.

"Unbuckle your gun belt," Koenig said.

Caleb did as he was told and his holstered Colt dropped to the ground. "How's my pa and brother Jethro?" he said.

"Jethro is as dead as a mackerel and your pa is the same way," Koenig said. "I figure by now they're stringing wire in hell, boy."

Caleb's chest was hollow, his shoulders hunched forward as he battled to absorb pain. But his bloodless lips were pale under his mustache. "I told pa we should shoot it out from the cabin," he said. "But pa wouldn't listen. He was a horseback fighter, a thing Bill Anderson taught him. So Bloody Bill done for him in the end."

Caleb untied the red bandanna from around his neck and shoved it between his wounded shoulder and shirt. "What happens to me?" he said.

Koenig smiled. "I haven't made up my mind."

Caleb said, "Let me go back to Cooke County and I won't bother you no more."

"I think that will depend on a judge," Jess said. A thin trail of blood trickled down his ear. He recalled the law book he'd read from cover to cover when he was snowed in at a Kansas line camp one winter and said, "You made an affray and resisted arrest with violence aforethought to say nothing of attempted murder."

"What the hell does that mean?" Caleb said.

"It means you're in a heap of trouble, boy," Koenig said. "You're Caleb, right? How old are you?"

"Sixteen, maybe seventeen, I don't rightly know."

Koenig nodded and stepped to Jeddah's body. He used his boot to roll the old man on his back and pa's pale, sightless eyes stared at the clouding sky. "The old buzzard was going to skin me," Koenig said.

"Pa skun men afore an' a Comanche woman one time," Caleb said. "But only after they was dead, him being a church deacon an' all."

"I'm sure he'll be sadly missed by his congregation," Koenig said. Then, "So what do I do with you, Caleb? If I let you go you're sure to come back one day and shoot me in the back. Ain't that so?"

The young man shook his head. "I'm never coming back here, mister. I should never have left Cooke County in the first place."

"Your sister killed herself over a tinhorn gambler," Koenig said. "Did you know that? Cut her wrists. Filled a damned copper bathtub with her blood."

"No, I never knew that," Caleb said.

"Well, now you do," Koenig said.

"I guess mistakes were made," Caleb said.

"And you made them," Koenig said.

"Let's take him back to town and get his shoulder seen to, Kurt," Jess said.

"One of my men lies dead on the ground," Koenig said. "I can't let that go."

"He's an accessory to murder," Jess said. "He'll spend a big chunk of his life in Huntsville."

Koenig shook his head. "No, I don't want that. Let's be sporting about this matter."

He stepped to his horse, slid his Winchester from the boot and said, "Caleb, are you a sporting man?"

"I don't know," Caleb said.

"Well, we'll find out, won't we," Koenig said. "Jess, see that stunted mesquite tree over yonder to the right? How far off would you say that is?"

Jess surveyed the flat land, then said, "A hundred paces. No less that that."

"That was my impression, about a hundred yards or so," Koenig said. He smiled like a cobra smiles. "Here's a lark, Caleb. I'll give you a twenty-yard start before I start firing. If you can reach the mesquite I'll cease fire and you can travel on to Cooke County unharmed."

Koenig racked a .44-40 cartridge into the chamber. "I can't say fairer than that."

Caleb Burns was steadily losing blood and his face was ashen. "And if I don't want to play your game?" he said.

Koenig raised the rifle until it pointed at the young man's belly. "Then I'll gut-shoot you and leave you here. You'll scream for hours, Caleb, and when death finally comes it will be a blessing."

Caleb Burns read Koenig's face and knew he was bucking a stacked deck. He swung his horse around and kicked the animal into a gallop.

Koenig let him go. Without hurry, he kneeled on the ground and took up a firing position. A flurry of rain swept across the grama grass and in the distance thunder boomed.

"Don't do this, Kurt," Jess said.

The big man ignored him.

Caleb Burns had almost reached the mesquite. Thirty yards . . . twenty . . . ten . . . He drew rein when he reached the stunted tree and looked back. Then a moment of bravado that cost him his life.

Caleb had not pegged Kurt Koenig as an expert rifleman. The big man was a named draw fighter, trained to shoot across the width of a card table. Making long-range rifle shots didn't enter into his thinking.

An old proverb says, "By ignorance we mistake, and by mistakes we learn."

Caleb made a mistake by turning his horse broadside to Koenig and raising his hat. But he would not live long enough to learn from it.

Kurt Koenig's bullet hit an inch to the left of Caleb's nose. It was deflected slightly by bone, punched through the young man's neck and smashed into vertebrae, cutting the spinal cord.

Luckily for him, Caleb Burns was dead when he hit the ground.

Jess Casey was appalled. Koenig had executed the young man, murdered him and had lied to him. But the big man was smiling as his surviving gang member slapped him on the back and told him he'd done good.

"Hell, boss, even Dan'l Boone couldn't make a shot like that," the man said.

Koenig saw the shocked look on Jess's face and

said, "He should have kept on riding instead of making a grandstand play." Jess was at a loss for words and Koenig stepped into the silence. "You did well today, Jess, stood your ground and got your work in. I won't forget it come bonus time." Then, dismissing him: "Johnny, round up the horses and strip the bodies of guns and whatever else they might have. We'll let the coyotes bury them."

"Sure thing, boss," the man called Johnny said, grinning.

To Jess it sounded like one murderous thug addressing another.

"I won't forget it come bonus time."

Jess Casey had sold himself for thirty pieces of silver and now he began to understand just what that entailed.

CHAPTER ELEVEN

"Big gunfight today, my friend, three men dead," Dr. Sun said.

Jess Casey watched the moths fluttering around the oil lamp in his office, and then said, "I had a hand in it."

"And now your hand feels dirty?"

Jess nodded. "You could say that."

"Why do you stay?" Dr. Sun said. "This is not for you."

Smiling slightly, Jess said, "Doc, a man reaches my age and he's all stove-up with years of cowboy ing and he looks ahead to a future bright with what? I can tell you, bright with nothing."

"So Kurt Koenig holds your future in his own dirty hand?"

"He's my ticket out of here with enough money in my poke to start my own spread. Sometimes a man has to bite the bullet."

"And sit down with thieves."

"Thanks for fixing up my ear, Doc. It doesn't sting near as bad."

"Take a walk with me, Sheriff," Dr. Sun said.

He'd swapped his colorful robe for a high-button suit, an oilskin cape and a bowler hat, though his long pigtail still hung down his back.

"All right," Jess said. "It's about time I made my rounds."

Dr. Sun said, "Tuesday night is a quiet time in the Half Acre. We can see the sights at leisure."

Jess rose from behind his desk and filled the empty chambers of his revolver, leaving the one under the hammer unloaded.

"Lead on, Doc," he said. Then, remembering, he asked, "How are Zeus and Nate Levy coming along?"

"Zeus is a strong man. He is recovering very well. Mr. Levy is older, but he has heart. He will be fine."

"Glad to hear it," Jess said. He shrugged into his slicker.

Main Street was much less crowded than usual, the rain and thunder keeping people inside. The sporting crowd and the hustlers were content to leave it alone and rest up for Wednesday, the middle of the week, when things started to snap.

In a steady downpour Jess and Dr. Sun walked only as far as 14th Street, where the little physician made a right turn past the Variety grocery store. After a stretch of dark, open ground the lamp-lit Du Louvre Hotel stood at the corner of 14th and

Rusk but Dr. Sun stopped short of the building and said, "Now we cross the waste. Be most careful of mud puddles."

Fastidiously, Dr. Sun carefully studied the ground before every tiny tread, his highly polished shoes hovering for just a moment before committing themselves to another step. For his part Jess walked boldly, a booted man having no such concerns.

Through the rain-swept gloom Jess saw a series of cabins, their iron chimneys smoking against the damp, then a larger structure with four windows on the wall facing them, each draped with red curtains.

"And here lies our destination, my friend," Dr. Sun said. "See the alley there? That's where we will gain entry."

Jess peered through the rain. "It's a pretty big place," he said.

"It should be. This house is owned by Mr. Koenig and he loves to do everything on a grand scale."

"What is this place?" Jess said.

"You'll find out soon enough," Dr. Sun said.

The house was situated in a vile-smelling alley that ran between rank, run-down tenements. "Those are where the poor of the Half Acre dwell," Dr. Sun said. "The tenements are places of poverty, misery and despair, of beaten women, abused children and drunken, violent men. Hear the wails, my friend, the female screams, the roar of drunkards, all of which Mr. Koenig helped create, since most of the tenements are owned by him."

Thunder roared, lightning flashed and Jess Casey

unbuttoned his slicker to free his gun. This was a
terrible place, a stinking slum he hadn't known
existed. It was hell on earth.

Dr. Sun rapped on the door with his cane and it
opened a crack, just enough to allow a Chinese face
to peer out. The man at the door smiled in recognition and beckoned the physician to come inside.
Jess, wary, followed him.

What he saw horrified him.

The entire building was a single, long room with
a low ceiling. The air was thick with brown smoke
that smelled like musky incense and lining both
sides were tiered wooden berths, like the crowded
bunks of an army barracks. Bodies lay stretched out
in the berths, both male and female with no attention to modesty, some of them Chinese but most
white. The room was dark but here and there the
red coals of long pipes winked first bright then
dull then bright again. Most of the smokers lay in
silence, their eyes closed, but others mumbled to
themselves and a few laughed at some joke they
heard only in dreams. A few stooped Chinese
moved among them, offered new pipes and spoke
in whispers.

"What is this?" Jess said.

"It is an opium den," Dr. Sun said. "People come
here to dream."

A tiny Chinese girl ran to offer Jess a pipe, but
Dr. Sun waved her away. The girl took no offense
but merely turned and vanished into the red-
winking gloom.

"I've heard of opium," Jess said. He realized he

was whispering and said louder, "But I've never seen anything like this before."

Dr. Sun said, "My friend, opium is a most wonderful drug, a gentle, caring lover who embraces you in angel wings and takes you to paradise, giving you a few years of warmth and affection. Then, without warning, one day the lover turns into a snarling beast that leads you down to the depths of hell. The dreams it imparts become nightmares."

"You've smoked the stuff?" Jess said.

"I was addicted to both opium and morphine," Dr. Sun said. "Together they almost destroyed me. Even now I yearn for a pipe or two or the needle. I want so badly to visit paradise again . . ." The little physician's black eyes glittered. He violently shook his head. "But there is no going back, not now."

"I'm starting to feel dizzy from the smoke, Doc," Jess said. "I've seen enough of this place. Let's get out of here."

"Wait, there is still something I brought you here to see. Step over here. Now, do you recognize her?"

Jess's eyes widened in shock. "Oh my God, yes, that's the girl who told me about Zeus getting beat up in the alley. Her name is Lillian Burke."

"And she's a morphine and opium fiend," Dr. Sun said.

The girl lay on her side, her eyes closed, the pipe smoking between her lips. Her expensive clothes were in disarray and her undone hair fell across her face.

Jess kneeled beside her berth and touched the

girl's naked shoulder. "Lillian, it's me," he said. "Sheriff Casey, remember?"

The girl did not respond though her parted lips moved slightly.

"She can't hear you, Sheriff," Dr. Sun said. "She is deep in dreams."

"I'm taking her home, out of here," Jess said.

"She won't thank you for it," Dr. Sun said.

A Chinese man tried to push Jess away from the unconscious girl, but Dr. Sun said a few sharp words in his own language and the man bowed and left.

Jess took the pipe from Lillian's mouth then lifted her in his arms. The girl's head dropped against his shoulder but she did not waken. He was surprised how light she was.

Jess walked to the door, pushed it open and stepped outside, deeply inhaling the clean, rain-washed air. When Dr. Sun stepped beside him, he said, "Where does her father live?"

The physician said, "No, take her to my home. Miss Burke's addiction is known to me and when she regains consciousness Mei-Xing will attend her. It is a service she has performed many times before."

"Should her father be told?" Jess said.

"Her father already knows. Lillian is twenty-two years old. He can't lock her away in a convent." Dr. Sun pushed an errant lock of hair from the girl's forehead and said, "Don't let what you've seen tonight influence your relationship with Kurt Koenig. It's too early to draw a line in the sand."

"I don't understand," Jess said. He did his best to protect the girl from the rain with his slicker. "I'm sheriff, of Hell's Half Acre at least. I can arrest him."

"And you'd be dead less than an hour later," Dr. Sun said. "No, that is not the way, at least not yet."

"Then what do you reckon I should do?" Jess said.

"For the moment just lie low and do your job. We will talk about this again very soon."

Lillian Burke stirred in Jess's arms and Dr. Sun said, "Come, we will go to my home now." Then, his face a study in suppressed anger, "Seventeen in three months, my friend."

"What does that mean?" Jess said.

"That is the number of drug fiends I have buried, and the toll still grows."

"And Koenig supplies the morphine?"

"Yes, and he's making himself rich in the process. Now come."

Jess carried the girl into the darkness. The rain fell on her face but there was not a thing he could do about it.

CHAPTER TWELVE

Scar Moseley needed a woman. Any woman so long as she was young. Well, youngish. Hell, not old.

The woman who'd just wrung the neck of a chicken and now stared at Scar from the coop would do nicely. She was youngish, thirty maybe, and plump. Her brown hair was pulled back in a bun and her large, motherly breasts strained against the thin stuff of her calico dress.

Scar watched the woman over the rim of the horn cup that he'd taken from the brick rim of the well. Nothing stirred in the sway-roofed cabin. Was she alone or were her menfolk asleep? "Hey, ma'am," he said. "You need some help around here?"

"Take a drink and ride on," the woman said. "We have nothing to give you."

"Having fried chicken for supper, are ye?" Scar said.

"That's none of your business," the woman said. She had brown eyes and under the hem of her dress her feet were large, bare and dusty.

"Your tone is not friendly," Scar said.

"We don't like strangers here," the woman said. Then, in a shout, "Henry!"

After a few moments the cabin door opened and a bald, middle-aged man stepped outside. "What is it, Effie?" Then his eyes locked on the tall, sinister figure of the man at the well. It was the last sight they ever saw.

Scar drew from his brass-studded holster and shot Henry through the heart.

The woman screamed, ran to her husband and in a flurry of white petticoats threw herself on his body. Behind her, a tall, gangly youth stood in the doorway, a shotgun in his hands. "Ma?" he said.

Then he saw the man dressed in black standing by the well. In his hand was a Colt trailing smoke from its barrel.

After a moment of confusion, the youth read the signs and lifted the scattergun. Scar shot him and the boy fell back into the cabin, triggering a shot that went into the air.

"Unfriendly folks, Effie," Scar said.

The woman rose and ran to her son. Scar, irritated, had to pull her out of the cabin by her kicking feet. "I like doing it outdoors, don't you?" he said to the now-terrified woman.

Then he threw himself on her.

Women were strange, Scar Moseley decided as he watched the naked woman washing herself with handfuls of dirt she'd scooped up from the yard. He hands, face and body were soon streaked with black, and that annoyed Scar greatly. It was as though she was trying to turn herself into a colored woman. Born to prejudice, he would not even touch a black woman, let alone screw one.

"Stop that," Scar said. "Go wash with water. We're riding soon."

The woman called Effie ignored him, rubbed dirt over her heavy breasts and softly sang something that sounded like a hymn.

Effie had gone to a distant place from where she'd never return, and Scar felt a twinge of disappointment. He'd planned on keeping her for a few months, but he was damned if he was taking a crazy woman to his place. He shot her with regret, not for her but for his ruined plan.

Scar retrieved his pocketknife. It was time to leave his *carte de visite* and ride on before anybody happened this way.

On the door of the cabin he carved his own profile, exaggerating the size of his nose as he always did, and then he added a livid, jagged scar that matched the one on his left cheek. Like an artist admiring his work, he stepped back and studied the carving for a while. Then, satisfied, he mounted his horse and rode away.

CHAPTER THIRTEEN

"What I just told you, Sheriff, I saw with my own two eyes," Len Hawley said. "Henry, Effie and their son, Thomas, all dead. Effie was nekkid and all covered with dirt and she'd been shot just like her old man and son."

"Was robbery the motive?" Mayor Harry Stout said, his face stern.

"Nothing taken that I could see," Hawley said. "Even the Clark's old plow horse was still in the barn. And there was a dead chicken lying in the yard."

"Dead chicken?" Jess said.

"Probably Effie had wrung its neck afore she was . . . well, you know."

Hawley, a puncher for one of the local ranches, reached into his shirt pocket and produced a page from his tally book. "And there was this carved into the door. I made a drawing."

Hawley tried to pass the paper to Jess Casey, but Stout, as bullying as ever, grabbed it out of his hand.

He studied the drawing and after a moment his face turned ashen.

"Oh my God, he's back," he said.

"Give me that," Jess said. He grabbed the paper and looked at it. It was a crude drawing of a man with a big nose, long hair and there was what looked like a scar on his cheek. "You know this feller?" he said to Stout.

"I know of him," Stout said. The fat man appeared shaken, his original complaint about the number of stray dogs in the Half Acre momentarily forgotten. "His name is Scar Moseley, a killer out of the New Mexico Territory. He's murdered and raped his way across Texas and last I heard he'd killed sixty people, men and women and children. He sometimes works as a gun for hire and he'll cut anybody in half with a shotgun for fifty dollars."

"You said he's back," Jess said. "Was he here in Fort Worth?"

"Yes," Stout said. "He worked for Kurt Koenig for a spell, but even Kurt couldn't handle him, so he fired him."

"Did Moseley take it hard?" Jess said.

Stout said, "Hell no. He and Koenig are two of a kind, ruthless and good with guns, and he got a good payoff, so he'd nothing to kick about."

"Then why is he back?" Jess said.

"I can't even guess," Stout said. "But I bet there's a wanted dodger for him around this office somewhere. Last I heard there was a five-thousand bounty on Scar's head, dead or alive." The mayor smiled. "If there's anybody crazy enough to try to collect it."

A brewer's dray trundled past the window with the name BURKE'S BEER painted on the side. A couple of ragged urchins rode on top of the barrels, a precarious and dangerous perch.

"Ah well," Stout said with the air of a man closing the matter, "thank you for the information, Len. I'll send out Big Sal with a burial party to bury the poor, hurting dead."

"Where is the Clark place?" Jess asked the puncher.

"About six, seven miles to the west of us, on the big bend of Bear Creek," Hawley said. "I reckon Big Sal knows where it is. She's buried folks from miles around."

The cowboy rose to his feet, touched his hat and left.

"Good man, that," Stout said after Hawley left. "And now to the business on hand, Sheriff Casey. I'm getting many complaints from merchants about the number of stray curs in the Half Acre and I want you to—"

"What about Scar Moseley?" Jess said.

Stout's florid face registered surprise. "What about him?"

"He just killed three people, a family."

"Let Scar be, Sheriff. He'll be brought to justice soon enough. You can bet that the Rangers are on his trail." Stout shook his head. "No, no, your responsibilities lie here in Fort Worth. Now about those curs—"

"I'm going after him, Mayor," Jess said. "I'm either a lawman or I'm not."

"Or you want the reward."

"I don't care about the reward."

"Damn it all, man, don't think for one moment you can raise a posse in this town," Stout said. "No one, and I mean no one, will take on Scar Moseley. He's . . . he's . . . an infernal machine."

Jess rose to his feet. "I'll bring him in, Mayor. You can hang him at your convenience."

Stout sighed and shook his head. "All right, maybe Kurt Koenig can talk some sense into you. Don't leave until we get back."

Alone in the office after the mayor stormed out, Jess tried to analyze his decision to go after Moseley. Was it the reward? He didn't think so. How about an act of bravado, trying to prove what a big man he was? Jess dismissed that thought immediately. Then there could be only one reason: he was taking his job as a peace officer seriously.

Jess considered that and could not dispute it.

He rode out of town a few minutes later. He didn't wait for Mayor Stout to return.

CHAPTER FOURTEEN

Big Sal had not yet visited the Clark farmstead on Bear Creek. The bodies were still there, buzzing with fat, black flies.

The cabin was situated on a pleasant spot, surrounded by stands of ash, juniper and wild oak. Jays quarreled among the trees and rainbow-colored butterflies fluttered among meadows of wildflowers.

Jess Casey brought sheets from the cabin and covered the bodies. He felt strangely ashamed that he had seen Mrs. Clark's nakedness, and for some reason his stove-up back and wrecked knees began to ache.

Jess was far from being an expert tracker, but the hoofprints left by a large horse were clear enough on the ground. Scar Moseley's trail headed north, into grass and brush country.

Groaning, Jess stepped into the saddle and followed the tracks. The sun was hot, the sky pale blue, all trace of the rain of yesterday gone. But the moisture had softened the ground and most of the time the tracks were well defined and deep. The drowsy day lulled Jess and once he almost dozed in the saddle. But his horse stumbled and he was startled awake.

All was still, the land around him silent but for the insects making their small music in the grass. Sweat trickled down Jess's back and he smelled only dust and sunbaked grass. There was no sign of Scar Moseley.

Thanking himself for remembering to fill his canteen at the pump behind his office, Jess drew rein and drank. He felt hot and sticky and his washed-out blue shirt clung to his back and shoulders. A fly buzzed around his sweaty face and he waved it away.

Jess kneed his horse forward then rounded a massive, humpbacked rock rimmed with cactus. Just fifty yards away, a saddled cow pony nosed for graze among the dry grama grass. He drew rein and his eyes scanned the area around the little paint and saw nothing more.

Jess dismounted and his hand on his Colt, he stepped carefully toward the pony. The little animal's head jerked up and it stared at him curiously for a few moments, then went back to cropping grass.

His foot in the stirrup, Jess got ready to mount again, but then he saw a boot sticking out of a patch of brush. He watched the boot for the space of a minute, wary of a trick, but then stepped carefully toward it. And then he saw the fallen man.

Sprawled on his back, his arms flung wide, there

was something familiar about the man. He wore a dull red shirt and a black-and-white cowskin vest. Len Hawley had worn such a vest.

It was the puncher, all right, and he was dead as he was ever going to be. There was a neat bullet hole between his open eyes and the middle finger of his right hand had been hacked away, leaving a bloody stump.

Taking a knee beside Hawley he noticed a white band of skin around the base of the dead man's sun-browned, severed finger. He'd worn a ring there that his killer wanted, and he'd been murdered for it. After a quick search of the body, Jess found nothing, indicating that Hawley had been robbed of whatever money and other valuables he'd carried. The tracks of a heavy horse and a man's booted feet were everywhere. They could belong only to Scar Moseley, since Hawley had been shot off his paint. Something turned over in Jess's belly. A man who could shoot like that was nobody to mess with.

The sun glinted on the silver star pinned to Jess's shirt, reminding him that for better or for worse he'd made himself a lawman. He had it to do.

Jess Casey wondered if Len Hawley was returning to his ranch when he met up with Scar Moseley. But if he knew about the five-thousand-dollar reward, had he tried to track him? Only Hawley knew the answer to that question and it had died with him.

Climbing into the saddle, Jess followed Moseley's

trail again, but this time more warily. Hawley's body had still been warm so Scar might be close, figuring he was safe.

Ten minutes later Jess smelled smoke. It was faint at first, just a trace in the wind, but as he rode the odor of burning wood grew stronger and with it the unmistakable tang of boiling coffee.

Jess swung out of the saddle and led his horse into a patch of juniper. He thought of taking his Henry but decided that if there was shooting it would be close-in work and he was increasingly confident about his newfound revolver skill. Besides, he'd never been any great shakes with a long gun.

Colt in hand he crossed about sixty yards of open ground that ended at the base of a gradual rise. Some twenty feet above his head the rise seemed to top off. More juniper grew on its crest and a thin trail of smoke rose from somewhere among the trees.

Moving as silently as he could, Jess climbed the rise. It was shallow enough that he reached the top easily. Lying flat on his belly he studied what lay ahead of him. Less than twenty yards away a tall black horse with four white socks was picketed near a clump of bunchgrass. To the left of the horse a man wearing a dark shirt sat with his left side to Jess. Smoke lifted from a small fire in front of him and the man was singing to himself as he studied the small object he turned in his fingers.

"Come on in," the man said without turning his head. "I've been expecting you, lawman."

Jess rose to his feet and said, "You're under arrest, Scar."

Now Moseley turned his head. "Is that a fact?" he said, grinning.

His belly lurching, Jess moved closer, then stopped and said, "I'm taking you back to Fort Worth, there to be hanged at Mayor Harry Stout's convenience. Get on your feet."

Scar Moseley didn't move. "Been watching you for quite a spell," he said. "First saw you when you put your horse into the trees. I was hunting wood at the time. I could have killed you real easy then, but I didn't. I knew I could do for you later . . . at Scar Moseley's convenience."

Advancing to within twenty-five feet of Moseley, Jess said, "I told you to get on your feet. I won't tell you again."

"You got the drop on me, huh?"

"Seems like."

"Then just don't shoot," Scar said. He grinned. "I've had a woman today and she relaxed me. Gettin' shot would spoil my mood, like."

"Get up, you damned scum," Jess said.

"Sure, lawman, sure," Moseley said. His dark, heavily browed face was evil. He got to his feet.

"Slowly now, unbuckle the gun belt, let it drop then step away from it."

"Anything you say, cap'n," Moseley said.

He went for his gun. His speed was incredible, fast as the snap of a bullwhip. Scar fired.

Jess felt the bullet thud into his chest and he fired back, way too slow, much too wild. But to his surprise he saw Scar stagger as a scarlet rose blossomed in the middle of his forehead. The man reeled, opened his mouth in shock then fell forward, his face raising flame and ash as it hit the campfire.

"Are you hit bad?"

Jess turned and looked into the handsome, concerned face of Kurt Koenig. The big man held a smoking Colt in his hand.

"I . . . I don't know," Jess said. He dropped to his knees. "He hit me in the chest."

"Let's take a look," Koenig said. Then he grinned. "When I bought that star for Hank Henley the jeweler told me the silver was so thick it could turn a bullet. He was right."

Koenig worked on the star for a few moments then pulled out a flattened bullet from its center. "Hold out your hand," he said. He dropped the lead into Jess's open palm and said, "You can show that to your grandkids. Make up lies about it."

Jess's chest hurt, as though he'd been hit by a sledgehammer, but he was otherwise unhurt. "Did I kill him?" he said.

"Hell no, I did," Koenig said. "I reckon your bullet is still traveling."

"Koenig, you saved my life," Jess said. "Damn you to hell."

The big man was taken aback, his face shocked. He said nothing.

"I don't want to be beholden to you, Koenig. I don't want to be beholden to you for anything," Jess said.

"Seems like you already are," Koenig said, his face stiff.

He stepped to the campfire, grabbed Scar Moseley's body by the back of the shirt and pulled the dead man's head out of the flames. Scar's face was blackened, just like Effie Clark's face had been. Koenig effortlessly dragged the man aside then stopped to pick up something. He studied it for a while then showed it to Jess. It was a silver band with a small oval stone.

"Yours?" Koenig said.

"It belongs to a dead cowboy," Jess said. "Moseley killed him for it."

Koenig said, "The dead man was Lonesome Len Hawley. He was a top hand for Abe Cameron and his Triple-T."

"I know his name," Jess said. "He came into town then reported the death of the Clark family."

"And went after Scar for the five thousand on his head? If he did it was a bad move. Well, now the reward is mine, but I'll remember you come bonus time, Jess." Koenig tossed the ring into the brush. "Cheap trash," he said.

"I don't want the reward and I don't want your bonus, Koenig," Jess said. "I plan to do my job."

The big man smiled and nodded. "Seems fair. Just don't plan too far ahead, huh?"

Without another word, Koenig stepped away. He saddled Scar's horse and then draped the dead man over its back. Scar's hanging hair moved in the wind like a mourning curtain and blood from his shattered head ticked on the grass.

Koenig mounted his own horse then gathered up the reins of the dead man's black. "Coffee's on the bile, Jess, get yourself some and bide awhile. I don't want to see you on my back trail."

"I'm no back shooter, Koenig," Jess said. "But don't underestimate me."

The big man smiled, his teeth very white. "I don't underestimate any man who's on the prod," he said. "Especially a broken-down puncher with a chip on his shoulder."

CHAPTER FIFTEEN

"How are you feeling, Nate?" Zeus said. A towering giant of a man, he leaned over the bed and stared down at the little man's battered face.

Nate Levy opened his eyes and sighed. "Oy, oy, oy, I'm dying and he's asking me conundrums."

Zeus grinned. "Nate, you'll never die unless you're tied down."

"What's the weather like?"

"Hot."

"Then why is this hotel room cold?"

"Because you've got no blood, Nate. You lost it all in the alley."

"How's that sheriff feller?"

"I saw him ride out of town this morning," Zeus said.

"He should keep on going. Fort Worth is no place for an honorable man. Besides coffee what did you bring me? What's in the poke?"

"A bacon and sourdough bread sandwich and a piece of apple pie. Hungry?"

"Why should I be hungry?" Nate said. "Am I lying in this bed near death and have had nothing to eat for days? And I'm a Jew. Can I eat pork?"

"It's bacon, Nate."

"I can smell it. But you're right, bacon isn't pork. I remember my mother saying to me, 'Nathanial, never eat pork because it's not kosher. But bacon, like shellfish, is all right in moderation.' Pass the poke."

"The pork poke," Zeus said, smiling. "The bacon bag."

"Damned impertinence," Nate said. "Now don't get uppity on me, boy."

As the little man ate ravenously, Zeus stepped to the window, his attention immediately caught by events in the street.

"Kurt Koenig's bringing in a dead man," he said.

"Is it the sheriff?" Nate said, his jaws suddenly still.

"No. Some ranny dressed in black with long hair."

"Don't know him," Nate said, going back to his food.

"Me, neither," Zeus said.

"Well, Koenig's always shooting somebody," Nate said.

Zeus said, "I'm going to see what happened. Do you need anything, boss?"

"Yeah, a new body. You got one of those? Oy, oy, oy, the damned bacon's given me dyspepsia. I told you I shouldn't eat pork."

* * *

Zeus, dressed in a gray suit that bulged over his huge arms and a plug hat of the same color, stepped onto the hotel porch and almost knocked into Dr. Sun.

The little physician touched the brim of his bowler and said, "Well met, Zeus. I'm on my way to check on my patient. How is he?"

"He ate bacon and now he has dyspepsia," Zeus said. His face was the color of polished mahogany, split by a toothy smile.

"I told him he could have the white of an egg and nothing more," Dr. Sun said. "He's not smoking cigars, is he?"

"Not while I was there, Doc," Zeus said.

"Then let him cope with indigestion for a while. It will serve him right. Now step over there and join me on the bench."

Zeus crossed the porch and sat and the little physician joined him and for a while Dr. Sun gazed into the waning day and said nothing.

"I saw Kurt Koenig bring in a dead man," Zeus said. His hands rested on his thighs, the knuckles the size of walnuts and deeply scarred.

"Yes, the bandit Scar Moseley. He's quite dead."

"Koenig plug him?"

"Yes, he did. Which brings me to the reason I wish to talk to you, my gigantic friend."

"Then talk away, Doc," Zeus said. "I've got cauliflower ears but I still hear pretty good."

"What do you think of our new sheriff?" Dr. Sun said.

"Well, I guess he saved my life, Doc. I owe him."

"One day he will go up against Kurt Koenig and his cohorts. We must assist him in every way we can."

"I'm a pugilist," Zeus said. "I know nothing about guns."

"And I am a swordsman," Dr. Sun said. He smiled. "One of my hidden talents."

"Fists and swords against Colts won't take us far, Doc. Well, maybe as far as the graveyard."

"As I said, we must do what we can. Will you support me?"

Zeus had no time to answer as a fracas that had just broken out at the Silver Garter across the street attracted his attention.

A sturdy man wearing an ill-fitting store-bought suit charged through the saloon's open doors. He had a woman by the arm and dragged her into the street. Then he turned and roared to someone still inside, "You leave my damn wife alone, Dickson."

Tall and as elegantly dressed as a gambler, the man called Dickson appeared, a nickel-plated Colt in his hand. "Be damned to ye for a scoundrel, Ed Manion, Ella has had enough of your abuse," he yelled. "She's living with me now."

"No, Alan, he'll kill you!" Ella, her hair in disarray, fled to Dickson and threw herself into his arms.

Manion drew a British Bulldog revolver from

under his coat and called, "Ella, you step aside, for I intend to kill that adulterer."

Frantic now, the woman stepped in front of Dickson and spread her arms wide. "No!" she shrieked. "Don't shoot my Alan. I love him."

"Then damn you, too," Manion said. He fired. His bullet hit Ella in the stomach and she dropped to the ground without a sound.

Dickson, his face black with anger, stepped back and took up a duelist's stance, right arm extended, revolver at eye level, left foot behind the right heel, his left arm held stiffly behind him, ending in a tight fist. He fired.

Manion took the hit high in his left shoulder, and a red rose blossomed on his suit coat as his collarbone shattered. But determined to see it through, he stood his ground and shot back. The .44 round hit the shin of Dickson's right leg and the elegant man dropped to one knee, cursing. He returned Manion's fire, shot once, missed, shot again. The second round was aimed true and Manion was hit again.

Manion, his blood up, sought to close the distance. He staggered across the muddy street and at a range of just ten paces Dickson shot him again. Losing his balance and nearly falling, he cursed Dickson for a lowlife and fired again, a clean miss. Dickson, yelling obscenities, tried to stand but he tumbled and fell on his back into the street. But an instant later he raised his Colt and he and

Manion fired at the same time, separated by just three feet of open ground. That exchange did great execution and both gunmen received mortal wounds. Manion took a hit to the chest and dropped to his knees, and Dickson, gut-shot, fell on his left side. The local newspaper later said that Ed Manion yelled, "Oh, I am slain." And that Alan Dickson uttered, "Yes, take that, you vile fiend."

But Zeus and Dr. Sun witnessed the gunfight and told the reporter that both men dropped without a sound. This was the truth of what happened—but it did not make good copy.

Dr. Sun was already on his feet and about to enter the smoke-streaked scene when the last act of the drama played out, dropping the curtain on a frontier Romeo and Juliet.

Ella dragged herself off the porch, leaving behind her a trail of blood like the track of a snail, and crawled to her lover. She took his gory hand in hers and said, "Alan, I think he killed the baby."

"Ella . . . Ella . . ." Dickson whispered, but then death took him and he said no more.

Dr. Sun stepped toward Ella, but the woman did something that shocked him and stopped him in his tracks. She grabbed Dickson's fallen Colt, aimed at her kneeling husband, who was gushing blood from his mouth, and fired. The bullet tore a great hole in Manion's chest and he whispered, "Ella," then collapsed flat on his face.

The woman then dropped the gun and was still

alive when Dr. Sun kneeled beside her and gently cradled her head in his arm.

"The baby?" Ella said. Her lips were as white as parchment.

Dr. Sun said, "The baby will be fine and so will you."

Ella smiled and then died and joined the baby within her.

Dr. Sun rose to his feet just as Kurt Koenig stepped outside the Silver Garter. He glanced at the bodies in the street then smiled. "So they finally had it out over Ella."

"Shot it out, Mr. Koenig," a small man with a red-veined face said. "Manion killed his own wife."

Koenig looked over at Dr. Sun. "They all dead?"

"Yes, all four of them," the physician said.

"I only count three," Koenig said.

Dr. Sun said, "Ella was with child."

"Too bad," Koenig said. "And too bad the shooting woke me from a sound nap." He turned to the red-veined man and spun him a silver dollar. "Rube, go bring Big Sal. Tell her to clean this mess off my doorstep."

"Sure thing, Mr. Koenig."

Koenig looked over Dr. Sun's shoulder and said, "Ready to fight again, Zeus?"

The big fighter nodded. "I'm always ready."

"Good. Tell your manager to come see me. I got a pug coming in from Chicago who'll give you a contest. He's a black boy like you. They say he has a killer left."

"I look forward to meeting the gentleman," Zeus said.

"Then so be it," Koenig said. He stepped back inside.

"Well?" Dr. Sun said after the man was gone.

"All the help we can give him," Zeus said.

"I thought you might say that, black boy," Dr. Sun said.

And both men grinned.

CHAPTER SIXTEEN

The day was shading into the night and the lamps were lit in Hell's Half Acre as Jess Casey brought in Len Hawley's body.

A couple of belligerent young punchers recognized the dead man and went immediately on the prod.

"Here, what happened to Len?" a freckled towhead asked as he grabbed Jess's reins. "He has friends in this town."

"I didn't kill him," Jess said. "Now take your goddamned hands off my horse or I'll shoot them off."

Jess was all played out, his nerves as taught as fence wire, and the puncher recognized it. He dropped the reins as though they were red-hot. "Just askin', mister," he said. "No offense intended."

Slightly ashamed for his outburst, Jess said, "He was killed by Scar Moseley for the ring he wore. Look at his left hand."

Both the young cowboys studied the stump of Hawley's finger and then the towhead, looking slightly sick, said, "I didn't know Scar was still around these parts. Did you do fer him?"

"No. Kurt Koenig did," Jess said. "Shot him between the eyes."

The puncher grinned. "Good ol' Kurt."

"Yeah," Jess said. "Good ol' Kurt." Then, "Now, will you give me the road?"

"Wait," the towhead said. He had pale blue eyes. "Len would want to be laid to rest on the Triple-T. We'll take him home."

Jess tossed the kid the reins of the paint pony. "Len died for nothing," he said. "See he's buried right."

"We will," the puncher said. "Me and Bill here will ride out right away afore it gets too late, see on account of how Len was always afeard of the dark."

"Well, he's in endless darkness now, isn't he?" Jess said.

Jess Casey took care of his horse then flopped behind his desk. He poured himself three fingers of Old Crow and built a cigarette, willing himself to relax. He'd made his feelings clear to Kurt Koenig and he was sure the big man would make the next move. But what might it be? Would he take his bullet-holed star and tell him he was through? That was the most realistic possibility, but exhausted as he was, Jess decided to postpone any thoughts on that topic until tomorrow.

He sipped the whiskey and drew deep on his

cigarette, eyes closed, his head resting against the back of the chair.

The door opened and he heard the rustle of skirts.

"The office is closed and the sheriff has gone fishing," he said without opening his eyes.

"I came to thank you."

Jess recognized the voice and jolted upright in his chair. "Miss Burke, what are you doing here?"

Lillian Burke smiled. "As I said, I came to thank you. May I sit?"

"Of course," Jess said. He rose to his feet and made a fuss of adjusting the chair before the girl sat. Lillian wore a dress of amber-colored silk that was as glossy as her hair. A small hat with a ship under sail perched on the top of her swept-up ringlets. She carried a long-handled parasol the same shade as her dress and it was as lacy and feminine as she was.

She'd been in an opium coma the night before, sweaty, babbling and disheveled, but now she looked as fresh as a spring morning, as though she'd just stepped out of a bandbox.

Lillian refused a drink then said, "Mei-Xing Sun told me what you did. You were very *galant*, Sheriff, a knight in shining armor, but I really didn't need rescue."

"But you were in that terrible place . . ."

The girl smiled. "The Green Buddha is not a terrible place. Once I enter I'm soon transported to wonderful destinations on the wings of dreams. It's a fabulous flight. Do you understand?"

"Miss Burke—"

"Call me Lillian, for heaven's sake."

"Opium is a drug."

"Of course it is and so is morphine, its bastard child, and I love them both. Have you slept with a woman, Sheriff?"

Jess was wary of a trap. "Yes . . . yes, of course I have."

"Opium is better." Lillian giggled. "Or so I'm told by my gentlemen friends." Still smiling, her face that of an angel, she said, "Please don't rescue me again or I'll be very cross with you." She rose to her feet. "I'm perfectly safe, you know."

Jess said, "Anyone, I mean . . . oh hell, I mean you could be taken advantage of in that place."

"Raped, you mean?" Lillian said.

"Yes. Exactly that."

"A man tried that at the Green Buddha once. He lay beside a dreaming girl and tried to have his way with her," Lillian said.

"Was it you?" Jess said.

"No. She was someone else, but a girl I knew. The man's name was Pettibone and later they found his body in Rusk Street, his manly parts in Houston Street and his head, well, his head has never been found."

Lillian stepped to the door, stopped and blew Jess a kiss from her beautiful scarlet mouth. "Bye-bye, gallant knight," she said.

Jess said, "Lillian, I'll do my best to shut that den down."

The girl smiled. "Oh dear, Sheriff, then Kurt Koenig will surely kill you."

The door slammed shut and Jess felt a great sense of loss. Never in his life had he seen a woman as beautiful as Lillian Burke and he knew he was falling in love with her. But she had another, greater love in her life that she would not forsake, an ardent but fickle lover named Opium.

Jess drained his glass, and poured another. He laid the drink beside him and buried his face in his hands. Somehow he'd lost his way and had ridden into a box canyon of his own making. Now there was nowhere to go but back the way he'd come . . . to a life without Lillian, a life without joy or purpose.

CHAPTER SEVENTEEN

Luke Short didn't like what was coming down.

The two Panther City Boys, big, belligerent and boozed up, were hunting trouble and they'd already scared off a dozen regular customers. It was the midnight hour and the White Elephant should be jumping, but it was as quiet as the city library and the piano player, threatened with death if he didn't play "Juanita" the whole night long, had slunk away.

The girls had tried their best, but the Panther City Boys, being employees of Kurt Koenig, the richest and most powerful man in Fort Worth, reckoned their exalted status entitled them to free ones. Mexican standoff had resulted. The four girls sulked at a table and the boys, hunting trouble, let them.

Short was not an even-tempered man and his rage simmered as he stood behind the bar and waited for customers who would never arrive. The last thing he wanted to do was offend Koenig and

get run out of town. But a man has his limit and
when the boys began to jeer, openly comparing
breast sizes and then tossing their empty glasses in
the girls' direction, he reached his.

Short disliked gun belts. He said they constricted
his bowel movements, and that night he carried
his fancy Colt in his waistband. He stepped from
behind the bar, eased closer to the two men and
said, "You boys pipe down and let the ladies alone."
Luke purposely separated himself from the two
thugs by about five feet of smoky air. Drunk as they
were, the Panther City Boys didn't pay his move any
heed but the regular bartender, a long-faced man
well used to witnessing shootings and cuttings,
knew what his boss was about and allowed a smile
to touch his lips.

The bigger of the two men, a violent, profane
brute called Whitey Dowell, grinned and said,
"Ladies? They're whores and they belong on a hog
ranch."

"That," Short said, "is a matter of opinion."

"It's my opinion," Dowell said. "And it's the only
one that matters in this dump."

"You tell him, Whitey," said his companion,
a vicious, slack-mouthed youth named Dopey
Dawson, who was wanted for murder and rape in
half a dozen states and territories. He slammed his
glass on the bar. "Fill this, bartender," he said.

"Dopey, you've had enough," Short said. "And
that goes for you as well, Whitey. Come back tomorrow when you've both sobered up."

Now, that was a reasonable request, but Dowell

and Dawson were not reasonable men, not that night or any other.

"You throwin' us out, Luke?" Dowell said. His face was stiff, his carrion-eater eyes glittering. He wore a holstered revolver as did Dopey Dawson, and they had both killed men before.

"No, Whitey, I'm just politely asking you to leave," Short said.

"Go to hell, you little runt," Dowell said. And Dawson smirked as they both turned to the bar and loudly demanded whiskey.

Short waited for a few moments then said, "Turn and face me, gentlemen. I have something to say."

Whitey turned, looking down on Short from his great height as though he were a dog turd on the boardwalk. "Then say it," he said. "And be civil or I'll tear this stinking whorehouse down around your ears."

Dopey Dawson, being of somewhat low intelligence, merely smirked again.

Luke smiled, always a bad sign. "I'll be as courteous as I can, boys," he said. "Now I'm not asking you to leave, I'm telling you."

In later years wise men talking around potbellied stoves in the dead of winter opined that Whitey should have remembered that Luke had gunned Jim Courtright and nobody thought Jim was a bargain.

Maybe Whitey did remember but didn't give a damn. We'll never know because he made the fatal mistake of drawing down on Short, so no one got a chance to ask him.

Whitey Dowell was good, fast on the draw and shoot, and actually got off the first shot. But he fired while his Colt was coming up and he missed low and to the left. Luke returned fire. It was said of Short that he was the undertakers' friend, because he shot his opponents where it didn't show. Maybe that's why he shot Whitey in the belly. Hit hard, Dowell took a step back, his mouth quivering. Luke directed his attention to Dopey Dawson, whose Remington was still clearing leather. He fired. The bullet hit Dopey's trigger finger and then ranged wild. Horrified, Dawson dropped his gun and stared at the bloody stump of his mangled digit. Luke saw he was out of it for now and he and Whitey exchanged shots. Neither scored a hit. The shock wearing off, replaced by pain, Dowell thumbed off three more rounds. One tore through the loose cotton of Luke's shirt but the other two were wide. Steadying himself, concentrating on the sights and trigger, Luke fired and his aim was true. The bullet hit Whitey high in the forehead and the man dropped, blood already staining his face.

"I'm done, Luke!" Dopey said. He had his hand on his right wrist and held up the gory stump of his finger for Short to see.

"Damn you, this is a shooting scrape," Luke yelled. "Pick up the gun in your other hand and get to your work."

Lily La Royale, formerly Bessie Baggett from Coldwater, Kansas, decided it was time to sum up the matter. She drew a Remington derringer from her garter and at a range of three feet shot Dopey Dawson in the head.

Big Sal later displayed both corpses in the window of her premises and expressed her irritation that Lily and Luke had shot them where it showed.

During those moments of ear-ringing unreality that follow a gunfight, Luke Short was appalled. The shooting deaths of two of his men was not a thing that Kurt Koenig would overlook or be inclined to write off as a misunderstanding. Now if Luke wanted to hang on to the White Elephant he'd have to fight for it.

Kurt Koenig stepped into the White Elephant just as Big Sal was leaving, a dead man in each arm. "They're yours, Kurt," she said.

"I know," Koenig said. "Whitey Dowell and Dopey Dawson, two good men shot down like dogs."

Big Sal hefted Whitey's bloody corpse higher under her hairy armpit. "They'll be sadly missed," she said. "Heaven has two more angels."

Angry as he was, even Koenig saw the humor in that. "I wouldn't bet the farm on it, Sal," he said.

"Nor me, either," the woman said.

Koenig stepped to the bar. He had four Panther City Boys with him, each wearing a deputy's star. "Where is he?" Koenig said.

The bartender thumbed over his shoulder. "Back room. He's expecting you."

"I bet he is," Koenig said. He turned to his men.

"One of you boys go get Sheriff Casey and bring him here. You others stay here at the bar, but I want you sober. Luke can be almighty sudden."

"I guess Whitey and Dopey learned that the hard way," one of the men said.

"And they're not the first," Koenig said.

He rounded the bar, ducked through a bead curtain, passing a half-naked girl on the way, and walked to the heavy walnut door facing him. "Luke!" he yelled. "It's Kurt Koenig. I'm coming in, so don't make any fancy moves."

"The door's open," Short said. "I want to see empty hands and a smile, like you were visiting kissin' kin."

"After what's happened I don't feel much like smiling, Luke," Koenig said.

"Then empty hands will do," Short said. "And remember, I can drill ya."

"I'm coming in, Luke." Koenig opened the door and stepped inside.

Short sat behind a massive oak desk facing him, a Colt steady in his hands. "They drew down on me, Kurt. I got five witnesses who'll say Whitey, God rest him, skinned his piece first." The Colt didn't waver. "That's how it was and I'm through talking about it."

"Do you ever offer a man a drink?" Koenig said.

Luke's Colt motioned to a row of crystal decanters on a table pushed against the far wall. Above the table, draped in black crepe, was a portrait of the gallant Custer. "Help yourself," he said.

Koenig nodded to the picture. "Looks like our new sheriff."

"Don't it, though," Luke said.

"I've sent for him," Koenig said as he poured himself a drink.

"Why's that?" Luke said.

"Keep him busy and out of my hair."

Koenig returned to the desk and sat in the overstuffed chair opposite Short. "I could burn this place down, Luke," he said. "With you inside it."

"You could try," Short said.

"Put that damned gun down and listen."

Luke opened a drawer, laid the Colt inside, then said, "I'm all ears, Kurt."

"I have a plan and we can avoid future unpleasantness if you'll agree to work with me," Koenig said.

"Jim Courtright wanted protection money," Luke said. "I refused to work with him."

"Nothing that crude, Luke. Come now, we're both businessmen."

Short sighed and said, "Then let's hear it."

"The White Elephant is not within the limits of the Half Acre, properly speaking," Koenig said. "It doesn't have the same, shall we say, stigma, of the Silver Garter. In other words, respectable folk come here."

"Most of them are, I guess. That is, until your ruffians showed up tonight and scared them off."

"A misunderstanding, obviously," Koenig said, waving a dismissive hand. He smiled like a cobra. "That is, if you agree to my proposition."

"Are you trying to blackmail me, Kurt?" Luke said.
"Yes."

"I figured that. So what's your proposition? If I dare ask."

"I want to sell opium in the White Elephant."

"Huh?" Luke said, shocked. "You mean turn my place into an opium den?"

"Yes. For the respectable folks of Fort Worth. And 'opium den' is so coarse, Luke. The upper classes prefer to call it a relaxation parlor. Before you object, let me say that with my funding we can renovate this place, plenty of brass and red velvet, gambling table, a score of pretty girls on hand, and we'll stock the bar with the best wines, spirits and cigars in Texas." Koenig leaned forward in his chair. "Now what do you say?"

"I say, what's in it for me?" Luke said.

"Forty percent of all monies taken," Koenig said. "Luke, I'm talking more than a hundred thousand a year. You'll be a rich man."

"What about the product?" Luke said.

"Opium arrives in San Francisco by sea from India and Burma and is distributed from there. Our supply is assured for years to come."

Luke Short rubbed his temples, then said, "Let me study on it for a few days, Kurt."

"I'll wait five days for an answer, Luke," Koenig said. "If you say yes, then we will become friends and business partners."

"And if I say no?" Luke said.

"Then we will be the bitterest of enemies."

"You sure lay it on the line, don't you, Kurt?"

"With so much money at stake, is there any other way?"

Luke said, "I reckon that's so."

He caught a glow of triumph in Koenig's eyes and it troubled him.

CHAPTER EIGHTEEN

"It's all over, Sheriff," Luke Short said. "The city marshal was here and agreed that it was self-defense. I've got five witnesses who will swear to it."

"City marshal. You mean Kurt Koenig," Jess Casey said.

"Marshal Koenig, yes," Short said. His eyes slid from Jess's face.

"What happened?"

"Two troublemakers drew down on me and I had to kill them both," Luke said. He said nothing about Lily's role in the affray, fearing that she might become a target of Panther City Boys out for revenge.

"Cut-and-dried, huh?" Jess said.

"I'm afraid so," Short said.

"Then why did Koenig want me here?"

"To carry out an investigation, I suppose," Short said. "I guess you'll want to talk to the witnesses."

"I don't think that will be necessary," Jess said. He had been wakened from bed and he was fatigued, his shirt hanging out of his pants and a two-day growth of stubble on his chin. "I'm sure Koenig covered everything."

"He did," Short said. "He's a very thorough man."

Jess looked at the little gambler as though seeing him for the first time. Short seemed agitated. Something was troubling him. Was he holding something back about the killings?

"Maybe I will talk to the witnesses," Jess said.

"My girls were four of them, but they've all gone to bed," Short said.

"Who is the fifth?"

"My bartender. His name is Gus Kelly."

Jess said, "Then I'll talk to him first."

"Whitey Dowell threw down on Mr. Short first, Sheriff," Kelly said. "Then Dopey Dawson—"

"Dopey? That was his name?"

"That's what folks called him on account of how Dawson was a little slow. Nobody knows what his real given name was. Anyhoo, Dopey pulled his gun and Mr. Short killed them both. It was a fair fight, Sheriff, if you consider two against one fair."

Luke stepped beside Jess. "Do you want me to wake the girls?" he said.

"I reckon not," Jess said. "They're all going to say the same thing."

"That's because they all saw the same thing," Short said.

Jess nodded. "Yeah, I guess they did at that."

* * *

Jess Casey made his way along the boardwalk, eager to return to his cot. A horned moon rode high in the sky and the coyotes yipped among the warehouses and yards along Houston Street where the rats lived. He had almost reached the sheriff's office when footsteps pounded behind him. Jess turned, his hand on his gun, but it was a woman who faced him, thin as a bed slat in a shabby cotton dress.

"Sheriff, you must come," she said.

"What's happened?" Jess said.

The woman frowned. "It's not what happened, it's what's happening. Tom Mulvane is beating up on his old lady again. I swear he's gonna kill her this time."

"Are you a neighbor?" Jess said.

"Yes, I am." The woman grabbed Jess's arm and pulled. "For God's sake, let's go. Hurry."

The woman led the way to a dilapidated tenement on 13th Street, a timber building that leaned badly to its right, as though the entire structure was drunk and ready to fall over at any moment. A knot of shawled women stood huddled together at the entrance to the common hallway that led to the stairwells.

"Are they still at it?" Jess's guide said.

"Oh, aye, Maggie," said a plump woman with a Scottish accent. "He'll do for her this time for certain. Poor wee lassie. Is that a constable you have there?"

"He's the sheriff," the thin woman said. She turned to Jess. "Annie Mulvane's place is on the third floor."

"Ye'll hear them before ye see them, I'll be bound," the Scottish woman said.

Tired as he was, Jess took the rickety stairs two at a time. A rat squealed and scurried out from under his foot and he almost tripped and fell. Above him on the next floor he heard a man shout and a moment later a woman shrieked. Jess reached the door, thought about knocking politely, but decided instead to force it open. The sickly stink of the squalid dwelling hit him like a fist, the loathsome stench of poverty.

A man in a collarless shirt held a woman against the kitchen wall and his fist was cocked back, ready to land another blow. The woman, who might have been pretty once, already had one eye swollen shut and a trickle of blood ran from her mouth.

Totally oblivious to Jess, the man said, "Where did you hide my damned money?"

"There is no money, Tom," the woman said. "I already told you."

The man pressed his forearm into the woman's throat. "Give me my money, Annie, or I'll kill you, by God," he said.

"You!" Jess yelled. "Get away from that woman!"

The man swung on him. "Who the hell are you?"

"The law," Jess said. "And you're under arrest."

Tom Mulvane's voice took on a whine. "She hid my money. I need it for whiskey."

Annie pushed herself off the wall. She flung open every cupboard in the kitchen, then she cried, "Look! There is no money! And there's no food! You've drunk away all our money, every last cent."

Mulvane lunged for his wife but Jess stepped between them. "You're coming with me, Mulvane," he said. "You can sleep it off in a cell."

"Damn you," the man said. "I need whiskey. I need it bad."

Jess grabbed Mulvane's arm, but the man wrenched away and threw a straight left at Jess's chin. But Jess had anticipated and he moved to his right, drew his Colt and slammed it into Mulvane's head. Half drunk, the man fell without even a whimper.

"I'm getting real good at that," Jess said, his voice flat.

"What?" Annie Mulvane said. She had beautiful brown eyes, startling in her bruised, hardship-ravaged face.

"Nothing," Jess said. He picked up Mulvane by the back of his shirt. This time the man groaned and a long string of saliva hung from his bottom lip. "How can you live with a man who treats you like this?" Jess said.

Annie said, "Well, he's a very good dancer."

"Maybe it's time you changed partners, lady," Jess said.

CHAPTER NINETEEN

Jess Casey released his prisoner the next morning after Tom Mulvane promised to abstain from demon drink and stop beating his wife. Promises easily made are easily broken and Jess didn't expect much, especially since Mulvane's wife was waiting for him at the sheriff's office door and the two walked along the boardwalk hand in hand.

For the next few days Jess was involved in routine police work.

A four-hundred-pound matron caught her equally obese husband in bed with their slim young maid. Irritated, the wife cut loose with a pepperpot revolver and pumped five .22 shorts into her cheating spouse. The man's fat slowed the little bullets some, but Dr. Sun had to pry them out of belly blubber with forceps, the fat man bellowing the whole time.

Two whores got into it at Jessie Reeve's Female Boarding House on 11th Street and one was cut up some. The assailant was fined ten dollars and warned to behave herself or she'd spend the night in the hoosegow. A vagrant was caught stealing a chicken from a coop on waste ground behind the St. John's Hotel. Jess gave him five dollars and told him to get out of town and never come back, adding that he'd shoot him on sight. There was a shooting scrape at the Saracen's Head saloon. No one was hurt but the combatants, one of them a church deacon, the other a warehouse clerk, were fined fifty dollars each.

Then on the third day three men robbed the Jewelry Exchange of Fort Worth and the female manager was shot and seriously wounded.

"It's in your bailiwick, Jess," Kurt Koenig said. "I'm giving you four of my boys to back you up, one of them a breed tracker. Bring those robbers in, dead or alive."

"Should I be grateful for your trust in me, Kurt?" Jess said.

"Nope. Maybe I'm hoping that you'll get your fool head blown off."

"Just so I know where we stand."

"Jess, I have big plans for this town and you can be a major part of them. It's time you saw reason," Koenig said.

"We've had this discussion before and my answer is still no. I don't want to profit from the human misery caused by opium and morphine."

"You know, you're still alive only because I like you," Koenig said. "Can you understand that? You make me laugh, Jess. I mean, a used-up cow nurse who looks like General Custer playing lawman is funny."

"You're easily amused, Kurt."

"Well, maybe so. But we'll talk again, Jess. I don't want to be your enemy."

"We'll talk again if I come back alive from this manhunt."

"You'll come back alive. Lost-in-the-woods pilgrims like you always do."

The breed, the result of a Kiowa woman's liaison with a Canadian trapper, led Jess Casey and his men directly to the jewel thieves.

The three young men had stopped in a dry wash ten miles west of town to divide the loot. Although they carried belt revolvers they didn't make a fight of it, the breed's scattergun intimidating them into surrender.

Two of the youths carried morphine syringes in velvet-lined Moroccan leather cases and all three were arrogant and not in the least penitent.

"Harm any of us and you'll answer to my pa," the oldest, a sneering redhead with freckles said. "He owns the only sawmill in town."

One of Koenig's men, a man with a black handlebar mustache, said, "The kid's name is Benny Locke and he's right about his pa. Adam Locke supplied the timber that built most of Fort Worth."

"What about the other two?" Jess said. Sweat ran from under his hat. The afternoon was hot and the deep, sandy wash was stifling.

"The one with the black hair is Manus Gallaher. His pa owns the Excelsior, the best hotel in town. The towhead over there with the bad attitude is called Tim Convery. He's Hank Convery the lawyer's son."

"You boys are in a heap of trouble," Jess said. "How old are you?"

"I'm eighteen," the redhead said. "The other two are both sixteen." He smirked. "How old are you?"

"Old enough that when I was your age I'd been up the Chisholm Trail and back four times," Jess said.

"My pa says you're not a real sheriff," the kid said. "He says you're just a stove-up old cowboy that Kurt Koenig keeps as a pet. I wish Mr. Koenig had arrested us. He's a real peace officer."

Jess nodded. "Yeah, and if the woman you shot dies, he's the one who will hang you."

"You talking about Addie Brennan?" Tim Convery said. "Who cares about that old prune?"

"I do," Jess said. "Now mount up; I'm taking you back to town."

"You'll be sorry, mister," Convery said. "Kurt Koenig isn't gonna like this."

He didn't.

"Jess, you arrested the sons of three of Fort Worth's most prominent citizens," Koenig said. "These are rich men, very influential in city politics."

"You told me to bring them back dead or alive," Jess said.

"That was before I knew who they were," Koenig said. "And hell, all the jewelry was recovered."

"Is Addie Brennan still alive?"

"Dr. Sun says she'll pull through. She's a tough old bird." Koenig stared hard at Jess, then grinned. "The boys' fathers are deeply ashamed at what their sons did and they say they'll make it up to Addie. Each of them is putting a thousand dollars into the pot."

"Addie gets three thousand dollars for getting shot by three rich kids out on a lark. Is that it?"

"Jess, Jess, Jess, boys will be boys," Koenig said, smiling. "Don't you remember your own boyhood?"

"I never was a boy," Jess said. "I was pulling my weight as a man on a two-by-twice farm from the time I stood knee-high to my pa."

Jess opened a desk drawer and tossed the two syringe cases on the table. "Did you know the boys were using morphine?"

"Says who?" Koenig said.

"Look on the desk."

"They could have found them. Boys treasure such things."

"Are they your customers, Koenig?"

"Friends don't call each other by their last name, Jess."

"They were probably drugged when they robbed the jewelry store and shot Addie Brennan. Who supplies their morphine?"

"It's easy to find morphine in the Half Acre."

"But you control the opium and morphine trade in the city."

"I don't know all my customers."

"What about the three boys I have in the cell? You seem to know them well enough."

"I don't know who sold them morphine. If anybody did." Koenig motioned to the cases on the desk. "That proves nothing. The boys found them, that's all."

"They won't tell me who pulled the trigger, but if Addie Brennan dies I'll charge all three of them with murder."

"You'll never get a jury to convict them in this town," Koenig said.

"A United States marshal could see things differently," Jess said. "He may say we can try them in some other town, probably Austin."

"You want to make things happen, don't you, Jess?" Koenig said.

"Yes, when it comes to law matters."

"What the hell do you know about the law? You're a damned cowboy and nothing else."

Koenig stomped to the door and flung it wide.

"Jess, you're walking a dangerous path," he said. "Don't push things any further than you already have."

"When you get hungry enough you'll eat it off the floor," Jess Casey said, looking around him at the three tin plates of beans and bacon that had just been tossed through the bars of the cell.

"The hell we will," Tim Convery said. "My pa is a lawyer. Why isn't he here?"

"I guess he thinks you're guilty as hell, huh?" Jess said, grinning.

"Of what? You can't prove nothing," Convery said.

"All we did—"

"Shut the hell up, Manus!" Convery said. "Tell him nothing."

"I'm planning to wire for a United States marshal," Jess said. "Maybe you'll be glad to talk to him."

Jess didn't know it then but he'd just uttered what he later realized was a foolish, empty boast.

CHAPTER TWENTY

The nice man at the door told Molly Brennan that she was wanted urgently at Dr. Sun's office regarding some new medication for her ailing sister.

"But I understood the doctor was coming here later tonight," Molly said. "He told me he'd drop in to check on Addie several times a day."

"Dr. Sun has been delayed," the man said. He had yellow hair and a nice smile. "I believe a difficult birth may delay him the rest of the night."

"Oh, the poor woman. I do hope she'll be all right," Molly said. Like her sister she was a middle-aged spinster who laid no claim to beauty.

"I'm sure she will be now that Dr. Sun is with her," the man said. "And we must always remember that the pain of childbirth is not remembered but the child is."

"What a perfectly sweet thing to say. Now I must get my coat," Molly said.

"Dr. Sun left the medication with his assistant,"

the nice man said. "Just knock on the door. She'll know who's calling."

"Have you seen that young girl's face?" Molly said. "Poor thing."

"Ah yes, but she has turned her scars into stars," the man said.

"What most singularly lovely things you say, sir," Molly said. "Are you a poet?"

"Alas, that is my cross to bear," the man said. "Now you must hurry."

"Yes, yes, of course," Molly said. She hurried into her coat, checked on her sister, and returned to the door. "Addie is sleeping comfortably. Dr. Sun said she'll pull through. What a perfectly awful thing to happen to her."

"Indeed," the nice man said. "And now, dear lady, I must wish you good night. And I will write a poem in your sister's honor this very night."

Molly quietly closed the door. "And then you must read it to me," she said.

"I will," the man said. "Be assured of that."

He and Molly walked together for a few yards and then parted ways. But after the woman was out of sight the man returned to the Brennan sisters' modest little home. He opened the unlocked door and silently stepped inside.

The door to the left of the short hallway was ajar and the nice man saw the flickering crimson flames of a fire reflected on the ceiling. He stepped into the bedroom.

Addie Brennan lay on her back sound asleep, and in the red-tinted semidarkness she looked almost pretty. The man smiled to see such a sight. It was, he considered, quite touching.

He then picked up the pillow that lay beside Addie and pushed it into her face. How softly he laughed as her kicks became more feeble until finally she lay as limp as a dishrag. The man removed the pillow and saw that dear Addie still looked as though she lay in peaceful sleep. He plumped up the pillow, stained with just a little saliva, and placed it gently beside her again.

Norman Arendale, the failed Shakespearean actor now considered to be the finest hired murderer in the nation, had claimed his one hundred and fifteenth victim.

Dr. Sun wakened Jess Casey from uncomfortable shallow sleep. He said, "Ha, you don't care to slumber with your prisoners?"

"They're a noisy bunch," Jess said, sitting up in his chair. "They'd make sure I was awake all night. What can I do for you, Doc?"

"Addie Brennan is dead. Her sister just brought me the news."

"I'm sorry to hear that," Jess said. "Then I will charge those three clowns with murder."

"Perhaps," Dr. Sun said.

"What do you mean, perhaps?"

"Addie Brennan was left alone tonight because a man, a nice man she says, told Molly Brennan to come to my surgery on a matter of some urgency regarding her sister's medication. I sent no such message."

"So Addie was alone for a while," Jess said.

"Yes, and that was when she died. But I think it could have been murder."

"You don't know?"

"I think she was suffocated with a pillow. It is a difficult diagnosis to make. The main telltale sign of suffocation is that the victim's eyes become bloodshot. Addie's eyes were very red."

Dr. Sun reached into a pocket of his coat and produced a piece of folded white writing paper. He opened it carefully and laid it in front of Jess. "What do you see?" he said.

"A hair," Jess said.

"That is all? You can't tell me more?"

"Well, it's fair, about three inches long. From the head of a man, I'd say."

"Indeed. I found it on Addie's pillow," Dr. Sun said. "But would Addie Brennan, who has black hair tied back in a bun, have entertained a fair-haired man in her bed recently? Or in fact at any time?"

"From what I hear, she and her sister are a couple of old maids," Jess said. "I don't think men entered into their thinking."

"Exactly, and they couldn't afford servants, blond or otherwise," Dr. Sun said. "I believe Addie was murdered by a man with light hair. But can I prove it in a court of law? Bloodshot eyes and a single hair will not impress a jury."

"If she was murdered, then the question is why?" Jess said.

"Think about it, Sheriff," Dr. Sun said. "It's not hard to figure out."

"To silence her. Addie could identify the three lowlifes I have in my cell as the men who robbed the store and tried to kill her," Jess said.

Dr. Sun said, "It's the most likely possibility."

"Do you think Kurt Koenig was behind the woman's murder?" Jess said.

"Everything points to him, but it's such a clumsy crime. One would think that Kurt would have handled it with a little more finesse."

"What does that mean?" Jess said.

The little physician smiled. "I really don't know. It's just that smothering a sick woman with her own pillow is not Kurt's style." Dr. Sun's smile grew wider and a network of wrinkles spread across his face. "Kurt would have shot her and then shot her again and to hell with the consequence. Addie's murder was expertly planned and carried out."

"If not Koenig, then who?"

"Sheriff, I have no idea," Dr. Sun said.

Jess sat bolt upright in his chair. "She could have had an assistant."

"I beg your pardon," Dr. Sun said. "I'm not following you."

"Did anybody else work in the jewelry store besides Addie?"

"Yes, in fact someone did," Dr. Sun said. "Dorothy Mills—she's what, sixteen or seventeen? The girl worked there but only part-time, two or three days a week. Dorothy has dreams of becoming an actress, another Lillie Langtry, that's why she worked in the jewelry store, to raise money for a trip to New York. But she probably wasn't in the store on the day of the robbery, since nobody mentioned her being there."

"Maybe, but I aim to find out for sure," Jess said.

Dr. Sun was silent for a while, then said, "Sheriff, have you ever been alone in the forest and sensed the presence of something very large, very evil?"

"You mean like a bear or a cougar?" Jess said. "Sure, Doc, plenty of times."

"No, I mean something larger, a creature without face or form that lurks in the darkness biding its time, waiting to strike."

Jess smiled. "No, can't say as I have."

"I sense it," Dr. Sun said. "I can feel its evil and its intelligence."

"Koenig?" Jess said.

"No, not Koenig. Something far worse and much more dangerous. And Jess, it means you great harm."

CHAPTER TWENTY-ONE

Dorothy Mills lived uptown in Jessie Reeve's Female Boarding House on 11th Street. The rambling, two-story timber building was painted yellow, allegedly to make it look like a prairie flower, and it had a neat green yard with a swing, a porch front and back, and was ruled with Teutonic strictness by Baroness Bathilda Von Wendt, the scion of an ancient Hessian family. There had never been a Jessie Reeve. The baroness thought that an American-sounding name would be better for business.

The thin, mousy little maid who answered Jess Casey's knock on the door never raised her eyes to his face.

Yes, Miss Mills was at home. Yes, she was allowed gentleman callers and no, he couldn't see her.

"Why not?" Jess said.

Visiting hours for gentlemen were after lunch, between two and four o'clock when a chaperone could be present, the maid said.

"I'm here in the name of the law," Jess said, aware that he sounded pompous. He pushed through the door and the timid maid told him to take a seat while she talked with the matron. Jess looked around at the uncomfortable straight-backed chairs and decided to remain standing.

The woman who swept into the hall in a rustle of black taffeta was as tall as a man. Her bosoms were enormous, strapped up high, and her black eyes were as sharp as obsidian. She had an angry expression on her face, so settled into permanent creases that Jess figured infuriated thoughts were her daily burden.

"I am Baroness Bathilda Von Wendt, the owner of this establishment," she said.

Jess thought she expected him to bow.

"*Whom* do you wish to see?"

"One of your young ladies," Jess said, playing the game. "Dorothy Mills."

"In what regard?" the baroness said, her heavy, Germanic jaw jutting a belligerent challenge.

"Police business," Jess said.

"Very well then, police business but no monkey business. *Eh?* I run a very respectable house with rules as strong as Krupp's steel."

"I'm sure you do, ma'am," Jess said.

"You may talk to Miss Mills here," the baroness said. "And of course I will be present at all times." Without waiting for Jess to speak she rounded on the timorous little rodent of a maid. "Ruby, don't just stand there, you silly creature. Ask Miss Mills to come down here on a matter of the greatest moment."

The girl curtsied and fled upstairs.

Baroness Von Wendt stood beside a potted plant that made her look like she was emerging from a jungle. She stared at Jess with intolerant aristocratic eyes, and made no effort to disguise the fact that she didn't care for what she saw.

"I take it you are the local sheriff," she said, her gaze switching to the star on Jess's shirt.

"Indeed I am, ma'am."

"Then stand up straight and don't slouch. It's a most unbecoming posture for both man and woman." The baroness laid a forefinger against her cheek. "You have a passing resemblance to the soldier who was slaughtered by savages. His name escapes me at the moment."

"General Custer," Jess said. He didn't think he looked anything like the great hero.

"No, not that silly fellow. Now I remember, I mean General Gordon, the one who was just killed by Fuzzy-Wuzzies in the Sudan. Surely you read about it in all the newspapers."

"I can't say I did, ma'am," Jess said.

"Well, it doesn't really matter. I've decided that you don't look like him in the least. He was very handsome. Ah, here is Miss Mills at last."

Dorothy Mills was a small, shapely blond girl with large, baby blue eyes, a Cupid's bow mouth and a little pointed chin. Jess decided she didn't seem very intelligent.

"You may proceed with your interrogation, Sheriff," the baroness said.

Jess asked the girl if she'd been present in the jewelry store the morning of the robbery.

"Oh yes, sir, I was working that day," Dorothy said. She seemed eager to please.

"Can you describe the men who carried out the robbery?" Jess said.

"Oh yes, sir, I can, just like I told the newspaper reporter and Mayor Stout. It was three black men, sir, one of them very big with bruises and cuts all over his face."

Jess felt his heart sink. The girl was describing Zeus.

"Which one of them did you see shoot Addie Brennan?" he said.

"The big one, sir." Dorothy brought out a scrap of handkerchief and dabbed her eyes. "He shot her for no reason, sir. No reason at all."

"Dorothy, how much were you paid to tell a pack of lies?" Jess said.

The girl refused to meet his stare. "I can only tell you what my conscience dictates," she said. Then, after a long pause, "I saw what I saw."

"It doesn't trouble your conscience that your lies will let three guilty men walk free and put a noose around the neck of an innocent black man?"

"The Negro did it," the girl said. "I . . . I saw him shoot Addie."

"What kind of gun did he use?"

"Gun . . . what . . ." the girl stammered, blushing.

"Yes, gun. Was it a revolver or a rifle?"

Dorothy hesitated, then said, "A revolver."

"Did he shoot once or twice? Three times maybe?"

Dorothy burst into tears. "I can't remember. I don't want to remember."

"Miss Miles, you're a damned liar," Jess said.

"Sheriff, that will do," the baroness said. "You have upset the poor child enough. Miss Miles told you what she saw, and now I want you to leave. Search for three Negroes and you'll have your bandits."

She put her arm around Dorothy's shoulder. "Go back to your room, child. I'll have Ruby bring you a nice cup of tea directly."

"Thank you, matron," Dorothy said. She threw Jess a wounded look then ran quickly up the stairs, hiking her skirts high.

"Your business is concluded here, *mein Herr*," the baroness said.

"The girl is lying through her teeth," Jess said. "She's been paid."

Baroness Von Wendt stared into space and her thin mouth flexed.

"Perhaps she has," she said.

CHAPTER TWENTY-TWO

It was yet early in the morning when Jess Casey made his way to the hotel where Nate Levy still lay abed. Jess's face was becoming better known in the Half Acre and people nodded to him and a few even smiled.

When he reached the hotel he found Levy's room empty, the bed unmade and the little man's clothes were gone. There was no sign of Zeus.

Worried, Jess stood on the hotel porch and surveyed the street. He saw the usual chaotic mix of people, wagons, and riders and a solitary puncher in a bright red shirt driving three steers toward the slaughterhouse.

Jess made his way through the noisy, jostling throng to his office and stepped inside. Sitting in the chair behind the desk was Nate Levy, looking pale and ill, and smoking a cigar. He looked up when the door opened, saw Jess and said, "They've taken him."

"Taken who?" Jess said, fearing the answer.

"Zeus. Some men busted into his room this morning and dragged him away. I heard a shot, but I don't know if Zeus was the target."

"Taken him where?" Jess said.

"If I knew that would I be sitting here instead of in my sickbed?" Levy said. Then, passing a piece of notepaper, "Read this. It was left on the desk for you."

The note got right to the point. The real killer of Addie Brennan was in custody and the innocent victims of the sheriff's bungling had been released. It was signed by Hank Convery and under his name the ominous addition: *and the Fort Worth Vigilance Committee.*

"'Vigilance Committee' is just a polite name for a lynch mob," Levy said. "I've seen the like a few times before in my life."

Jess walked past Levy to the cells. The door of the holding cell was flung wide open and his ripped-up mattress and bedding had joined the bacon and beans on the floor.

He returned to the front of the office and said to Levy, "I'll help you back to the hotel. You're still too weak to be out."

"What about Zeus?" the little man said.

"I'll have words with Mr. Convery."

"Jess, I love that boy as though he was my own son," Levy said. "Find him."

"He's your meal ticket, Nate. You know it and I know it."

"You think you've got your hand on it, huh?"

Levy said. "Well, you're wrong. I love that big pug and I don't want any harm to come to him."

Jess stood at the window, his mind racing. Where was Zeus? Who had paid Dorothy Mills to lie? Convery? Koenig? Somebody else? Luke Short maybe?

He had plenty of questions with no answers and now Nate Levy asked him another. "Jess, did you ever find out who paid that Porry McTurk feller to kill you?"

"I reckoned it was Kurt Koenig," Jess said. "Or Luke Short."

"Koenig does his own killing and so does Luke."

"Why are you asking me this?" Jess said.

"Because maybe it was Convery. He sure doesn't seem to have any liking for you."

"Not liking a man is hardly a reason for killing him," Jess said.

Levy said, "It's been plenty enough reason in the past."

"I'll hear what Convery has to say," Jess said. "And now you're going back to bed and I'm confiscating that cigar."

"The hell you are," said Levy. "At my age it's about the only pleasure I have left."

Hank Convery's law office was a converted yellow and gray house with a wide porch and a stone chimney at its gable end. The porch was unfurnished, no chairs or even a potted plant. The house gave off a hostile energy as though visitors were unwelcome.

But since Half Acre lawyers like Convery dealt with the dregs of society maybe his clients weren't encouraged to linger.

But even more unwelcoming was the broken-nosed bruiser who stepped out the door just as Jess was coming up the steps to the porch.

"What the hell do you want?" the man said. He had small, tight eyes and his stubbly blue chin was the size and shape of a split cannonball.

"I'm here to see Convery," Jess said.

"Mr. Convery ain't seeing clients today, so beat it," the man said.

When Jess reached the porch, the man towered over him like a massive oak growing next to a willow tree.

"Give me the road," Jess said, his anger spiking.

The big man shot out his hand and grabbed Jess by the throat. He grinned, hoisted him three inches off the ground and shook him like a terrier with a rat.

"You don't listen too good, mister," he said.

Jess Casey's mind was in an extremely delicate state and he was not in the mood to suffer bullies gladly. He reached down, skinned his Colt, judged where the man's left foot would be and fired.

It was a well-judged shot. A first-rate piece of work.

The big man roared as the bullet crashed into his foot and neatly severed his pinkie toe and the one next to it.

Jess left the agonized tough to perform a dervish

dance on the porch and stepped through the door into the office. A slim, efficient-looking woman sat behind a desk, an opened register in front of her. Ignoring the recent shot and the animal bellows of the tormented thug on the porch, she said, "Do you have an appointment?"

"Where is Convery?" Jess said.

But it seemed that the gunshot and the roaring thug had indeed affected the woman. She quickly said, "The door at the end of the hallway."

"Thank you most kindly," Jess said.

"You're quite welcome, sir," the woman said. Her eyes were cool and gray.

Jess stomped down the hallway, his spurs ringing his wrath, and kicked in the door. Jess was pleased that the glass panel with HENRY CONVERY, ATTORNEY-AT-LAW picked out in gold paint, shattered into a hundred pieces.

It was a pity that Convery had chosen the moment of Jess's dramatic entrance to make his own entrance into the woman who was bent over his desk. His pants around his ankles, the lawyer stood frozen for a moment then made a fast dive for his open desk drawer.

Jess was aware of the woman fleeing the room as he quickly crossed the floor, slapped away the Colt .30 caliber belly gun in Convery's hand and landed a right hook to the man's chin. Staggered, the lawyer squeezed off a shot into the ceiling before he fell flat on his back and his revolver skittered away from him across the polished floor.

Jess bent and pulled the man to his feet. Convery had bit his tongue and blood and saliva pooled at the corners of his mouth.

"Where is he?" Jess said.

Convery spoke around a painful tongue. "Where is who?"

"You know who. Where is Zeus?"

"I don't know where he is."

Jess shook the man. "Damn you, tell me where he is or I'll beat you until you can't stand."

"All right, all right, I'll tell you," Convery said.

"Where is he?" Jess said.

"We left him with the mayor. He's locked up somewhere in City Hall."

Beside himself with rage, Jess drew his Colt and shoved the muzzle into Convery's bloody mouth. "The truth," he said. He thumbed back the hammer. "Where is he?"

"I told you the truth," Convery said, desperation in his eyes. "We knew if we locked up him in your cell you'd free him. So we took him to City Hall."

"We? Who's we?" Jess said.

"Me . . . me and the Vigilance Committee."

"If you're lying to me, Convery, I'll come back and kill you."

"It's the truth. I swear it."

"Who paid Dorothy Mills to lie about Zeus?"

"I don't know what you're talking about."

"She said three black men robbed the jewelry store. You know that's a lie."

"It's the story the girl told the newspaper in the

presence of Mayor Stout as a witness," Convery said. "I was glad to go along with it because her testimony freed my son."

"Who paid her to lie? Tell me."

"I don't know. It wasn't me. Damn you to hell, Casey, and listen to me. I didn't pay the girl to lie but I'm glad she did."

"You'll stand by and watch an innocent man hang?" Jess said.

"Hell, he's only a nigg—"

Jess Casey's punch put Convery to sleep and hurt his hand.

CHAPTER TWENTY-THREE

Fort Worth's City Hall was a two-story brick building at 2nd and Rusk. It housed the fire department and there were rumors that a regular police department would be located there sometime within the next ten years.

Jess Casey knew he didn't have the authority or the manpower to storm the huge place and conduct a search for Zeus. All he could do now was talk to Mayor Stout and hear what the fat man had to say. He'd probably deny that Zeus was there.

Jess made the effort and spoke to one of Stout's aides.

"No, you can't talk to the mayor," the aide said. "He is very busy with city business. Try again tomorrow."

When Jess said he had reason to believe Zeus was in the building, the aide said, "He's not. Nor are any other of the Greek gods."

Jess fought down the urge to punch the man and returned to his office where he spent the day cleaning the cell area and repairing his mattress and bedding.

After an uncomfortable night Jess washed at the pump and strolled along the boardwalk to the restaurant for breakfast. He was on his second cup of coffee and fourth cigarette, waiting for his order of fried steak, six eggs and four biscuits, when the door opened and Dr. Sun stepped into the steamy interior.

He stopped for a few moments at a table where a pasty-faced man pointed out different parts of his anatomy that were causing him discomfort. Dr. Sun lingered long enough to give the man some hope-fully sage advice and they parted with smiles on both sides. The little physician, dressed in a prissy celluloid collar and striped tie, sat at Jess's table.

"Coffee, Doc?" Jess said.

"No, thank you, I just had tea," Dr. Sun said. He stared into Jess's eyes for a moment then said, "I treated a patient yesterday who had just lost two of his phalanges and I harbor serious doubts about a third."

"Phalanges?"

"Toes. He told me the sheriff shot them off and that his lawyer—"

"Hank Convery," Jess said.

"Plans to sue you and the city for damages."

"He was notified," Jess said. "But he refused to cease and desist, as my law book says."

"You were trying to find Zeus?" Dr. Sun said.

"Convery says he's locked up in City Hall somewhere. He's in danger and I'll find him."

The physician shook his head. "He who is drowned is not troubled by the rain."

"What does that mean?" Jess said.

"It means that the fate of Zeus has already been settled. He is a dead man."

"You heard something?" Jess said, his shocked face expressing his concern.

"No, I heard nothing. But the evil I spoke of yesterday will not let Zeus live. Jess, see to your own safety. Now you are in the greatest danger. You know who was really responsible for the death of Addie Brennan and you know that Dorothy Mills was paid to lie about who robbed the jewelry store. Someone is protecting the sons of rich, influential men and he won't let you discover who he is."

"I know who it is. It's Kurt Koenig. He takes a cut from every business in the Half Acre, and that includes Matt Gallaher's hotel, Adam Locke's sawmill and Hank Convery's law business. Of course he'll do favors for men who pay him protection money, and that includes the odd killing."

Dr. Sun had several times checked his watch. Now he snapped it shut and said, "Jess, come with me."

"But I haven't had my breakfast yet," Jess said.

"That can wait." The physician rose to his feet. "Come with me."

"Where are we going?"

"The Texas and Pacific railroad station," Dr. Sun said.

Dr. Sun led Jess Casey past the ticket office onto the platform. "My friend Baroness Von Wendt visited my surgery early this morning and told me that the young lady planned to catch the 9:05 and then connections east," he said. "Bathilda is aware of my concern for Zeus."

Dorothy Miles stood on the platform, a suitcase at her feet. She was dressed in traveling clothes and carried what looked like a packed lunch in a paper sack. The only other passenger was a thin, sallow man with yellow hair. Despite the growing heat of the morning he wore a tweed overcoat. He had a pleasant face and seemed nice.

Jess stepped to where Dorothy stood. "You're leaving us, Miss Miles?" he said.

The girl was surprised and a little fearful. "I have no reason to stay in Fort Worth," she said. "My future lies elsewhere."

"Isn't testifying at the trial of the man you accused of shooting Addie Brennan reason enough to remain in this city? But I thought you'd want to stay for the trial."

"No, the sworn statement I dictated in front of Mayor Stout and City Marshal Koenig and then signed was quite sufficient, especially since the black man has already admitted his crimes."

"They told you that?" Jess said.

"Of course they did, and also Mr. Convery the lawyer, who was also present."

The locomotive in the siding vented steam and then clanked slowly forward. It pulled only two passenger cars, a boxcar and a caboose.

"Now, you must excuse me," Dorothy said. She smiled sweetly. "I must embark on the first stage of my new career."

Jess was caught flat-footed. From what little he'd read of his law book he had no grounds to hold the girl.

"Who paid you off, Miss Miles? You're leaving so there's no harm in telling me."

"I can't," the girl said. Then realizing her slip, she said, "See, you're confusing me and you're scaring me. Now I must go."

The yellow-haired man stopped and said, "May I help you with your valise, young lady?"

"Why yes, thank you," Dorothy smiled. "You're so nice."

Jess stood on the platform, seething with frustration. He watched the girl take a window seat in the car and the man sat beside her. Stepping to the edge of the platform, Jess pounded on the window and yelled, "Who paid you, Miss Miles?"

But the yellow-haired man reached out and pulled down the shade. The locomotive huffed into motion and pulled out of the station. Jess stood with his hands on his hips and watched it go.

CHAPTER TWENTY-FOUR

The Silver Garter was open for business but given the early hour most of the saloon customers sat around reading the newspapers and drinking coffee. But a few lingered over their morning bourbon and conversed in the hollow voices that men always seem to have around breakfast time.

Jess Casey asked the bartender, who was polishing the French mirror behind the bar, for the whereabouts of Kurt Koenig.

"He's around," was the man's laconic reply.

In the event, it was Koenig who found Jess. "Over here, Sheriff," he called from the shadows. "I hope this is a social visit. I'm not up for gunfights and the like this early."

Jess followed the sound of the voice and stepped into a dark corner where Koenig sat at a table drinking coffee.

"What can I do for you, Jess?" the big man said.

"You can tell me where Zeus is," Jess said.

"You mean the fighter? I have no idea. You can

lay to that, matey. Headed out of town on a fast horse, I should imagine."

"He was dragged from his hotel room by armed men and according to Hank Convery was taken to City Hall," Jess said. "Were they your Panther City Boys, Kurt?"

"I don't know what you're talking about," Koenig said. He stopped a passing waiter. "Bring another cup, Sam. The sheriff here has a brain fever. Maybe coffee will help."

"Who paid Dorothy Miles to lie about the robbery?" Jess said. "I want the truth."

"The truth is somebody did, but it wasn't me," Koenig said. He took the cup from the waiter. "I've got nothing against Zeus. He cost me money but so have other fighters, and horses."

"You wanted Tim Convery and the others released," Jess said.

"And I told you why," Koenig said, pouring coffee into the cup. "I owe their fathers favors. Those three men are movers and shakers in this town. They can make or break a man's business. Now sit down and have some coffee and maybe a brandy, huh? You need to steady your nerves, Jess. You're all a-fluster."

"You're willing to let Zeus hang so you can repay favors?"

"Hell no, he won't hang. I'll get the big pug out of here, give him a few bucks and shove him and Nate Levy on a train to Hicksville. All right? Now drink your coffee. Cigar?"

Jess sat and built a cigarette. He drank coffee,

reminding himself how hungry he was. "Dr. Sun thinks Addie Brennan was murdered," he said.

Koenig was surprised, a thing Jess noticed. "I thought the old dear had died of the gunshot wound."

"She was suffocated, Dr. Sun said. By a man with strong hands and yellow hair."

"And I fit the bill?"

"Seems like. I mean, yellow hair and strong hands."

"I don't murder old women, Sheriff. I don't murder young ones, either."

"Then who did? Or paid to have it done?"

"Beats me," Koenig said. "I have no idea. I don't much care, either."

"Convery, Locke, Gallaher, any one of them, or all of them, could have done it to save the necks of their worthless sons. Silence Addie, pay off Dorothy Mills and blame the shooting on a black man and suddenly there's no case against them."

"Convery maybe. The other two, no, they're just not the violent kind," Koenig said.

"What about Luke Short?"

Koenig laughed and said, "Luke's a lady-killer all right when he twirls his mustache and cuts a dash. But he doesn't suffocate old ladies. What would be in it for him? He doesn't give a damn about the sons of our fair city's prominent citizens."

Jess drained his cup and got to his feet. "One more question. The first night I got here somebody paid Porry McTurk to kill me. Was it you?"

Koenig took that with a smile. "No, Jess, if I wanted you dead that night I'd have shot you myself. Now Luke Short might have done it. The word around the Half Acre is that he doesn't like you all that much."

"The feeling is mutual," Jess said.

Koenig shook his head. "You sure want to be a lawman, don't you, Jess? I hear you did some bang-bang yesterday, shot three toes off Tom Lurker. Then you beat Hank Convery senseless. I heard he's going to sue."

"Yeah, and so is Lurker," Jess said

"Tom Lurker won't sue you. He'll shoot you in the back, Jess," Koenig said. "Just a warning between friends."

"I'll keep it in mind," Jess said.

CHAPTER TWENTY-FIVE

In the early afternoon Jess Casey got word that train robbers had held up a Texas and Pacific cannonball and several men were feared dead. A puncher brought the news, but it was a garbled account since he'd seen the train at a distance, heard shots and saw a couple of men dead on the ground. He hadn't stuck around to investigate further. According to the cowboy the train was stopped about two miles up the line in the flat brush country.

The news was brought to the Silver Garter, not the sheriff's office, and Jess joined a thirty-man posse that had already formed. Kurt Koenig was the man in charge.

In the West at that time train robbery posses were easy to round up, mainly because the bandits were seldom caught so the risk was minimal and usually with all the riding and taking pots at shadows a good time was had by all.

But when Jess and the others arrived at the stalled train most everyone aboard was half drunk and the apple of everyone's eye was the surly gunman Wilson J. Tucker out of the Pecos River country.

The guard, helped by passengers eager to get a word in, told the story, while Tucker listened, his morose face expressionless.

"Marshal, four bandits stopped the train, climbed on board and demanded the strongbox," the guard said to Koenig. "I told them there was only about ten dollars in the box but they made me open it anyway."

"At gunpoint," a passenger said.

"Yeah," the guard said. "One of them had a gun to my head the whole time. Well, sir, there only being ten dollars made them angry so they decided to rob the passengers."

"And that was a bad mistake," a middle-aged woman said. She waved a hand toward Tucker. "They told this gentlemen that they wanted his wallet and watch and—"

"Instead he gave them lead," said an eager man with shining brown eyes.

"Mr. Tucker killed two of the bandits inside the car and the other two outside as they tried to escape," the guard said.

"Four shots, four dead outlaws, Marshal," the eager man said.

Koenig nodded, then said, "Howdy, Wilson. I thought you never left the Pecos."

"Hard times, Kurt, a man has to move where the work is. I heard you'd been hung by the Rangers, but I guess I heard wrong."

"I guess you're right about that. Getting hung is not the kind of thing that slips a man's mind. What brings you to this neck of the woods?"

"Like I said, work," Tucker said. He wore a belt gun in a cross-draw holster and a second tucked into the waistband of his pants. Dressed in a gray suit, elastic-sided boots and a low-crowned, flat-brimmed hat he looked like a hard-faced fire-and-brimstone preacher.

"Wilson, I don't want you in the Half Acre," Koenig said. "Everywhere you go you bring trouble and that's something I can do without right now."

"What's coming down, Kurt?" Tucker said.

"Nothing I can't handle."

"I'll stay out of your hair."

"Stay out of the Half Acre. I mean that."

"I wired Luke. He's expecting me."

"You doing a job for him?"

"I never disclose the identity of my clients, Kurt. You know that. But Luke isn't hiring me. He owes me and I'm calling in the favor."

"You still use that Holland and Holland elephant gun for long work?" Kurt said. "I recollect seeing you blow Sandy Glower's head clean off with that cannon."

The passengers had craned forward, all ears, as Tucker said, "Sandy was a named revolver fighter, you recall. I wasn't real sure I could shade him on the draw and shoot. To answer your question, I left the Holland and Holland to home. City work doesn't need long guns."

Jess stepped back into the car and Koenig looked at him, a question on his face. "The two outside both killed with one shot, just like the ones in here."

"Back or front?" Koenig said.

"That's hurtful, Kurt," Tucker said.

"Front. Right through the heart," Jess said. He turned his attention to Tucker. "You know how to shoot, mister."

"He should. He's been hiring out his gun ever since he got out of short pants," Koenig said. Now it was his turn to study the gunman, then added, "Welcome to Fort Worth, Wilson. But I mean what I say—stay the hell out of the Half Acre."

Tucker said, "And I mean what I say. I won't step out of line."

Koenig shook his head. "Who the hell in Fort Worth would hire a gun like you, Wilson? You don't come cheap and you never come friendly."

The gunman managed a slight smile. "If I do my job right, Kurt, you'll never know."

"Or never know what hit me," Koenig said.

"Kurt, you're way down on my list of men I'd like to kill," Tucker said. "So let's hope it doesn't come to that."

* * *

A wild wind was blowing, kicking up clouds of dust, when Jess and the others rode onto Main Street. Wilson Tucker had retrieved his horse from the boxcar of the stalled train and rode between Jess and Koenig.

His head lowered against the stinging wind, Koenig drew rein and pointed along the street, busy with only commercial traffic because of the stinging sandstorm.

"You ride that way, Wilson, and when you pass 12th Street you're out of the Half Acre," he said, yelling above the howl of the wind. "The White Elephant, Luke Short's saloon, is up that way."

Tucker touched his hat. "Much obliged to you, Kurt. See you later."

"See me never, Wilson," Koenig said. "I don't want you anywhere near me."

The gunman glimmered his slight smile, rode away and Koenig watched him go. He shook his head and said to Jess, "I don't need Wilson Tucker in my life."

"He seems like he's a good friend of yours," Jess said, holding on to his hat.

"Wilson has no friends. And if he ever did, they're all in hell."

Once back in his office Jess Casey made up the fire in the stove, tossed a fistful of Arbuckle into his brand-new coffeepot and put it on to boil. Outside the sandstorm raged and Main Street was deserted. All along the thoroughfare hanging store signs tossed and jangled on their chains, screen doors banged and the dogs, upset by wind and driving sand, barked their dismay.

When the coffee was good and ready, bitter and black as mortal sin, he poured a cup and sprawled behind his desk and let the questions form in his head.

Why was Zeus being held in City Hall?

Why did a known contract killer suddenly appear in town?

Who hired him?

Who paid off Dorothy Mills?

And, thinking back to Porry McTurk, who wanted him dead when he'd been in town only a few hours?

The questions could have gone on and on but since he had no answers to any of them he let the matter rest and concentrated on building a cigarette.

The office door, caught by a wind gust, slammed open and Jess rose to shut it again. That move saved his life. A bullet shattered through the side window and drove splinters from the back of his chair . . . where his head had rested just a moment earlier.

Without thinking, knowing only that he had to get out of his office, where he was an obvious target, he drew his Colt and stepped through the door. Jess made a quick right turn and then crouched low beside the office wall. To his left, the direction from where the shot had been fired, a row of six flatbed wagons were parked on open ground. One still bore a cargo of cotton bales and the one farthest away was loaded with a few empty crates. Jess screwed up his eyes against the cartwheeling sand and gusting wind and his blinking, blurred gaze reached out among the wagons.

He saw nothing but the movement of the storm.

Expecting a bullet at any moment, Jess straightened then weaved his way toward the closest wagon, his gun tucked inside his shirt to keep sand out of the action. When the shot came it surprised him. With a vicious *whap!* the bullet kicked up an exclamation point of dirt just an inch from his right boot. Jess caught a drift of smoke that immediately got tangled in the wind. The smoke seemed to come from the last wagon in line and he snapped off a shot in that general direction. He knew he wouldn't hit anything but it would at least keep the bushwhacker honest.

As a second shot roiled across the open ground, Jess rolled to his right and fetched up hard against a wagon wheel. His unhealed shoulder wound thudded against its steel rim and Jess cried out as a vicious pain stabbed at him. The pain made him angry and he got to his feet and ran around the front of the wagon under the raised tongue. He threw himself behind the next flatbed in line, the one piled with cotton bales, then stood, his Colt up and ready.

Jess had invited a shot and he'd heard its crack as he ran. A quick glance around the wagon told him that the smoke drifted from the same spot, behind the last flatbed. Either the bushwhacker liked that position or for some reason he was immobile.

The loss of three toes could slow a man, keep him from moving too much, and Jess decided with certainty that it was the vengeful Tom Lurker who was trying to kill him. He smiled to himself. It was time to make hard times come down for ol' Tom.

Windblown sand gusting around him, Jess scrambled onto the cotton wagon and then scrambled to its rear, tossing down bales in his haste. He measured the distance then jumped to the next flatbed, and then scrambled away from Lurker's line of sight and made a leap to the next wagon. This time the flatbed rocked and creaked and Jess lost his balance and fell hard. His breath coming in ragged gasps, he jumped again and this time the wagon held firm.

As he'd hoped, the crates on top of Lurker's wagon blocked his field of fire. Jess was way to his left and to bring his rifle to bear he needed to get out from behind the wagon. Lurker hobbled to his right, his rifle ready at his shoulder. When he had a clean view of the wagons he and Jess spotted each other at the same time.

Both men fired.

Lurker hurried his shot and missed. But Jess

Casey, a less confident marksman, took an extra moment of time and then thumbed off an aimed shot. Lurker gasped in pain and surprise as he took the hit. But his hand slapped the Winchester's trigger guard and he cut loose another shot.

But Jess was already moving.

He threw himself onto the wagon bed and as Lurker's bullet cut the air a foot above his head, he raised his Colt in both hands, got a quick sight picture and fired.

This time Tom Lurker was hit hard and his face was frozen into a grimace of hate and shock. He staggered a little but managed to bring the rifle up and Jess heard the report as the man fired.

But Jess was firing steadily. He got off the last three rounds in the Colt and each one of them hit Lurker . . . in the right wrist, his left knee and a killing shot that hit the man dead center in the chest.

As a final gesture of defiance Lurker tried to throw down on Jess one last time, but the Winchester dropped from his grasp and he fell on his face. The uncaring wind tore the hat from Lurker's head and sent it tumbling along the ground and the thin hair danced on his scalp.

Jess stared down at the bullet-torn body. Koenig had been right. He surely did want to be a lawman. But the cost of his baptism by fire was proving way too high.

CHAPTER TWENTY-SIX

It was fixing to be a bad morning for Sheriff Jess Casey.

His gunfight with Tom Lurker had drained him emotionally and physically. Stiff, achy all over, his dicey knees throbbing, it took him several minutes to get out of his cot and shuffle to the stove.

The little calico cat that had decided to adopt him, stared at Jess with accusing eyes.

"Kept you awake all night, huh?" he said. "Well, I was hurting last night. Maybe something to do with the weather."

As a breed, cats do not accept apologies gracefully. The calico walked to the front door and scratched to be let out.

"Right," Jess said. "Go catch a mouse for breakfast and catch one for me while you're at it."

Disdainfully the cat stepped through the door and merged with the early morning hubbub on Main Street.

Jess made up the fire, set the coffee on to heat,

made a short toilet and dressed. He was sitting behind his desk, drinking coffee and smoking his first cigarette of the day when the door opened and a large man in a loud checked suit and red vest stepped inside.

"Are you the new law?" the man said. He had great bushy sideburns, a florid face and an abrupt manner. He might have been a jolly man but he wasn't that morning.

"Sheriff Jess Casey. "What can I do for you?"

"You are a son of Erin?" the big man said.

"Way back, I guess."

"Good. Then that is a point in your favor."

Jess tried again. "You have a problem . . . Mister . . . ah . . ."

"Burke's the name. Patrick Burke. Burke by name, Burke by nature, my late wife always said."

"Are you Lillian Burke's father?" Jess said, surprised.

"I am. And that is why I've come to see you."

"Coffee?" Jess said.

Burke stepped to the stove, picked up the coffeepot in a speckled hand the size of a ham, lifted the lid and sniffed. He made a face and said, "No, thank you."

"Then please take a seat," Jess said.

"I will stand on my own two feet," the big brewer said. "What I have to say will not take long. My daughter has disappeared."

Alarmed, Jess sat forward in his chair. "When?"

"Two nights ago. Lillian left to visit a girlfriend and never came back."

"Who is her friend?"

"It doesn't matter. I spoke to the girl, she's of a respectable family, and she told me she hasn't seen my daughter in at least a week."

"Is there anyone else she might have visited?" Jess said.

"No one that I know of," Burke said.

Jess fought a mental battle with himself and decided to keep quiet for now about Lillian's opium addiction. A man like Burke could go off half-cocked and cause more harm than good.

"I'll look into it," Jess said.

"Sheriff, since her mother died, Lillian is all I've got," Burke said, shedding his brusque manner like a suit of armor. His voice breaking, he said, "If anything has happened to her . . . I . . ."

"I'll find her, Mr. Burke," Jess said.

"And may Jesus, Mary and Joseph and all the saints in heaven aid you in your endeavors," Burke said. "Sheriff Casey, bring my child home to me."

The big man's pride would not let Jess see tears in his eyes. He turned away quickly and rushed out the door.

Jess rose to his feet. He sniffed the coffeepot as Burke had done, shrugged and poured himself another cup. His first stop that morning would be the opium den off Rusk Street. It was entirely possible that Lillian Burke was still there.

Even early in the morning there were several addicts dreaming opium dreams, but Jess Casey found no trace of Lillian Burke and his questions about the girl's whereabouts were met with empty faces and blank stares. He left the den, crossed the waste ground and headed to Dr. Sun's house.

The harsh morning light was not kind to Mei-Xing. When she opened the door the network of scars across her face stood out in stark relief. As she opened the door and allowed Jess inside, he smiled at her and she shyly smiled back.

"I have not seen Lillian Burke since the night we visited the opium den," Dr. Sun said. "Could there be a lover involved?"

"Possibly," Jess said. "She had a young man with her the night I first met her."

"Do you know him?" the physician said.

Jess shook his head. "He looked to be like a clerk of some kind. I doubt I'd even recognize him if I saw him again."

Dr. Sun said, "Zeus a captive, Miss Burke missing, strange things are happening in Fort Worth, are they not?"

"Could Kurt Koenig have anything to do with Lillian's disappearance?" Jess said. "He deals in women."

"Women of a sort, Jess. I doubt he grabs young girls off the street and forces them into prostitution."

"I think he's capable of anything," Jess said.

"Yes, but kidnapping the daughter of the Half

Acre's only brewer would hardly be good for his saloon business."

Jess nodded. "I guess you're right about that. Then where is she?"

"I don't know the answer to that," Dr. Sun said. "But there are forces at work in this town I don't understand. Yet I fear them."

"Doc, have you ever heard the name Wilson J. Tucker?"

"No, I can't say I have."

"He's a contract killer, a fast gun for hire. Somebody in this town sent for him. The money must be big because Koenig says Tucker never leaves the Pecos River country."

"I have no idea, Jess," Dr. Sun said. "Gunmen come and go all the time in this town."

"Not gunmen like Wilson Tucker," Jess said.

On his way out Mei-Xing laid her tiny hand on Jess's arm and whispered, "Opium costs money and so do diamond brooches, Sheriff. Yet Lillian told me her father is an old skinflint."

"But—"

The door closed on him and Jess stood on the step, pondering what the girl had just told him. The brooch was expensive, he was sure of that. The diamond was huge. To his surprise he recalled the words on it, as though the violent events of that night were seared into his consciousness. *Toi et Nul*

Autre. What the hell did that mean? Jess had some book learning but he figured at the time they were just fancy words he didn't know. He thought about knocking on the door again to ask Dr. Sun, but decided against it. He didn't want to get Mei-Xing in any trouble for telling tales behind his back.

But maybe the brooch was a clue to Lillian's disappearance.

Fighting down his distaste, he knew that the one man in town who might know was Kurt Koenig. He would ask him.

As it happened, Jess had to send someone to roust Koenig out of bed. He kept a room at the Silver Garter where he slept most nights.

"What the hell time is it?" Koenig said. He looked rumpled and out of sorts. His cotton nightgown reached to his hairy ankles.

"Nearly seven," Jess said. "I have a question to ask you."

"Damn you, Jess, you don't ask a man questions at seven in the morning," Koenig said. "Don't you ever sleep?"

"It's about a brooch," Jess said.

"About a what?"

"A brooch. It's got words on it and I need you to tell me what they mean."

Koenig was stunned. He tried to talk a few times and when he finally found his tongue he said, "Jess, I said I liked you, but this time you've gone too far. You'd better get out of here before I shoot you."

"I wrote the words down just as I remembered them," Jess said. He tore a page out of the tally book he always carried and showed it to Koenig. "What does that mean?"

"I'm gonna shoot you, Jess. By God, I mean it."

"What do the words mean, Kurt?"

Koenig sighed and glanced at the slip of paper. "Despite your large, illiterate scrawl, I can read them," he said. "It's a French saying and it means 'you and no other.' Now get the hell out of here."

"One more question, Kurt."

"You're killing me here, Jess."

"How much would a brooch with a diamond the size of a five-dollar gold piece and those words in emerald stones cost?"

"More than a lawman will earn in a lifetime," Koenig said. "Now get the hell away from me."

Koenig turned on his heel, threw some choice cuss words over his shoulder and tramped back upstairs to his room.

Jess stood in the middle of the empty saloon, his head bowed in thought. If Lillian's father was a tightwad would he spend a small fortune on a diamond brooch? But perhaps it was her mother's and Lillian had inherited it. There was only one way to find out. He'd have to speak to Patrick Burke again.

CHAPTER TWENTY-SEVEN

Patrick Burke's office was directly above the brewery and was redolent with the rich, malty smell of beer. The walls of his office were decorated with animal heads and a thick Persian rug lay on the floor.

"You have news for me?" Burke said, his face hopeful.

"Only questions, I'm afraid," Jess Casey said.

"What kind of questions?" Burke said.

"Did Lillian own an expensive diamond brooch?"

"Not that I know of."

"You didn't buy a brooch for her or give her one that was left by her mother?"

"What tomfoolery is this?" Burke said. "I brew beer. Do you know what my profit margin is? Damned little. I don't have the money to buy my daughter diamonds or her mother before her, either."

"Was Lillian walking out with any rich men friends?"

"No. The only man she brought home regularly was some accounting clerk who writes poetry on the side. He's as poor as a church mouse."

"Do you recall his name?"

"Of course. His name is Lester Ward and he works for the Chartered Exchange on 10th Street. Does he have anything to do with my daughter's disappearance?"

"I don't think so, but I'm following every lead I can get, Mr. Burke."

"Then go follow them, Sheriff," Burke said. "Find my daughter."

In the aftermath of the sandstorm, the sky bore the promise of a bright day as Jess rode north along Main Street, a favor to his horse, who hated to be cooped up in his stall all day. To his surprise, people began to acknowledge him. Men touched their hat brims and ladies smiled and fluttered their eyelashes. Jess was not one to cut a dash and he assumed the Half Acre had begun to accept him as its peace officer. If that was the case, it was indeed a gratifying thought.

The Chartered Exchange was a grim building of gray brick with a myriad of small, dusty windows that looked onto 10th Street.

When he asked to speak to Lester Ward, the

young man was called from a room full of pale, bent-backed clerks and Jess was told by some kind of fussy manager that he could interview Ward in the hallway but to be quick about it since clerks worked from only seven in the morning to seven at night and as it was "there were just not enough hours in the day to get the work done."

Ward was a personable young man and it seemed he had nothing to hide. He said he and Lillian walked out together now and again, but she showed little interest in him as a possible husband.

When Jess asked him if he'd given Lillian Burke the diamond brooch he said, "Sheriff, I could never afford jewelry like that on a clerk's salary. But I did ask her who gave it to her and all she'd say was, 'It's a gift from a secret admirer.'"

"Have you any idea who that might be?"

Ward shook his head. "No, I haven't."

"Did you know that Lillian Burke was an opium fiend?" Jess said.

"Yes, and she used morphine," said Ward. He shook his head and frowned. "I tried to warn her away from it, but she wouldn't listen. Recently another drug made from opium has made its way into Hell's Half Acre. I don't know if Lillian was using that or not."

"Where would she get the money to spend on drugs?" Jess said.

"Not from her father, I can tell you that. He

keeps Lillian on a very strict budget. I've done his books a few times and Mr. Burke is quite wealthy, but he pleads poverty all the time."

"Have you any idea where Lillian could be?" Jess said.

The young man shook his head again. "None. But I'm worried sick. In many ways she's a very vulnerable young lady. She was only twelve when her mother died quite horribly of cancer and I don't think she ever got over it. She's not a stable person, Sheriff."

The prissy manager showed up in a state of high agitation and Jess thanked Ward for his help and left.

As he rode back to his office all Jess had determined was that Lillian Burke had a rich secret admirer and that she was sinking deeper into her drug addiction. He was willing to bet the farm that it was Kurt Koenig who'd introduced it into the Half Acre.

As nightfall came to Fort Worth Jess Casey decided his investigation could wait until tomorrow. For some reason the post of sheriff generated a lot of paperwork, most of it dealing with routine stuff like the amount of fines to be levied on the owners of loose dogs and a five-page memo from Mayor Stout on how vagrants, boxcar hobos and dance hall loungers were to be treated.

Such low persons must be taken to the city limits and warned to stay out of Fort Worth. Any reoccurrence of their offense must be dealt with harshly by a sentence of ten days in the city jail on bread and water. Where possible, such vagabonds must be put to work to pay for their food and accommodation. {See addendums IV, VII, X, XII, and XV listed below.}

Jess sighed and bent to his task, plowing through a ream of paperwork created by City Hall clerks with nothing better to do.

CHAPTER TWENTY-EIGHT

As Jess Casey signed endless memos with a sputtering steel pen, across town Wilson J. Tucker killed a man.

It was a two-bit shakedown that had gone wrong and it cost the lives of a tinhorn gambler who went by the name of Frank Poteet and his six-foot-tall lady friend, an actress and sometime hooker the sporting crowd called High Timber Tess.

The rules of the shakedown were simple and Poteet and Tess had played the game many times. But that night they tried it on the wrong man. Wilson J. Tucker didn't play by the rules.

The Alamo Saloon and Sporting House was a two-story dive on Houston Street next to Battles Cotton Yard. Everything about the place was third-rate. The booze was watered, the whores one cut above those found on a hog farm and the nightly entertainment was provided by a drunken fiddler who played fast and loose with the music.

Tucker didn't just wander into the place. He'd

been sent to find out why opium and morphine had been duly delivered to the Alamo but no monies were forthcoming in return.

The proprietor of the place, Larry Kemp, a swarthy, greasy-looking man, apologized profusely and vowed that, pending a good Friday and Saturday night, he would gladly pay what was owed.

"Even if you have a bad Friday and Saturday night, you'll pay up," Tucker said. "Otherwise you'll be in real danger of trying to get around on two broken knees." The gunman smiled. "Is there anything about what I just said you don't understand?"

Tucker stood under a gas lamp and his hard eyes were in shadow. Kemp blinked and said, "I understand. Good or bad, I'll have the money come Sunday morning." And then, the devil in him, he said, "You can pick it up on your way to church."

Tucker liked that, a man with spunk. He'd been thinking that he might leave Kemp with a reminder, a broken wrist maybe or a cut, but he decided against it.

"Good idea, Kemp," he said. "I'll stop by Sunday and read to you from the book."

"A drink, mister, on the house?" Kemp said. He was relieved that the tall hard case had not taken umbrage at his remark.

"Yeah. And get the bottle from under the bar."

Tucker, his eyes on the proprietor, making sure he got a bottle with a label on it, didn't see the exchange between a seedy-looking gambler and the woman who stood watching him.

Almost imperceptibly, Frank Poteet nodded his

head in Tucker's direction and the woman smiled. High Timber Tess could lay no claim to beauty, but she had large, well-shaped breasts just visible under the filmy stuff of her camisole and a wide, expressive mouth, painted bright scarlet. In all, she was a desirable woman to a man just off the trail.

Tess waited until Tucker got his whiskey, then she pushed her breasts against him and said, "In the mood for some company tonight, honey?"

"I don't pay for it," Tucker said. "I've never paid what you got to offer, girlie."

At first Tess was frightened by the man's eyes, ice blue, cold, merciless, the eyes of a killer. She turned and glanced at Poteet, but he nodded in Tucker's direction, irritably this time. The woman was experienced, had entertained hundreds of men and she overcame her revulsion.

"Honey child, what I got to give, all of it, is free for a big, strong man like you," she said. "Come upstairs and go exploring in the high timber country."

Tucker smiled. "All right, why not? It's been a while since I had a willing woman."

"Well, big boy, you found one now," Tess said.

Tess played the game well. She made a tease of disrobing in the mean little candlelit room and eagerly, or so it seemed, got into bed naked beside Tucker.

Now it was all up to Frank.

The well-worn Colt that Tucker placed on the upended wine crate that served as a table gave her pause. "Honey, I didn't think you were armed," she said.

"I wouldn't feel undressed without it," Tucker said.

"May I see it? I do love a man with a big gun."

"Well you found one now," Tucker said. He took the woman in his arms and Tess became frantic. *Damn it, where was Frank?*

The rules of the shakedown were simple. Poteet must wait outside the door until the bed started to rock. Then, playing the outraged husband he must charge into the room, gun in hand and yell, "What are you doing in bed with my wife?" Or words to that effect. The last rule was that the mark must be aghast, beg for forgiveness not to be shot, and gladly pay up to soothe the cuckolded husband's dangerous rage. The take varied from a few dollars to hundreds if the mark was a married man and a pillar of society who wanted no scandal.

Frank Poteet thought that the man in bed with Tess looked prosperous enough for a good haul. When the bed began to creak rhythmically, Poteet pulled his face into a ferocious expression and charged through the door.

"You bounder! What are you doing—"

The words died in Poteet's mouth. Tess sat up in bed, her breasts uncovered, and she looked horrified. Tucker, naked as a jaybird, held his Colt in his right hand and made the bed creak with his left.

"The oldest game in the book," Tucker said, grinning. He shot Poteet in the chest but as the gambler fell he managed to squeeze off a shot. The bullet hit Tess between her breasts. She cried out in shock and pain, fell on her left side and her long brown hair cascaded in glossy waves to the floor. As feet pounded on the stairs, Tucker dressed hurriedly and shoved his revolver back into his waistband.

Larry Kemp rushed into the room, took in the carnage at a glance and said, "What the hell happened?"

"They tried a shakedown play," Tucker said. "The man had a gun so I shot him. He shot the woman."

Kemp caught on immediately. "His name is Frank Poteet. He's worked the angry husband thing before."

"And the woman?"

"She called herself High Timber Tess. I don't know what her real name was. She and Poteet shacked up together and he pimped her out when the cards turned against him."

"A charming couple," Tucker said. The ivory butt of his Colt showed under his coat.

"Hell, mister, how did you know?" Kemp said.

"In my line of work a man looks at nothing but sees everything," Tucker said. "I saw Poteet give the woman a nod and I figured they planned to make a shakedown play."

A couple of bruisers stepped into the room and Kemp said, "Boys, get them bodies out of here. Dump them in Battles's yard. I sure as hell don't need the law poking around my place."

After the bodies were carried out, Kemp said, "What's your name, mister?"

"Wilson J. Tucker."

Kemp was stricken. "Oh my God," he said.

"Heard of me, huh?" Tucker said, smiling without warmth.

Kemp swallowed hard. "Tell the big man I'll pay his score on Sunday," he said. "Tell him I won't fail."

Tucker nodded. "I'm sure you won't."

CHAPTER TWENTY-NINE

"Both killed by a single shot to the chest, Jess," Dr. Sun said. "It looks like somebody gunned them both." He looked around him. "How did they end up here?"

"That's what I'd like to know," P. J. Battles said. "Bodies bleeding all over my cotton is bad for business."

Jess Casey's eyes lifted to the Alamo. "They could have been killed in the saloon and dragged into your yard, Mr. Battles. Or they were shot right here but that seems unlikely."

"Rats," Battles said. He saw the question on Jess's face and said, "Cotton bales crawl with rats at night. Nobody would come in here unless they were forced."

"They were pushed in here at gunpoint and then shot," Jess said. "It's a possibility."

Big Sal and her scrawny assistant stood by like vultures. The woman said, "The dead man is Frank Poteet, a two-bit gambler, shell game artist and pimp. The woman, God rest her, is Tess Rambler. She called herself High Timber. She and Poteet lived together in a shack behind the Germania boardinghouse."

"You knew them, Sal?" Jess said.

"I saw them around a time or two and talked. Poteet was a right sociable man."

"Did they visit the saloon there on the corner?" Jess said.

"Visit? They were there all the time. Poteet was a crooked gambler and he was banned from every saloon in town but this one."

"Who owns the place?" Jess said.

Battles said, "A lowlife by the name of Larry Kemp. He did ten hard in Leavenworth for bank robbery and when he came out he bought the Alamo. I guess he'd buried his loot somewhere and went back for it."

"Let's go have words with him," Jess said.

Walking into the Alamo first thing in the morning was like stepping into an outhouse in summer. The place stank of human sweat, vomit, piss and spilled beer and the not unpleasant incense smell of burned opium.

Larry Kemp was quick to deny that Poteet and Tess had been killed in his saloon. "I run a strict house here," he said. "No funny business, if you catch my drift."

"Who supplies your opium?" Jess said.

That caught Kemp off guard. He hesitated a

moment, blinked, then said, "I don't sell opium. Beer, whiskey, gin punch, but no opium. Never."

Jess, unnerved by the deaths of the gambler and his woman, snapped. "You're a damned liar," he said. "This dive stinks of the stuff."

Kemp's face took on a sly cast. "Be warned, Sheriff, the man who supplies the opium and morphine is big, so big that he can crush you and your little Chinese friend underfoot, like a booted man steps on a cockroach. Now just turn around and toddle out of here before you get hurt." Then, "Riker! Sims! Get over here."

Two huge men who'd been lounging against the bar drinking coffee stepped toward Jess and Dr. Sun. Huge in the arms and shoulders with broken simian faces, they were a pair to be reckoned with.

"Show the gentlemen the door," Kemp said.

Jess expected a strong-arm play but to his surprise the bigger of the two bruisers pulled a switchblade. "You heard the boss—out!" the man said. He stepped closer, the knife ready, and Jess's hand dropped to his gun.

Dr. Sun wore a plain black robe that fell to his ankles. Quickly his right hand shot inside an opening in the gown and he drew a broad, single-edged sword, a bright green tassel hanging from the pommel.

He was incredibly sudden. The blade flashed in an arc and neatly severed the knife-fighter's hand at the wrist.

For a heartbeat the man stared at his bleeding stump, then he shrieked in pain and horror and for some reason he ran outside, bellowing for help. His companion, appalled, took a step back and reached for the gun under his vest. Dr. Sun advanced on him, his steel blade bloody, and the big man lost interest in the fight. He turned on his heel and fled. His booted feet pounded all the way to the back of the building and then a door slammed.

Jess holstered his Colt. Kemp's horrified eyes were fixed on the hand lying on the floor, the switchblade still in its grasp.

His voice low and flat, Jess said, "Who supplies your opium, Kemp?"

Dr. Sun's blade rippled in the morning light as he flicked the point under the man's chin. "The sheriff asked you a question, my silent friend," he said. His words sounded like the hiss of a snake.

Kemp was scared. Really scared. He-pissed-himself scared.

"I don't know," he said, standing in a puddle. "The opium is delivered, I pay for it and I've never been told who supplies it. I know he's big, a very important man in the Half Acre, and he kills without even thinking about it."

Dr. Sun said, "Mr. Kemp, have you ever seen the *jian* take off a man's head? The blade is so quick, it is an exquisite thing."

Kemp wailed, "I'm telling you the truth. I don't know who he is."

"Is it Kurt Koenig?" Jess said.

Kemp didn't hesitate. "I told you. I don't know."

Jess tried a long shot. "Does Lillian Burke, the brewer's daughter, ever come here?"

Kemp shook his head. "Not as far as I know."

"Jess, are we finished?" Dr. Sun said.

Jess nodded. "Yeah. I don't think we're going to learn any more from Mr. Kemp."

"Then I must go look for that poor man I disabled. He needs help. Give me his hand, Jess. He might want it."

"Doc, get it yourself," Jess said. "I'm not touching it."

Dr. Sun picked up the severed hand and left and Jess said, "Clean up this mess, Kemp." He looked at the man's wet pants. "And for heaven's sake take a bath."

CHAPTER THIRTY

There were three men in the Silver Garter when Jess stepped inside.

Kurt Koenig, Luke Short and Mayor Harry Stout sat at a table, a silver coffee service and china cups between them.

The mayor's face was black with rage and Jess heard him say, "An outrage, I tell you. I never thought the day would come when I'd be exposed to such villainy."

Koenig looked up, saw Jess and grinned. "Ah, the law has arrived. Now we'll get to the bottom of this."

Jess nodded to Short, who ignored him, and then to the mayor, who said, "Good morning. Did you hear what happened?"

"Hear what?" Jess said. "I've been investigating a double murder."

He looked for a reaction from Koenig, but the expression on the man's face hadn't changed and still showed only a slight amusement.

"Murders, sir?" Stout said. His florid face was almost crimson. "As though murders are anything new in Hell's Half Acre. My dear boy, I'm talking about thuggery of the highest order, a vicious attack on civilization itself, by God."

"Is anybody going to tell me what happened?" Jess said. Without being invited he picked up a cup and poured himself coffee, an I-don't-give-a-damn move that wasn't lost on Koenig, who looked surprised.

Stout said, "In the early hours of this morning, when decent Christian folk were asleep in bed, a band of armed men broke into City Hall and removed the murderer who calls himself Zeus. As far as I can tell the night watchman turned the other way, the rogue."

The news hit Jess like a fist. He said, "What does the watchman say?"

"He says he was making his rounds when he was hit on the head and remembers nothing more," Stout said. "I don't believe a word of it."

Luke Short said, "Black men are dragged out of jails and lynched all the time. Why make such a fuss, Your Honor?"

"Because the man was taken from the jail cell in City Hall by vigilantes," Stout said. "Such an act of savagery cannot stand." He glared at Jess. "Conduct an immediate investigation, Sheriff, and report to me personally. Do I make myself clear?"

Jess didn't answer that. He asked a question of his own. "Who would want Zeus dead?"

"Hell, that's easy," Luke said. "You heard the

mayor, they were vigilantes. Addie Brennan was well liked in this town."

"No, she wasn't," Jess said. "I've been told she was a mean old biddy who never had a good word to say about anybody. A woman who wasn't well liked in life would hardly be regarded as a saint in death."

Koenig said, "Then what's your take on it, Jess?"

"I think Zeus had to be silenced," Jess said. "But for what reason I don't know. I believe we're already talking about a dead man."

"Who's going to take a black man's word for anything?" Luke said. "You're talking nonsense. A bunch of vigilantes took him out of the jail and strung him up someplace because he shot Addie Brennan. Use your brain, cowboy."

Mayor Stout gave Jess a long, speculative look then said, "Report to me, Sheriff, as soon as you find out something. Now I must go and see if I can undo the damage done. If a man cannot feel safe in City Hall then where can he feel secure?" He shook his head. "This will not set well with the voters who've come to trust Honest Harry Stout."

After the mayor left, Luke Short said, "Making a mountain out of a molehill, ain't he?"

Koenig shrugged. "Like Stout said, it won't look good to the voters." His eyes moved to Jess. "And to what do we owe the honor, Sheriff?"

Jess laid his empty cup back on the table. "Don't sell any more opium to Larry Kemp. I'm shutting him down."

Koenig seemed surprised. "Kemp sells opium in his dump? First I heard of it."

"You don't supply him with opium and morphine?" Jess said.

"The hell I do. I did for a while, but he never paid on time and I cut him off."

"What about this new drug, Kurt?"

"Haven't heard of it. What the hell is it?"

"It's made from opium. It's supposed to be much more powerful. It kills people, Kurt."

"Then I won't sell it, if it even exists," Kurt said. "I wouldn't want to kill off all my customers." The big man smiled. "You're just in time to congratulate Luke and me—we're going into business together. I'm supplying the White Elephant."

"With opium?" Jess said.

"Of course. There's a big market for it outside of the Half Acre."

"No, you're not, Kurt," Jess said. "Luke, if you turn your saloon into an opium den I'll shut you down. The plague has spread far enough. For now I'm content to confine it to the Half Acre, but soon I aim to crack down on any establishment that sells it."

By nature Luke Short had an explosive temper and Jess had pushed him over the edge. "You damned upstart, try to close me down and I'll kill you."

"If you don't want to go out of business then don't sell opium," Jess said.

"Damn you!" Luke yelled. He jumped to his feet and got belly to belly with Jess, just as he'd done with Jim Courtright. His hand reached behind him for the gun he kept in his back pocket.

Jess screwed the muzzle of his Colt into Short's side. "Luke, skin that piece and I'll scatter your liver all over the sawdust," he said.

Short was taken aback by the speed of Jess's draw. He let his gun hand fall and took a step back. His eyes were ablaze with a killing light.

"Luke! Let it go," Koenig said. The big man was on his feet. He wore his gun. "Jess, you're stepping over the line."

"I mean what I say, Kurt," Jess said. Then, "Where is Lillian Burke?"

"Pat Burke's daughter? How the hell should I know?"

"You own the Green Buddha opium den?"

"Sure I do."

"Lillian goes there regularly. She's hooked."

"I never go near the place," Koenig said. "It stinks."

"Not even to collect the money? Does the money stink as well?"

Koenig said nothing, but Luke Short was mad and it showed.

"Luke, turn around real slow," Jess said, sensing the danger.

"The hell I will," Short said. The light was still in his eyes. Even though Jess had his gun in his hand, Luke was going to attempt a draw.

Jess took a step forward and slammed his Colt into the side of the little gambler's head. Luke dropped without a sound. Jess rolled him over on his belly and removed the fancy Colt from his leather-lined back pocket.

"Tell him he can get it back at the usual place," Jess said. He shook his head. "That man never learns."

"Jess, you've just declared war," Koenig said. "You won't come out the winner."

"I've declared war on the Half Acre's opium trade, Kurt," he said. "I'm real sorry you're such a part of it."

"Jess, I'm seriously thinking of drawing down on you," Koenig said.

"Don't, Kurt," Jess said. "I don't want to kill you."

It was a moment of truth for Kurt Koenig. He'd given Jess Casey the job of sheriff almost as a joke. But now the joke was on him. All he'd done was create a monster.

CHAPTER THIRTY-ONE

Dr. Sun counted seventeen bullet holes in Zeus's huge body and evidence of a shotgun blast to his face at very close range.

"He was shot to pieces," he said. "Tied up and blasted into doll rags."

Jess Casey stared at the body, once so strong and vital, now a torn and dead thing. "It took a lot of lead to put him down," he said.

"There's rage here," Dr. Sun said. "Somebody hated this man. When the face is disfigured like this it's always because the victim was murdered in hot blood."

The rising wind tugged at Jess's clothes and hat brim. The blue bandanna around his neck fluttered like an imprisoned bird. "Who would hate Zeus that much?" he said.

Dr. Sun adjusted the position of the sword under his robe. "Some white people hate blacks," he said.

"I don't see it that way, Doc," Jess said. "This wasn't a lynching, it was a revenge murder. Look at the tracks. Four booted men dragged Zeus here and a fifth arrived later. He was wearing shoes. I'd be willing to bet that he carried a scattergun and fired the last shot into Zeus's face."

Dr. Sun looked up at the sky, where white clouds raced like a flock of sheep. "There is great evil in Fort Worth," he said.

"Who? Or what?" Jess said.

The little man shook his head. "I have no answers." He looked at Jess. "Perhaps you should have remained a cowboy, my friend."

Jess smiled. "Too beat up to be a cowboy, too scared most of the time to be a lawman. What do I do?"

"I have seen many brave men in my time and I have seen many cowards," Dr. Sun said. "Jess, you are neither one nor the other. You're just a man doing the best job he can."

"And not doing it very well," Jess said.

"That remains to be seen," Dr. Sun said.

Zeus was buried in the wind-torn Fort Worth cemetery. A parson said the words and Jess, Dr. Sun and an ailing Nate Levy were at the graveside. Big Sal and her assistant hovered close by, waiting to do what had to be done when the praying was over.

To everyone's surprise Kurt Koenig joined them, wearing a black mourning gown. "Zeus was a fighter," he said. "I'm here to pay my respects."

After the praying and the singing of hymns, the preacher left and Koenig took Jess aside. "We have our differences, Jess," he said, "but Zeus's murder was none of my doing."

"I didn't think it was," Jess said. "But I aim to find out."

"Jess, stay away from Luke Short," Koenig said. "He's a proud man and you've humiliated him twice. There won't be a third time. Go slower, Jess, go slower."

"Kurt, I'm shutting down the Alamo and the Green Buddha," Jess said. "I plan to stop the spread of opium and morphine in this town, and the new drug, if it appears."

The mourning robe flapped around Koenig in the wind as he said, "I don't supply the Alamo with opium. I told you that."

"And I believe you. But I think closing down the Alamo will bring whoever is out from under his rock." Jess locked eyes with Koenig. "Kurt, you get a cut from every dirty business in town and you run whores and sell bad whiskey in the Silver Garter. You're already a rich man, so when do you say enough is enough? You don't need the opium."

"Leave the Green Buddha alone."

"I can't do that."

"Jess, you're sheriff for only as long as I say you're sheriff," Koenig said.

"You firing me, Kurt?"

"Not quite yet. But I'm thinking about it."

The Alamo would have to wait. Jess Casey had more urgent business at City Hall. Nate Levy, who was still weeks away from recovering from the vicious beating he'd taken, insisted on accompanying him. He wore a plug hat and long black coat, a Colt .44-40 self-cocker in the right pocket.

"You any good with that Colt, Nate?" Jess said as they walked along the boardwalk.

"Good, bad, how am I to know? I've never shot the thing," Levy said.

"Perfect," Jess said. "Just what I wanted to hear."

The wind remained strong and gusty, coming in from the east, and Jess fancied that it had traveled all the way from the tropics and had smelled of fragrant flowers before it picked up the scent of horse dung and cattle pens.

"Something smells good," Nate Levy said. Just ahead of them a street vendor sold hot sausages and little meat pies from a handcart. "Let's stop, Jess," he said. "I'm hungry."

"Not the kind of food for an invalid," Jess said, smiling.

"'Invalid,' he says. Says me, I'm starving to death. Broth and boiled eggs isn't fit food for a sick man. We'll stop."

He and Jess each sampled a sausage and a pie and Nate declared it was the best grub he ever ate. But when City Hall came in sight he was already complaining of dyspepsia.

"Sheriff, why did you let me eat that damned greasy sausage?" he said. "You should have told me it was not the kind of fare for an invalid."

Another stop had to be made while Nate stepped into a candy store where he bought peppermints to settle his stomach. And Jess began to wonder if allowing the little man to tag along was more trouble than it was worth.

At City Hall Jess learned that the night watchman, a man called Dave Feeney, had already left and would not be back until seven that night. But the clerk at the reception desk said Dave Feeney lived alone in a shack behind the French Hotel on 15th Street.

Nate Levy had not come inside and when Jess joined him again the little man was gazing intently at something in the palm of his hand.

"Catch a bug, Nate?" Jess said, grinning.

Nate shook his head. "No, it's a little jewel, an emerald by the look of it."

Jess took Nate's hand and studied the stone. "Where did you find it?" he said.

"Over there by the doorstep," Nate said.

Jess said, "I would never have seen that."

"I'm closer to the ground than you," the little man said. "I don't think it's real. But it looks like it was in a setting."

"Lillian Burke has a brooch with emeralds like that," Jess said. "Could it possibly be hers?"

"She's the brewer's daughter who's gone missing?"

"Yes, she is."

"I don't think this is a real emerald," Nate said. "I mean, it could be, but I don't think so. It's small so it's hard to tell."

"Can you find out?"

"When I get back to the hotel I'll look at it closer with a magnifier. My father was a jeweler and he taught me how to tell real from fake."

Jess's enthusiasm waned. "Probably a lot of women in town have fake emerald jewelry," he said. "And the stone could have been lost years ago and today it was uncovered by the wind."

Carefully, Nate Levy put the gem in his pocket. "Well, I'll take a look and tell you what I think," he said.

There were several frame and tar-paper shacks behind the French Hotel, the abodes of some of the city's poorest. Each had a sagging roof, boarded-up windows and a rusty stovepipe sticking through the wood shingles. The area was covered in empty bottles and other trash, probably the reason all the windows to the rear of the hotel had closed shutters.

A ragged old woman throwing bottles into a sack looked up when she saw Jess and Nate. Her eyes went to the battered star on Jess's shirt. "Plannin' to arrest somebody, sonny?" she said.

Jess smiled. "Not today, ma'am. I'm looking for a feller, name's Dave Feeney."

"Ha!" The woman grinned, revealing toothless gums. "He's always one of three ways, drunk, sleeping or working."

"And what is he today?" Jess said.

"Sleeping probably and you'll have a hard time waking him. He works nights, you know."

"Which house is his?" Jess said.

The woman cackled. "House! Is that what you call it?" She assumed a genteel accent. "The Feeney mansion is right in front of you, sonny. Knock and the butler will answer." Still cackling, she went back to scavenging for bottles, her burlap sack clinking.

Jess rapped on the door and set it rattling on its hinges. "Mr. Feeney, are you to home? It's Sheriff Casey. I'd like to talk to you."

Jess got no answer. He waited a while then tried knocking again, louder this time. The shack remained silent.

"Maybe he's a sound sleeper," Nate said. "Or drunk."

"Or he isn't to home," Jess said.

He walked around the shack but the boarded windows blocked out any sign of life and there was no sound.

"I guess we try later, Nate," Jess said.

"This is later enough," Nate said. He stepped around Jess, lifted his leg and kicked the door open. Then, immediately, "Sheriff, you'd better come see this."

There was a sagging beam at the V of the roof and to this was attached a rope. A dangling noose neatly fitted around Feeney's neck but the man had strangled to death. His bloodshot eyes had popped as large as pool balls and his tongue lolled out of his mouth. An overturned chair lay on the floor.

"Hung himself," Nate Levy said. He looked around the mean shack. "Poor man didn't have much, did he?"

Jess said nothing. He quickly searched the cabin and then, holding down his revulsion, checked the dead man's pockets.

"Where's the money?" he said.

Nate's expression asked a question and Jess said, "Feeney was paid to look the other way when Zeus's killer came for him. He should have the money. Where is it?"

"I guess he drank it all away," Nate said.

"He's had no time to do that," Jess said. "He should have had some money, but he hasn't, not a dime."

Nate said, "Well, he hung himself so we'll never know."

Jess smiled. "I wish I had a Pinkerton close by."

"Why?" Nate said.

"Because I think this man was murdered."

"Looks to me like he done himself in," Nate said. "I'm not a Pinkerton but it seems kind of obvious."

"But why? Feeney had a steady job and was earning money for whiskey. Why would he kill himself?"

"Because he couldn't live with the shame of betraying my boy Zeus," Nate said. "I don't want to talk ill of the dead, but that's a possibility."

"I don't think even you believe that, Nate. A man who would step aside and see another human being slaughtered had no shame."

Jess opened his Barlow knife, cut the rope, and Feeney's lifeless body thudded onto the dirt floor.

"No point in keeping him hanging there," Jess said. "I'm not a detective but I'm sure, like Zeus, he was murdered to silence him."

"Hell, then who done for him?" Nate Levy said.

Jess shook his head. "I just said I'm not a detective, Nate, so the answer is I don't know."

CHAPTER THIRTY-TWO

Nate Levy showed up at the shcriff's office two hours after Big Sal had taken Feeney's body away. She told Jess Casey that the man was a well-known drunk but she had nothing else to add.

But Nate brought news of the emerald.

"It's a high-quality stone," he said. "It's small but very finely cut."

"How much is it worth?" Jess said.

"On its own, not a great deal," Nate said. "But it would add value to a piece of jewelry. There's no doubt about that."

"Like a diamond brooch," Jess said.

"Exactly," Nate said. "And one more thing, I don't think it was in the ground for long. I saw no sand abrasion of any kind through my magnifier."

Jess sat back in his chair. If Lillian Burke had lost the emerald, what was she doing at City Hall? On an errand for her father perhaps? He was one of the city's most prominent merchants and would often have business there. And the girl could have lost it days or even weeks before she disappeared.

"I don't think the emerald tells us much, Nate," he said. "Except that Lillian Burke was at City Hall sometime—"

"Within the past couple of months or so, no longer," Nate said.

"Dead end, don't you think?" Jess said.

Nate Levy had no time to answer that because the unexpected arrival of Luke Short, roaring drunk and ready to burn powder, stopped all conversation.

The little gambler kicked the door open, charged inside and cut loose at Jess with a Colt shopkeeper's model.

Nate Levy dived for the floor and Jess followed him. Luke's drunken state and the shortness of the Colt's barrel combined to make his shooting less than accurate but he put his last two rounds into Jess's empty chair before he yelled, "You won't buffalo me again, Casey!" He turned to the cowering Nate and said, "Now you can bury him."

Luke staggered out the door and Jess rose to his feet.

"Did you get hit?" Nate Levy said.

"Hell, no. He's as drunk as a skunk."

Jess ran to the door and saw Short staggering down the boardwalk, his empty gun dangling at his side. There were too many people around to shoot, so he yelled, "Luke Short, get back here, you bushwhacking, low-down son of a bitch!"

But if Luke heard, which was doubtful, he ignored Jess and kept on staggering homeward.

"Go after him," Nate said. "Put a bullet in him or he'll give you no peace."

"He's drunk," Jess said. "I'm not going to shoot a man with the devil in him."

Nate, pale, wizened and worried, said, "Jess, this is Hell's Half Acre, remember. Saints don't last long in this place. Now go gun him like I told you before you lose him."

"I'll see him tomorrow when he's sober," Jess said.

"Well, that's just crackerjack," Nate said. "Tomorrow when Luke's sober he'll shoot straighter."

CHAPTER THIRTY-THREE

Luke Short could wait. Jess Casey had more urgent business at hand.

Just after first light he walked to Simon Hall's carpentry business and lumber yard on 13th Street, where the man was already at work repairing a broken chair.

"I have a job for you," Jess said, after the customary handshake. "I need a couple of doors and some windows boarded up."

"I have that capability," Hall said. "When do you want the work done?"

"Now," Jess said.

"Well, I'm kind of busy—"

"You bill the city," Jess said.

Hall's face lit up. "In that case I'll get right on it." Then, "Jack, get out here. We have a job."

A gangly young man came out of the workshop, and Hall said, "Hitch the mare to the wagon and be quick about it."

It took just ten minutes to get the horse into the

traces and load the wagon with lumber and ladders. When Jess told Hall where they were headed, and why, the man raised an eyebrow but made no comment. He and Jack, a carpenter apprentice, jumped on the back of the wagon and dangled their legs as Hall drove to the Alamo.

Because of what had happened to his bruisers, Larry Kemp made little objection as Jess rousted out the early-morning patrons from the saloon. One rooster, already drunk, swung at Hall, and the robust carpenter laid him out with a neat crack to the jaw.

"Front and back door and all the windows, upstairs and down," Jess told Hall. Then, to Kemp: "These premises are officially closed until such times as repairs are carried out to the structure. At the moment the Alamo is in dangerous condition and it's a fire hazard."

"You're closing me down because I sell opium here," Kemp said. "I don't need your fancy talk about structures and fires."

"Who supplies you, Kemp?" Jess said.

"Go to hell."

Jess stood outside the saloon as the sound of hammers echoed throughout the building. Kemp stood watching and seethed with rage. Finally he sidled up to Jess and said, "Sheriff, you'll hear that sound again when they're hammering down the lid of your coffin."

"Who supplies your opium?" Jess said. "And, Kemp, give me some sass and back talk. I need an excuse to shoot you."

The saloonkeeper read Jess's eyes and didn't like what he saw. "I don't know."

"Who do you pay for the stuff?"

"Usually a man comes and collects it, occasionally a woman."

"Kurt Koenig's woman?"

"Hell, no. Some old hag who always picks up my empty bottles while she's here."

Jess remembered the old woman he'd met at Feeney's place. Was it her? And who did she deliver the proceeds of Kemp's ill-gotten gains to? He would look for her later. First he had to see the Alamo shuttered . . . and then move on to the Green Buddha.

A few of the patrons and a growing number of passersby expressed their concern that the Alamo pleasure palace was shutting down. Kemp, smiling broadly, reassured them. "I'll be open for business in a day or two," he said. "I've got powerful friends in this town."

"Good for you, Larry," a woman said. She glared at Jess. "And you, for shame, trying to put an honest man out of business."

That met with growls of approval, and a couple of burly fellows spoke darkly about a certain lawman getting his teeth kicked in. Simon Hall got on with his work, but he looked uneasy. His apprentice, enjoying the spectacle, grinned and pounded harder with his hammer.

The Alamo was located in one of the most

dangerous, violent neighborhoods on earth and Jess was aware that things could rapidly get out of hand. The crowd that had gathered was growing increasingly hostile and Kemp stoked their anger. He played the martyr to the hilt and crocodile tears reddened his eyes.

"I was never one to turn a hungry man away from my door or refuse a few dollars to a widow woman or an orphan," he wailed. "And now I'm being driven out."

This incensed the crowd, which conveniently forgot that Larry Kemp was never known to give anyone a free drink, let alone feed the hungry and care for orphans.

"You're a victim, Larry," a woman yelled. "That's what you are, a victim of the law."

Kemp nodded and spread his hands, "Yes, a victim. While villains like Kurt Koenig prosper."

"The damned sheriff is on Koenig's payroll, Larry," one of the burly men said. "That's the real reason you're being shut down. Koenig thinks you're too much competition."

That last was met with a roar of approval and the burly man said, "Rip the damned timber off those doors! I'm a Panther City Boy! Who's with me?"

"And free drinks for everybody when it's done," Kemp said, in a moment of madness.

The situation was fast getting out of hand and Jess decided to up the ante. He drew his Colt and said, "I'll kill any man who goes near the doors."

The burly man and his companions were skull,

fist and boot fighters and the gun in the sheriff's hand gave them pause. Jess took advantage of their hesitation.

"You, Panther City Boy, try to pull the timbers off the door and see what happens," he said. "Go ahead, we're all waiting."

The big man didn't like that one bit. The slender, hard-eyed sheriff was as significant as a stiletto blade and he saw no back-up in him.

Jess thumbed back the hammer of the Colt. "Damn you! Try it!"

"Don't, Andy boy," a woman said to the big man. "He's crazy."

"Kemp, if anyone moves toward the door you'll be the first one I kill," Jess said.

Kemp swallowed hard, then said, "We'll let my friends deal with this outrage. I'll be open for business tomorrow."

This raised cheers and the crowd's mood swung from hostile to happy. The big bruiser called Andy stabbed a thick finger at Jess and said, "I'll remember this."

But the moment was past. Andy knew it and so did Jess. The sound of hammers started again and the crowd drifted away.

"Kemp," Jess said, holstering his gun. "Go away."

"Go where?" Kemp said.

"Anywhere I don't have to see you."

"You'll regret this, Sheriff," Kemp said. But he skedaddled, constantly looking over his shoulder.

* * *

To Jess Casey's surprise, the Green Buddha was closed and padlocked. A note pinned to the door read:

OUT OF BUSINESS
—BY ORDER OF SHERIFF

Jess was puzzled. Had Kurt Koenig got religion or was he avoiding a confrontation? Neither seemed likely.

Simon Hall tapped his ball-peen hammer on the horny palm of his hand. "You still want it boarded up, Sheriff?" he said.

"Huh?" Jess said. He'd been lost in thought.

"Do we board up the doors and windows?"

"No, leave it," Jess said. He smiled at Hall. "Thank you for your help. Send your bill to City Hall."

"It will be a big one," Hall said. "I'm adding hazard pay."

Jess nodded. "You should. For a while back there things got tense."

Hall, a dour man, managed a smile. "That's one way of saying it. I reckon it got downright dangerous."

"If you still want it, I'll have more work for you soon," Jess said.

"You know where to find me," Hall said. "Working for you, Sheriff, is an adventure."

CHAPTER THIRTY-FOUR

"I'm not catching your drift," Kurt Koenig said. "I didn't shut down the Green Buddha."

"Then I withdraw my thanks," Jess Casey said. "But shut down it is."

"What the hell?" Koenig said. He was genuinely confused. "Who did that?"

"Me, if the sign on the door is to be believed," Jess said. "The place is padlocked."

"But you'd nothing to do with it?" Koenig said.

Jess smiled. "Not a thing. Somebody beat me to it. I planned to board up the dive, had a carpenter standing by and everything."

Koenig pushed his coffee cup away from him as though he'd suddenly lost the taste for it. "This is a declaration of war," he said.

"Seems like," Jess said, enjoying this.

Koenig got to his feet and his eye rested on a man who was trundling a beer barrel behind the bar. "Sikes!"

"Yeah, boss?"

"Call a meeting of the Panther City Boys. I want them here at seven tonight. I don't care what you have to do to get them here, but I want all of them, present and correct and armed."

"Sure thing, boss," Sikes said. He wore an eye patch made from a piece of rawhide.

Koenig said, "Leave the beer barrel. Let the bartender do that. Go round up the boys and tell them we're at war."

"Sure thing, boss," Sikes said, calmly, as though a gang war was declared every day.

"I think it's high time I visited the Green Buddha," Koenig said.

"I'm coming with you," Jess said. Then, "You know your friend Luke Short tried to kill me last night?"

Koenig brushed it off as though it was a matter of no account. "Luke was drunk. He does silly things in drink."

"I could charge him with attempted murder," Jess said.

"No need for that. I'll talk to him."

For the moment, Jess decided not to push the matter. Solving the mystery of the Green Buddha had to come first. The last thing he needed in the Half Acre was a full-scale gang war.

When he reached the Green Buddha the first thing Kurt Koenig did was tear the note off the door, the second was to turn the air blue with curses. "The low-down rats used my own padlock," he said. "That adds to the insult."

Privately Jess didn't quite see why, but he kept quiet as the big man fished in his pants pocket and came up with a bunch of keys. "Rats," he said. "Dirty rat scum, motherless riffraff, every last one of them."

"Who do you think did it, Kurt?" Jess said.

"How the hell should I know?" Koenig said.

He opened the door and stepped inside. The place had been trashed. Everything that could be broken was broken, everything that could be torn was torn and black paint had been splashed over the walls.

But there was worse . . . much worse.

Jess found the first body, a small Chinese woman dressed in a dragon robe. She'd been shot in the forehead at close range, the skin around the wound blackened by powder. Koenig said she was one of his helpers. The rectangle of daylight that shafted through the open door revealed seven more bodies, five men and two women. Lillian Burke was not one of them.

Soothed by the opiate, the smokers had died without fuss. Shot in the head, several still had the pipe in their mouths and one woman's dream smile was frozen on her lips. The place was silent and still, the dead making no sound, no stir.

Like Jess, Kurt Koenig was horrified. He looked around him at the carnage, then stared at Jess, his face unbelieving. "Who . . ."

"I don't know, Kurt," Jess said. "I wish I did."

Koenig brushed past Jess and stepped outside. Gun in hand his eyes searched the wasteland around him. He was looking for a target, anyone or anything that could be connected with the attack on his place. He saw nothing but bunchgrass, cactus and a few struggling wildflowers. He heard the hum of busy Main Street and the rush of the wind and felt the *thump-thump* of his racing heart beating.

Reluctantly he pushed back his frock coat and holstered his Colt.

"Wilson J. Tucker works like that," he said. "Fast kills. No fuss."

"If it was Tucker, somebody ordered him to do it," Jess said.

"Yeah, somebody gave the order," Koenig said. "A somebody who wants to put me out of business."

Jess thought for a few moments then said, "He's clearing the way for something. Maybe that new drug we heard about."

"Or he wants to take over the Half Acre and I'm in the way."

"Apart from Tucker, is there anybody new in town, Kurt?" Jess said. "Somebody with money, talking big."

Koenig said, with a slight smile, "Only you, Jess. You talk big. But you don't have any money so that lets you out."

"Have you heard of anybody else?" Jess said, refusing to be baited.

"No. People move in and out of Fort Worth all the time. Who can keep track of them? That Doc

Holliday feller was in town for a month before I found out about it."

"Then it could be some ranny who's already here," Jess said.

"Yeah, a man who talks big and has a lot of money," Koenig said. "You know how many men there are in this town who fit those shoes? I could sit down here and name a hundred right off."

"Don't reopen this place, Kurt," Jess said. "Raze it to the ground."

"Playing sheriff again, Jess?"

"That's about the size of it, I guess."

"Now the Green Buddha is a damned tomb," Koenig said. "Do what you want with it."

CHAPTER THIRTY-FIVE

"When I drink I get mad at people and when I get mad at people bad things happen," Luke Short said. "I didn't mean you any harm, not really."

"Four bullets in my roof and walls and two in my chair say otherwise," Jess said. Short said nothing and Jess said, "I could hang you, Luke, or see you sent to Leavenworth for thirty years."

Short groaned and ran his fingers through his thinning hair. "I told you I was drunk. A drunk is not responsible for his actions. I'm more to be pitied than sanctioned." Another groan, then, "I think I'm going to die anyway. So there's not much more you can do to me."

"How much whiskey did you drink last night?" Jess said.

"Too much."

"Drunk or not, when a man tries to kill me I take it real seriously, Luke," Jess said.

The White Elephant bartender clinked a glass

and the little gambler yelled, "Quit that racket!" He held his head in his hands. "Ooooh . . . I shouldn't have done that."

"Did you hear what I said, Luke?"

"Yeah, I heard." Short shoved out his wrists. "Put the chains on me and then hang me, Sheriff. I don't give a damn."

Jess sat back in his chair. "I'm not going to hang you, Luke. I call it doing you a favor."

"Sure, sure," Luke said.

"Do you owe me a favor, Luke? Look at me and tell me if you do or you don't."

"I owe you a favor," Luke said.

"I'm going to call it in."

"When? Now?"

"No, sometime soon. Anytime I feel like it."

Jess took Luke's Colt from his waistband and shoved it across the table. "I'm giving you your gun back, Luke. You didn't do too good with the one you had last night."

"What kind of favor?" Luke said. He reached out his hand to take the revolver but Jess clamped it down with his hand.

"Does it matter? A favor is a favor."

"All right, you got it, Sheriff. I'm a man of my word."

Jess lifted his hand from the Colt. "And so am I. Renege on your word and I'll have you in the hoosegow so fast you won't know what hit you."

"You're a hard man, Casey," Luke said. "I never thought that about you before, but I think it now. I won't go back on my word. In the West or anywhere else it's the most valuable thing a man possesses."

"Did you hear about the Green Buddha?" Jess said.

Luke shook his head, then winced.

Mindful of Luke's delicate condition, in as few words as possible Jess told him about the murders. "Any idea who would do a thing like that?" he said. "Kill eight people, three of them women?"

Luke said, "Yeah, Kurt Koenig, but he wouldn't do it to his own place."

"Anybody else in town that'd kill like that?"

Luke rested his thumping head on the palm of his hand. "I only know it wasn't me."

Jess got to his feet. "You should go see Doc Sun. He'll give you something to make you feel better."

"A bullet in my brainpan is the only thing that will help," Luke said.

"When I call in the favor you owe me, you may get your wish," Jess said.

Jess left the White Elephant and made his way to the Feeney cabin through the early-afternoon crowds. The door hung open and whatever mean possessions the man had were looted.

"You're back again, lawman, huh?"

The old bottle lady stood watching Jess after she gave him a bad start. "You surprised me," he said. "I didn't hear you."

"I surprise a lot of people," the woman said. "Maybe I'll surprise you, lawman."

"You live around here?" Jess said.

The woman turned her upper body and pointed to a cabin that looked even worse than the Feeney hovel. "That's my house. That's what you call these mansions, ain't it? You call them houses."

"I'd like to talk to you, ma'am" Jess said. "I'm Sheriff Jess Casey."

"I know who you are, sonny. Death stands at your right shoulder. Did you know that? He's a terrible sight. As cold as ice, that one."

Jess felt a shiver but resisted the urge to turn his head and look.

"But maybe he doesn't want you," the woman said. "He knows that you bring death to others and he stands patiently, like a dog waiting for scraps to fall from your dinner table."

Jess glanced at the blue sky and enjoyed the warmth of the sun. "Can we talk in your . . . cabin?" he said.

"What about?" the woman said. Her eyes slanted and looked sly.

"Just a few questions," Jess said.

"No," the woman said. "We'll talk here. Death will follow you and I don't want him to cross my threshold."

"Well, then we'll do it out here," he said. He took the makings from his shirt pocket. "May I beg your indulgence, ma'am?"

"Please do. I have always been partial to the smell of a gentleman's tobacco."

Jess heard a distant echo of what this woman once was, an upper-class young lady schooled in the proper etiquette of the Southern belle. "May I ask your name?" Jess said.

"I have no name," the old woman said. "I had a name once, but in these many years I've heard it so seldom I forget what it was. But you may call me Dixie if that pleases you, or nothing at all, if that pleases you more."

"I'll call you Dixie," Jess said. He lit his cigarette then said, "Larry Kemp—"

"That damnable piece of white trash."

"Larry Kemp said you sometimes picked up money from him to pay for the opium he used in his saloon."

"The Alamo," Dixie said. "Yes, I did. But not often."

"Who hired you to do that?"

"A man who wished to keep his identity secret. He'd give me five dollars and then wait here until I brought Kemp's money to him. He did it only when his regular courier was sick, or so he told me."

"Can you describe this man, Dixie?" Jess said.

"Fairly tall but not as tall as you. He was a pale, pasty-faced gent who dressed quite well. I always took him for a clerk of some kind."

"Did he ever give you his name?"

Dixie stared at Jess. Waiting.

"Will five dollars jog your memory?"

"It might. It very well might."

Jess reached into his pocket . . .

And then Dixie's head exploded.

CHAPTER THIRTY-SIX

Blood, bone and brain splattered scarlet across Jess Casey's face, followed an instant later by the flat report of a high-powered rifle.

For a moment Jess stood there stunned, frozen in place. Then as Dixie dropped at his feet he dived for the ground, his Colt in his hand. He saw nothing. If there had been a drift of smoke the gusting wind had taken it away.

Slowly, his gaze probing into the distance, Jess rose to his feet, his gun up and ready. But there was no second shot. A heavy bullet had done terrible things to Dixie's head and the old woman had been dead before she hit the ground. The rifleman, whoever he was, had accomplished his task. Like Dave Feeney before her, Dixie had been silenced.

Wilson J. Tucker was the proud owner of a fine Holland and Holland elephant gun. He'd told Kurt Koenig that he hadn't brought it with him to Fort Worth, but English rifles were easily taken apart and could be stored in a relatively small case that

Tucker could have hidden in his bedroll. And the gunman was skilled enough to make an accurate head shot at distance.

There was no doubt in Jess's mind that Tucker was the killer.

Hell's Half Acre was a town used to the sound of gunfire and no one came running to see what had happened. Suddenly ashamed that he had brought about Dixie's death, Jess picked her up in his arms and carried her to the cabin. There was a cot, a collection of bottles on the floor, and one other thing—yellowed with age, but lovingly preserved, a lacy, white parasol stood in a corner, the relic of a bygone age when Dixie had been young and beautiful.

Deeply touched, Jess laid the old woman on the couch and covered her with a sheet. At least when Big Sal came for her it would look as though another human being had cared enough to lay her out as a Southern belle of good family deserved.

"I hope you stay around, Sheriff," Big Sal said. "You're good for business." The huge, masculine woman seemed to fill Jess's small office.

"You took care of Dixie?" Jess said.

Big Sal nodded and then said, "The rumor going around about Dixie was that she was born to a rich plantation family in Alabama. The war ruined them and they fell into poverty."

"It's as good a story as any, I guess," Jess said. "She had a parasol in her cabin."

"Yeah, I know," Big Sal said. "I'll bury her with it."

"Thanks," Jess said.

The woman was silent for a few moments, then said, "Big story doing the rounds, Sheriff. Seems there's a new opium drug that somebody wants to push in the Half Acre."

"I heard that myself," Jess said. "I reckon it's true."

"If it's as popular as some folks think it might be, somebody could make millions selling it."

"What else have you heard, Sal?" Jess said.

"That's about it. What about that Lillian Burke gal? She show up yet?"

"No, not yet."

"She's real sassy, ain't she?" Big Sal said. "A pretty bird to keep in a gilded cage."

"You think somebody kidnapped her?" Jess said.

The woman smiled. "Hell no, Sheriff. Little Miss Lillian is playing dollhouse with some rich man. You can bet your bottom dollar on it."

"I hope that's the case," Jess said.

Sal gave Jess a wave and stepped to the door. But she turned and said, "I heard Luke Short cut loose on you with a .45."

"He was drunk," Jess said.

"Ah, then that explains it," Big Sal said.

CHAPTER THIRTY-SEVEN

Hell's Half Acre was the most claustrophobic town in the West, more like the slums of Calcutta than part of a booming frontier town.

Jess Casey patrolled the streets and alleys as part of his duties and the rickety buildings along Main, Houston and Rusk Streets seemed to close in on him, threatening to crush the life out of him. At night the darkness was kept at bay by the blaze of gas and oil lamps, and the throngs of people on the boardwalks continually drifted from light to shade and back again.

On the evening of the day he saw Dixie buried he was on the corner of Rusk and 12th investigating the report of a cutting in the Nance Hotel and Saloon. It was a modest establishment and its only claim to fame was that Long-Haired Jim Courtright had dropped in every now and then for a hot gin punch.

The cutting was of a minor nature, a woman who spiked her husband in the ass with scissors because he was drinking all the rent money. Jess warned both parties to behave and sent them on their way.

But before he left a shabby-looking man in a long black overcoat and bowler hat sidled up to him and said, "I seen something, Sheriff. Heard something, too."

Jess stared at the little man. He had a thin black mustache and expressionless eyes the color of Mississippi River mud. "What did you see?" Jess said.

"Buy me a drink and we'll sit at a table and I'll tell you," the man said.

"If you're wasting my time you'll be scratching your name on the jailhouse wall tonight," Jess said.

"I don't know what my information is worth, but it's at least worth a whiskey," the man said.

"We'll see," Jess said. But he bought the man his drink and then crossed the floor with him to a shadowed table. The saloon smelled of boiled cabbage and sour beer, but there was no hint of opium.

Jess lit a cigarette, watched the little man sip his whiskey. Finally the man sat back in his chair and licked his lips as though about to say something. A vein pulsed in his neck. He stayed silent.

"Tell me what you saw," Jess said. His gaze slid over the dozen or so working-class men standing at the bar. Nothing there alarmed him.

"What's your name?" Jess said.

"Michael."

"All right, Michael. Tell me what you saw."

"What I seen wasn't here in the Half Acre, it was up near the stockyards where all them big houses are," Michael said. "I did some yard work for Mrs. McClelland—you know Mrs. McClelland? No? Well, anyway it took me the whole day and then she gave me corn bread and buttermilk, so it was dark when I finally set out for home. I live on 13th Street, you see."

"So what did you see, Michael?" Jess said, sighing out the words, slightly irritated.

"Like I said, I was near the stockyards and I heard the sound of running feet, light feet, like a woman's," Michael said. "And it was a woman, or a girl, because I heard her sobbing. Then I heard a man yelling at her to stop and a second man shouted out to her, calling her a very bad name."

"What did he call her?"

Michael looked over his shoulder, then whispered, "He called her a whore. A black man's whore."

Jess nodded. "Then what?"

"I was scared, so I crouched down behind a fence post and then I saw the woman fall. She was nicely dressed but her clothes were torn. The two men grabbed her and a man, a big, powerful man, slapped her across the face and she went limp and almost fell again."

"Then what happened?" Jess prompted.

"Well, then, I think it was the big man, called her a whore again and they carried her away."

"Did you see where they went?" Jess said.

"No, sir. I was too scared to stay around. I ran all the way home and bolted my door."

"When did this happen?" Jess said.

"The night before last, Sheriff. I'll never forget it."

"Did you get a good look at the men? See their faces?"

Michael shook his head. "No, they were in shadow. I just saw their shapes."

"Recognize their voices?"

"I thought the big man's voice sounded familiar, but I don't know. I couldn't place it." Michael's muddy eyes were hopeful. "I hope what I told you was useful, Sheriff."

Jess nodded. "It was." He reached into his pocket and gave the man five dollars. Dixie's dollars. "You be careful," he said. "Keep what you told me to yourself."

Michael swallowed hard. "Do you really think I'm in danger?"

"Yes, I do. You were seen talking to me and that's enough. Take my advice, buy a bottle, go home and bolt your door. Don't answer it to anyone."

Jess rose to his feet. "Wait until ten minutes after I leave before you go outside. Understand?"

The little man nodded. He looked scared.

The little man's name was Michael Hannah. He'd been a nonentity all his life, an odd-job man who eked out a meager living doing menial tasks nobody else would do. But suddenly he saw a way to make himself important, to be a somebody, for a few hours at least.

He stepped to the bar, put his five dollars on the oak and loudly ordered whiskey. "I'm celebrating tonight," he said. "I just helped the sheriff solve a very important case, a mystery about a beautiful kidnapped girl."

There were men at the bar who wanted to hear the story, but there was another man who already knew the story and how it would end.

He could not let Michael Hannah, suddenly the cock of the walk, live for too much longer.

CHAPTER THIRTY-EIGHT

She could have been a whore who had crossed her pimp, Jess Casey reckoned, and had been beaten up and dragged back to the brothel.

Or had Lillian Burke attempted to flee her gilded cage, and had the men Michael seen and heard chased after her? But Lillian was not a whore. She was not a black man's whore or a white man's, for that matter. Why did the big man call her that?

Big man. Could Kurt Koenig be the one who had decided to make Lillian his kept women? It was possible, but unlikely. Destiny Durand was Kurt's steady gal and from what little Jess had seen of her she was not the type to stand idly by and let Koenig replace her. Unless it had been Destiny at the stockyards that night. Had she run away from Kurt?

Jess rose from his desk and stared out at the morning. A cattle herd had crossed the Trinity at first light and had been driven through town to the pens. The signs of its passing were littered all over the street.

Jess shook his head, clearing his thoughts. Later he would talk to Dr. Sun and get his opinions, but first a routine matter required his attention. A landlord had reported a murder at his boardinghouse on 13th Street.

The realization hit Jess like a fist. The little man called Michael lived on 13th Street.

Jess saddled his horse and made his way through the Half Acre's heavy traffic, an almost immobile sea of freight wagons, carriages, handcarts, riders and heedless pedestrians. He saw two drivers get into it over the right of way and rode around them as they exchanged both punches and curses. A woman walked among the crowd with her baby on top of her head. The child didn't seem to mind, peeking out of his blankets and looking around at the sights.

The boardinghouse on 13th Street was one of the earliest three-story structures in Fort Worth and its age showed. It was a ramshackle building held together with rusty nails, string, and prayers and above the main entrance a wit had hung a painted sign that read: ABANDON HOPE ALL YE WHO ENTER HERE.

Just a few short weeks before Jess would have left his horse in the street. But growing wise of the ways of the Half Acre he hired a passing urchin to guard his paint with the promise of a dollar if it was still there when he got back.

* * *

The man called Michael had not died easily.

His small room off the top story hallway was spattered with blood. The little man's tongue had been cut out and laid on top of his chest, prompting the owner of the building, a big-bellied, blue-chinned man wearing carpet slippers to gloomily observe that the tongue was probably severed while the victim was still alive.

That was also Jess's opinion. The little man's throat had been cut but he'd been made to suffer terribly before he was killed.

"His name was Michael Hannah, Sheriff," the blue-chinned man said. "He wasn't much, but why kill him like that? I mean, so much pain and blood."

"He talked too much to the wrong people," Jess said.

Before he returned to his office, Jess rode to the stockyards where the bellowing herd was now penned up, and scouted around the area. There were a few large houses nearby and he'd read in the newspaper that even bigger homes were to be built on a rise just north of the yards that the press had already christened Quality Hill.

After an hour of fruitless searching, Jess swung into the saddle and that's when he saw a man walking purposefully toward him. The man was short, stocky and wore a gun as though it were part of him. There were many gunmen of one sort or another in

Fort Worth, but this man had the arrogant stamp of a seasoned professional.

Jess watched him come and some instinct told him that this was not going to end well. Horseman-style, his Colt rode high on his waist just behind the hip bone and was unhandy for the draw and shoot. Jess reached behind him, eased the gun from his holster and rested it on the saddle pommel.

The man stepped to within twenty feet of Jess and said, "You the local sheriff?"

"I reckon I am," Jess said.

"I thought so," the stocky man said. He smiled . . . and skinned it.

As the gunman made his draw Jess was already falling out of the saddle, but a bullet burned across his ribs on the left side and a second cracked the air beside his ear. He hit the ground with a sickening thud and most of the air was knocked out of his lungs. Luck always plays a part in a gunfight and Jess Casey was lucky that day.

Startled, his horse, never trained to stand in the presence of gunfire, reared and swung to its right. The gunman's third bullet, aimed at Jess as he tried to scramble to his feet, slammed into the paint's left flank. The horse screamed, turned and ran in the stocky man's direction. He jumped to the side, cursing, then turned and looked for Jess.

But he was too late. Jess Casey was on his feet and firing. His first bullet slammed into the gunman's chest and then Jess stepped toward him, thumbing off shot after shot.

"Do you like it?" Jess yelled. At that moment a little insane, all the stresses and strains he'd kept buried inside him flaring to the surface. "How does it feel to be on the receiving end, you miserable, low-down son of a bitch."

The gunman dropped to his knees, his face shocked that this was happening to him. He said as much. "This can't be . . ."

"Damn you, it can," Jess said as he fired his last round into the gunman's belly.

The man rose, backed up one staggering step and the Colt slid from his dying fingers. He tried to speak again, but the words choked in his throat and then his knees buckled and he pitched forward on his face.

There were several cowhands hanging around the pens and they quickly gathered around the dead man. "Hell, I know him," a lanky man wearing shotgun chaps said. "He's Earl Broadwell out of San Antone. He killed Jeff Link down on the Brazos that time, remember? Jeff rode with Bill Bonney and his hard crowd. They say he just got out of the New Mexico Territory ahead of a hemp posse."

"What has he done since?" Jess said.

"Hired out his gun. Some say Earl killed eighteen men, but I don't hold with that. I figure he gunned ten or eleven, tops."

"Is that all?" Jess said.

But his irony was lost on the puncher. "Earl got started late. He was a lawman for a spell."

"Sheriff, we saw it all," another puncher said. "He drew down on you and you defended yourself. Pity about the horse."

Jess had been staring at his dead mount. The paint had been a good little horse. Never complained much.

"He had you marked, Sheriff," the lanky man said. "He's been planning to kill you fer sure. I'd say he followed you here." The cowboy had just built a cigarette and Jess took it from his fingers. "I need that more than you do," he said.

"Smoke away, Sheriff," the puncher said. He had an open, good-natured grin. "The man who killed Earl Broadwell deserves a cigarette. Earl was a real bad man. No mercy in him, if you catch my drift."

Jess nodded. "Well, Big Sal will be pleased."

"Huh?" the puncher said.

"Nothing. Talking to myself." Then, to the puncher again, "Wilson J. Tucker is in town. What does that tell you?"

The man grinned. "It tells me this is a bad time to be a lawman in Fort Worth."

CHAPTER THIRTY-NINE

The lanky cowboy and Jess Casey rode two up back to the sheriff's office. The puncher said he'd bring the saddle on his way back out of town.

Dr. Sun was waiting for Jess when he stepped back into the office.

"You've been shot," the physician said.

"I got burned across the ribs," Jess said. "A man, a hired gun, tried to kill me."

"Tucker?" Dr. Sun said.

"No, a man called Broadwell," Jess said. "He wanted to kill me real bad."

"Where is he now?"

"He's dead."

Dr. Sun said, "Your shirt is ruined."

"I know. And it's my best," Jess said. "My dress-up-go-to-prayer-meeting shirt."

Dr. Sun removed the shirt and then opened the bag he always carried. "You're not hurt badly. This salve will help." Then, "But I've got some bad news, Jess."

"I'm dying, right?"

Dr. Sun's smile was tight. "No, not that. The Alamo Saloon has reopened by order of the mayor. It's selling opium again and maybe the new drug that's starting to scare me real bad."

"The mayor? You mean Mayor Stout?" Jess said.

"Is there another mayor I don't know about?" Dr. Sun said.

"Who told you this?"

"Told me? Nobody told me. I was there to treat a broken leg, the result of a fall by an inebriated patron."

"Why would the mayor do a thing like that?" Jess said.

"Larry Kemp took great pleasure in telling me that the closure was in violation of the city charter, whatever that means," Dr. Sun said.

"It means Mayor Harry Stout didn't want to lose his cut of the Alamo profits," Jess said.

"That could be," Dr. Sun said. "I wouldn't put a clean shirt on until the salve dries."

"It stings bad," Jess said.

"If it didn't, it wouldn't do you any good. In China we have an old saying that goes, 'For cuts and bruises, the sting is the thing.'"

Jess smiled. "Do you have any sayings for doctors who just make things up?"

"No," Dr. Sun said. "But I'm sure there are some."

"Doc, have you ever treated the mayor or his family?" Jess said.

"Horny Harry has no family, unless you count

the whores he visits regularly. And yes, I have treated him."

"For what?"

"I am not at liberty to say."

"Where does he live?"

"Come now, Jess, you're not talking about doing him an injury over the Alamo?" Dr. Sun said, his face concerned.

"No, nothing like that. I'm just curious."

"He has a house up by the stockyards and he's thinking of building another."

Jess was silent for a while. Then, "I wanted your thoughts on something, Doc. An incident that happened the night before last and ended in a dead body being found this morning."

"That sounds intriguing, Sheriff Casey," Dr. Sun said. "We shall have a whiskey and you can tell me all about it."

After Jess stopped speaking, Dr. Sun smiled and said, "Now I know why you asked me where Mayor Stout lives. But the man Michael Hannah saw only silhouettes in the darkness. There are many large men in Fort Worth. And he couldn't identify the girl."

"Why did they call her a black man's whore?" Jess said.

"Presumably because she was just that. It seems she was unfaithful to someone."

"Could it have been Harry Stout?" Jess said.

"The emerald that may have fallen from Lillian

Burke's brooch was found outside City Hall, and the girl, whoever she was, was chased and abused near his home."

"And Stout is a big man."

"Yes, those are clues that point in His Honor's direction, but they are not proof. But remember that Kurt Koenig is a big man and his record with young women is, well, spotty at least."

"But why would Kurt want Lillian Burke? He has plenty of women at his disposal, including Destiny Durand, a rare beauty if a little bit hard."

"And why would Harry Stout want her? He has his whores. But perhaps he wanted something different, an innocent, pretty virgin to mold into his ideal woman. When she told him she'd slept with a black man his dream was shattered and he couldn't bear the pain."

"Did he kill her that night?" Jess said.

"Perhaps." Dr. Sun smiled. "That is, if Stout is really our man."

"But what you say makes sense, Doc," Jess said.

"Of a sort," the little physician said. "But again, where is the proof?"

"Somewhere in this town is a hired thug who knows what happened to Lillian," Jess said. "And as God is my witness, I'll find him."

"Perhaps even Wilson J. Tucker," Dr. Sun said. "All things are possible."

"Then I'll talk to him first," Jess said. He winced as he shifted position in his chair. "Now my ribs are really starting to hurt."

"Enjoy the pain, Jess," Dr. Sun said. "It means you're still alive."

After the physician left, Jess thought he was done with visitors for the night. But the door opened and Luke Short stepped inside.

"Don't you ever knock, Luke?" Jess said. "And show me your hands."

"I'm unarmed and sober," Like said. "I heard you got shot today. You were lucky. Earl Broadwell was a shootist."

"How long has he been in town, Luke?" Jess said.

"For a few weeks but he's been lying low, especially after Wilson Tucker rode in. Those two were happy to step around each other in the past, but then you never know, do you?"

"Who hired Broadwell to kill me, Luke?"

"I've no idea, Sheriff. It wasn't me."

"Why are you here?" Jess said.

"Well, when I heard you'd been shot I hurried down here to see if you wanted to call in the favor I owe you. Or if you were dead."

"I was shot hours ago."

"Yeah, well I don't hurry very fast." Luke motioned to the glasses on the desk. "You got a drink for me or did the Chinaman drink it all? I don't like him and never will."

"You'll have to use his glass," Jess smiled, "or wash it under the pump out back."

"Whiskey kills all germs, even Chinese ones. Pour it, Sheriff."

After Luke was seated with a drink in one hand, a cigar in the other, Jess said, "What's your opinion of Mayor Stout?"

"I don't like mayors. They've thrown me out of too many towns."

"I mean as a person," Jess said.

"I told you, I don't like mayors."

"Is Stout capable of kidnapping a young woman and keeping her in his home against her will?"

Luke was genuinely surprised. "Horny Harry? Hell, no. He likes whores. He sees using whores as a business arrangement that keeps him free of emotional entanglements. For men like Stout it's all about power, and a full-time woman would do her best to undermine that power. You're an innocent, Sheriff, but I hope you're catching my drift."

"Is he capable of murder?" Jess said.

"Any man is capable of murder under the right circumstances, but Harry Stout?" Luke shook his head. "I don't think so."

"Is he mixed up in the opium racket?"

"Like Kurt Koenig, Stout gets his cut to turn a blind eye to it." Short grinned. "What is this, Casey, a question-and-answer session? I came here to see if you wanted to call in the favor I owe you, not exchange gossip."

Jess said, "I believe somebody wants to introduce a deadly new drug into Fort Worth and I think Mayor Stout is behind it."

"Right now this city has all the drugs it needs— Stout knows that," Luke said. "You're listening to too many rumors."

"Are you going into the opium business with Kurt?"

"I haven't decided yet."

Luke Short drained his glass and rose to his feet. "Casey, the thought of owing you a favor is keeping me awake o' nights. Until you call it in, I'll be your shadow."

"Nice of you to say so, Luke," Jess said. "But we'll let things play out and see what happens."

"And for God's sake, change your shirt," Luke said. "You've got blood all over it."

CHAPTER FORTY

There was little by way of mindless violence that could horrify the people of Hell's Half Acre, but the manner of Lillian Burke's death did.

Jess Casey, the entire left side of his chest stiff and sore, sat at his desk drinking his morning coffee as he gazed out the window at a sky the color of tarnished brass and wood smoke. The wind gusted in the street and a few random drops of rain ticked on the roof.

Jess was on his second cup of coffee when the door opened and several men and a couple of women stepped inside. The men seemed stunned, the women were pale, their lips white.

Jess sensed something bad and he let them speak.

A man wearing a cloth cap and workman's clothing said, "Sheriff, you'd better come."

"What happened?" Jess said.

"Mother of God, come," a woman said. Her dark eyes were haunted.

"Where?" Jess said.

"The graveyard. Come," the woman said.

Jess stubbed out his cigarette and rose to his feet. He glanced at the bruised sky and shrugged into his slicker, a move that caused him considerable pain.

When Jess stepped outside it seemed the entire town was headed in the direction of the cemetery. People moved like automatons and clergymen walked among them, reading aloud from the Book . . .

"Yea, though I walk through the valley of the shadow of death, I will fear no evil: for thou art with me; thy rod and thy staff they comfort me . . ."

"What the hell happened?" Jess said to a man walking close to him.

"I don't know how to say it, Sheriff. Something terrible."

"An evil thing," a woman said.

And Jess gave up asking.

A slender rain fell on the city graveyard like a mist and the crows that had sought shelter in the wild oaks quarreled incessantly and sent down showers of leaves. There were no shadows but darkness lingered in hollow places as though the night had been reluctant to leave.

Jess followed the crowd to where a large wooden cross with a carved Jesus had stood over the mass grave of two pioneer families killed by Comanches. But the Jesus figure was gone, replaced by what had once been a living human being . . . the bloody body of Lillian Burke.

The girl had been nailed to the cross in a grim parody of the suffering Savior. She was naked and the huge nails had been driven through her wrists and feet. Jess pushed people out of his path and studied the ground around the base of the cross. As he expected the soil had been dug up and then replaced, indicating that Lillian had been crucified before the cross was raised. Jess hoped fervently that she'd been dead before it happened.

The crowd was hushed around the cross, only small sounds could be heard, the murmur of prayer and the click-click of rosary beads through trembling fingers.

Jess scouted the area but onlookers had trampled the ground to mud and there were no tracks. It shamed him to draw close to Lillian's body and raise his eyes to her nakedness. She was as white as bone. Her head hung onto her breast and Jess thought he could detect the signs of bruising on her neck, but the cause of her death would be determined by Dr. Sun. Mercifully, then, he could not see her back.

Jess forced himself to do what had to be done. He turned to a responsible-looking man and said, "Bring Simon Hall the carpenter here." Then, the words sticking in his throat, "He has the tools."

The man left, replaced by a woman who held

a bundle of clothing in her arms. "I think these belonged to the dead girl," she said.

Before he could object, she thrust the clothes into Jess's arms. He identified white underclothes and a plain dress of blue and white gingham. The dress was ripped, as though it had been torn from the girl's body, and so was the underwear. Her perfume lingered on the dress, but when Jess lifted it to his nose he could not identify it. He knew he'd smelled it before, but it wasn't the flowery scent he recalled Lillian wearing. Had another woman been involved in her murder?

"Sheriff, look at this."

A man held out a small object and dropped it into Jess's palm. It was Lillian Burke's brooch. It looked as though it had been torn from her dress. The fastening pin was bent and a scrap of blue fabric still clung to it. One of the emeralds was missing from the *You and No Other* motto.

That missing stone had been found outside City Hall, a pointer to Mayor Harry Stout as Lillian's abductor and murderer. As Jess stood in the soft rain he recalled that one of Stout's henchmen had called Lillian a black man's whore. Was he behind the framing of Zeus for the jewelry shop robbery and the shooting of Addie? Had he bribed Dorothy Miles to lie? Was he enraged because Lillian had slept with a black man? And yes, that man had to be Zeus. That was why he had to die.

Jess's mind was still racing when Simon Hall arrived, Dr. Sun riding in the back of his wagon.

"Get her down from there and off the cross, Hall," Jess said. He was about to say, "And don't hurt her," but realized how foolish that would sound. Instead he said, "Be gentle with her."

Hall, stone-faced, nodded and then he and his apprentice went about their grim task.

"Poor child, I'll examine her when she is freed," Dr. Sun said.

"I think she was strangled, Doc," Jess said.

"We'll see," Dr. Sun said.

Lillian Burke's back was a nightmare.

"She was lashed, many times," Dr. Sun said. "By a man who was in a rage at the time. He wanted to hurt her, repay the girl for all the grief she'd caused him. Then he strangled her. I don't think she was pregnant."

"I think she told Stout that she'd slept with Zeus and that drove him into a killing rage," Jess said. "He framed Zeus for the jewelry store robbery and then had his thugs drag him out of City Hall and execute him."

"An excellent deduction, Sheriff, and one we should definitely explore," Dr. Sun said.

"I think I'll arrest him and at least put him out of the girl-killing business for a while," Jess said. He watched Hall spread a tarp over Lillian's body.

"Not yet, my friend," Dr. Sun said. "Let me conduct

my own investigation first. I have ways of getting information that you don't."

"Sheriff, I can take her to Big Sal's place," Simon Hall said.

"Yes, please do," Jess said. "And Simon, thanks. You left her with some dignity in death."

"She was a beautiful girl," Hall said.

"She was all of that," Jess said.

Dr. Sun, lost in thought, said nothing.*

*The above account is loosely based on the 1887 murder of a prostitute known only as Sally who was found nailed to an outhouse door in the Acre. Her identity was never discovered and her murderer never found. This killing brought on a major reform campaign by real-life Mayor H. S. Broiles and County Attorney R. L. Carlock. But even as late as the 1890s, the Acre continued to attract gunmen, highway robbers, card sharks, con men and shady ladies, who preyed on out-of-town pilgrims and the local sporting crowd.

CHAPTER FORTY-ONE

Kurt Koenig, wearing a holstered gun under his gray frock coat, walked into Jess Casey's office and said, "I heard what happened this morning."

"Be glad you didn't see it, Kurt," Jess said.

"I had nothing to do with the girl's death," Koenig said. "I hope you don't think otherwise."

"Kurt, I don't blame you for everything bad that happens in the Half Acre, just most of it."

Koenig pulled the chair over with the toe of his boot, then sat. The chair creaked under his weight. "Somebody's pushing a new drug, Jess. Yesterday a beef squad walked into the premises of one of my best customers. They told him that from now on he had to push a new product and to quit buying opium and morphine from Kurt Koenig. My man says, 'Why, I always buy from Kurt—he gives me an honest deal. And I buy my booze from him as well.' One of the hoodlums says, 'Not any longer, you don't, or you'll see this place blown sky-high and you with it.' What do you think of that?"

"Kurt, I won't put my stamp of approval on your illegal activities," Jess said.

"Well, that's no matter. I've got some of my Panther City Boys guarding the place." Koenig sniffed, then said, "But I want to know who's selling the new opium drug."

"I have my suspicions, Kurt, but I can't reveal them at this time."

"Well, suspicion this, Sheriff, one of the hoodlums said that my shadow will not fall on the Acre for much longer." He sniffed again. "Now that's a death threat if ever I heard one." He sniffed again. "What the hell is that stink? It smells like a Shanghai brothel in here."

"Those are Lillian Burke's clothes over there in the corner," Jess said. "I think that's what you're smelling."

Koenig was horrified. "You're keeping them?"

"Doc Sun says we should hold on to them as evidence."

Koenig got to his feet, walked to the corner and sniffed. "That's incense, the stuff the Chinese burn. Hell, I've smelled it a thousand times."

Realization dawned on Jess. "Yeah, I knew where I smelled it before. At Doc Sun's place."

"There are Chinese living all over Fort Worth," Koenig said. "She probably picked up the smell in one of them backroom opium dens."

Jess considered that. Had she been returning from some opium dive when Stout's men grabbed her? No, that didn't make any sense. Why would they if she was already living with the mayor?

Unless . . . Jess figured it out and he tried it on Koenig.

"I believe that Lillian Burke was living with Harry Stout," he said. "She'd been at some opium den as you say and when she returned to Stout's house he accused her of having sex with Zeus."

"Zeus?" Koenig said. "That's a stretch."

"Hear me out, Kurt. Fearing for her life Lillian fled from the house but Stout's hired thugs brought her back. Later the mayor murdered her."

"And nailed her to a cross," Koenig said. "I doubt that Harry has that much imagination."

"Then what do you think?" Jess said.

"Maybe she was living with Harry and he knocked her up. She went to Doc Sun to confirm her suspicions and picked up the incense smell on her clothes. Somebody murdered her on her way back to Harry's place."

"Doc Sun says she wasn't pregnant," Jess said.

"Well, it doesn't really matter. I'm trying to explain the incense smell on her clothes."

"It's thin, Kurt, real thin."

"And so is accusing Horny Harry. Jolly fat men don't go around nailing young ladies to crosses. Just not their style."

Koenig stepped to the door. "Jess, this job is getting to you, driving you nuts."

Jess glanced out the window and saw a shadow flick across the oil lamp that always burned in the window of the hardware store across the street. He would not normally have attached much importance to such a thing if it were not for the death threat Koenig had received.

Koenig's hand was on the door handle. He pulled it toward him. Jess yelled, "No! Down!"

Koenig, a man with fine-tuned reflexes and an instinct for survival, threw himself on the floor. A split second later a bullet crashed through the half-opened door where he'd been standing just a moment before.

Gun in hand, Jess blew out the office oil lamp and then ran to the door. Koenig was already on his feet. "You or me?" he said.

"I reckon it was meant for you," Jess said. He rushed out the door but the boardwalk opposite was deserted, black with shadow.

"See anything?" Koenig said. He had his Colt ready.

"Not a damn thing," Jess said. "Whoever he was, he's gone."

"Damn, that was a big gun," Koenig said. "Sounded like a ship's cannon." He stepped back into the office, examined the wall and then did the same in the cell area. "Bullet went right through the place like it was paper and it's probably still going. Look at the wall. What kind of bullet makes a hole like that? I could put my fist in there."

"A Holland and Holland elephant gun," Jess said.

"Wilson Tucker has one of those, but he told us he left it behind," Koenig said.

"He didn't," Jess said. And he told Koenig about the death of the old woman named Dixie. "Almost blew her head off," Jess said. "It was a big bullet from a big gun." Then, "Did Harry Stout hire Tucker?"

"Hell, get Harry out of your head," Koenig said. "He wouldn't even know how to hire a killer like Wilson Tucker, he doesn't have the smarts or the connections. Harry's mind never rises any higher than his crotch, remember that."

"Then who did?" Jess said.

"Whoever wants to sell a new drug in Fort Worth and make his fortune."

"That could be a lot of people," Jess said.

"Damn right it could," Koenig said. "And that's what bothers me."

His handsome face was troubled.

The incense smell in the office was suddenly very strong and Jess wondered at that. Was Lillian Burke trying to tell him something?

The little calico cat jumped onto the desk beside him and then stared fixedly at the pile of torn clothing on the floor. She didn't blink.

Was the kitty also trying to tell him something he should know?

CHAPTER FORTY-TWO

"There's something you should know, Sheriff," Destiny Durand said.

Jess Casey smiled. "Then tell me."

He decided that once you got around the slightly hard cast of the woman's features she was stunningly beautiful. And her body . . . well, he didn't want to think about that.

"Kurt doesn't know I'm here," Destiny said. "And I'm sorry it's so late. I heard the City Hall clock strike eleven just as I stepped into your office."

"Then I won't tell Kurt you were here, and I don't feel much like sleeping anyway," Jess said.

"You've never taken his money," the woman said.

"No. And I never will," Jess said. Then, "You have something to tell me?"

"Maybe it means nothing," she said. Her French perfume clung to her like an embrace. "It could be just idle gossip."

"Let me decide that," Jess said.

"Before she disappeared Lillian Burke came to

ask Kurt for a position. She made it clear that what she had in mind was a job where she'd sit at a desk, not lie on her back."

Jess smiled but said nothing.

"Sometimes Kurt just takes a liking to people, as he did you, and he seemed to like Lillian. Well, like her enough to offer her a clerical job. He has a lot of paperwork keeping track of all his businesses, you know."

"Paperwork. Well, that surprises me," Jess said.

Destiny's eyes searched for the sarcasm, but Jess's face was empty.

"Well, anyway," Destiny said, "that was on a Friday and she was to start the following Monday, but she never showed."

"This was before she disappeared?" Jess said.

"Yes, before," Destiny said. She shifted in her chair and her gold silk dress rustled like autumn leaves. "I met her in the street, that would be on the Thursday, and asked her why she hadn't showed up for work. She said her circumstances had suddenly changed. What an odd thing to say: 'My circumstances have suddenly changed.'"

"And had they?" Jess said.

"Well, she said so. Lillian was wearing an expensive brooch. Kurt never bought me anything like that, the skinflint."

"Destiny, what do you think of Harry Stout?" Jess said.

"I never think about him."

"If you did, what would be your opinion?"

"Horny Harry? Well, he's very outgoing, the

typical hail-fellow-well-met local politician on the make. He's also as dumb as a wagonload of rocks. On his best day Harry doesn't have enough smarts to spit downwind."

"Could Lillian Burke have played house with him?"

"Anything is possible, Sheriff, but I doubt it. Harry is not a one-woman man, that's why he keeps all the whores in Fort Worth in business. Besides, Harry is not that rich. If Lillian wanted a meal ticket she could have found better. She was an attractive girl. Sheriff, are you wearing perfume?"

Jess smiled. "No. The incense smell is from Lillian's clothes over there in the corner."

Destiny was horrified. "The clothes she—"

"Yes. Dr. Sun says he needs to examine them."

"Then why didn't he take them to his place?"

"He'll be here for them tomorrow, I guess."

"Harry Stout doesn't burn incense. He probably doesn't even know what it is."

"I think Lillian Burke may have visited an opium den before she was murdered," Jess said.

"Or Dr. Sun's place," Destiny said. She rose elegantly from her chair. "One more thing, General Custer, thank you for saving Kurt's life tonight."

"I'd have done the same for my worst enemy," Jess said.

The woman smiled. "Sheriff, Kurt Koenig is not your worst enemy, not by a long shot."

CHAPTER FORTY-THREE

Jess Casey could never have explained why he returned to the graveyard the next morning but he felt drawn, as though there was a clue he'd missed, something vital he'd overlooked.

He carried his breakfast in his hand, a fried bacon sandwich made with excellent sourdough bread. The wind talked in the trees and the early birds greeted the new aborning day with an endless variety of songs. A cobalt blue sky promised no rain, only sun and heat.

The cross was standing again and the crucified Jesus was back in place. Jess stared up at the carved, aesthetic face and saw only suffering, sadness maybe, but no indication that the Savior was about to impart some essential information.

Jess sat on the flat tombstone, finished his breakfast and then built and lit a cigarette. How hushed and tranquil were the dead. He took the brooch from his short pocket and studied it, as though it could impart the information he needed. *You and*

No Other. Four little words packed with a wealth of meaning. Was Horny Harry Stout capable of such a sentiment?

Jess rose and searched the ground around the cross again. Perhaps he hoped to find a note that read, *Yes, I done it,* signed *Harry Stout.* But he saw nothing, only a thin layer of mud, covered here and there by blown leaves. The sun was beginning its climb into the drowsy morning and a short ways off a covey of bobwhite quail exploded from a patch of creosote bush. Jess Casey hit the ground in a flat dive.

Boom!

He heard the authoritative bellow of the big-bore rifle and rolled to his left behind a granite headstone.

Boom!

Jess tried to make himself small, curling his body into a tight ball as the second bullet chipped the top of the stone and then shattered a glass vase into a thousand shards. Drawing his Colt, Jess stuck it around the side of the headstone and thumbed off two quick shots, firing blind.

There was no answering fire.

Jess rubbed his suddenly dry lips with the back of his gun hand. Where was the rifleman? Was he even now on the move, seeking a better firing position? But all seemed still as Jess looked around him. Nothing moved but the restless wind in the trees. His palms sweaty, he wiped his gun hand on his shirt and took up the Colt again. He had to move. He was too exposed where he was.

Ten yards to Jess's left was a roughly built dry-stone wall about four feet high. At the base of the wall grew thick brush and a thin strip of shadow where a man could lose himself. Ten yards was a long way, but he had to do it. Jess got his legs under him and ran.

He dived into the brush at the base of the dry stone, and then rolled, trying to lose himself in shade.

"Well, that move was about as useless as teats on a boar hog."

Luke Short stood at the gravestone Jess had so recently left. He had a gun in his hand and a scowl on his face. "How the hell have you managed to live this long, cowboy?"

"He's gone?" Jess said from the cover of the brush.

"Yeah, he's gone. Wilson Tucker is an ambush killer and he don't stick around when things turn bad."

Jess got to his feet and stepped into sunlight. "I fired at him," he said. "Did I scare him off?"

"Hell, no. He saw me coming up the hill, hoping to do you a favor, and decided this wasn't his day." Luke turned his upper body and pointed north. "He went thataway." He grinned. "See that tomb over yonder. I reckon Wilson planned to set there and nail you as soon as you ran like a scared rabbit from this here headstone. You should've stayed right where you were at and let him come to you."

Jess holstered his gun and said, "I guess I just called in the favor I owe you."

"Hell no, you didn't, more is the pity. All I did was leave my breakfast and follow you up the hill and that wasn't a favor. Truth is if I'd known it was Wilson up here with a hunting rifle I would have stayed home."

"It was him who tried to kill Kurt Koenig last night, huh?" Jess said.

"Wilson wasn't trying to kill Koenig, Sheriff. It was you he wanted. Kurt was in the wrong place at the wrong time and he got in the way."

Jess shook his head. "They say Wilson Tucker is the best there is. Somebody must want to kill me real bad."

"Seems like," Luke said. "Well, you can cross them three young fellers you locked up in your jail off your list. They're already on a train bound for the New Mexico Territory, thanks to their rich folks. Seems like their fathers weren't happy about a certain nosy sheriff walking around asking questions."

"Then they got away with murder," Jess said.

"Those three have criminal tendencies and they're rich-kid arrogant," Luke said. "Boys like that don't last on the frontier. Some tough lawman who doesn't take any sass will plant them in boot hill before too long."

"Luke, who is giving Wilson Tucker orders?" Jess said.

"I don't know."

"Could it be Mayor Stout?"

Luke shrugged, an expressive gesture of his. "Why would Harry want you dead?"

"Maybe he's heard that I suspect him of murdering Lillian Burke," Jess said.

"He'd certainly screw her, but murder? I don't see Harry doing that."

"Then who?"

"Sheriff, I owe you a favor. I don't owe you my opinion. But I'll say this, I have no idea who wants you dead and I don't much care. You're not one of my favorite people and owing you a favor is aging me rapidly."

"I think you may have saved my hide this morning, so thank you anyway," Jess said.

"Casey, take my advice and go back to cowboying," Luke said. "You just ain't cut out for this kind of life."

CHAPTER FORTY-FOUR

Dr. Sun came by the sheriff's office in the early afternoon to pick up Lillian Burke's clothes. "They may tell us something, but more likely they will remain silent," he said.

"I guess you heard what happened this morning, Doc," Jess said.

"It's all over the Acre, mostly because Luke Short was involved. He's a desperate man."

"I reckon Luke saved my life," Jess said.

"But he won't always be around to save you," Dr. Sun said. "That is what worries me."

"I can take care of myself, Doc," Jess said.

"As I told you before, there is evil afoot, and it is directed at you, Jess. You are too good a man to remain here any longer."

"What are you telling me?" Jess said.

"That you should leave and leave now," Dr. Sun said. "Don't linger here another day, Jess. Your life is in danger."

"Do you think Harry Stout is behind all this?"

"I don't know for sure, not yet," Dr. Sun said. "But you must get out of this town and leave the investigation to me." The physician's smile was sympathetic. "You lingered in Fort Worth because you want to earn enough money to buy your own ranch, is that not so?"

"That is my intention, Doc."

"I am not a rich man, Jess, but I can advance you the money to buy a place."

Jess opened his mouth to speak, but Dr. Sun held up a silencing hand. "No, it's not charity, Jess. If you wish, you may make me a partner in the enterprise. I can't ride a horse or herd cows, but I am very good with books, you know, profit and loss."

"Doc, that's very kind of you," Jess said, "but I have a job to do in the Acre and I'll see it through."

Suddenly Dr. Sun seemed angry. "No! You must leave. You can make a life for yourself away from Fort Worth. Don't be a fool, Jess, listen to what I tell you before it's too late."

Jess smiled. "Doc, don't worry about me so much. I'll be just fine."

"You won't be fine. You'll die, Jess, shot down in the street."

Jess shivered. "Hell, Doc, now you're scaring me."

"I'm trying to scare you." Then, in a high-pitched tone, "Get out! Get out! Get out!"

With that, Doc Sun turned on his heel, picked up the bundle of clothes and charged out of the door.

Jess was stunned. What had gotten into the man? Or was Dr. Sun himself scared. Was the evil he'd talked about also directed at him?

Suddenly Jess was angry, angry at Horny Harry Stout, whose unbridled lust had brought all this trouble upon him. The man had to be brought to justice and soon. Jess wanted to see his fat carcass swing from a noose.

The little old lady was distraught over her lost Pekingese.

"She's so tiny, Sheriff, just an itty-bitty thing. I'm so worried that a ferocious stray dog will get her. Please help me find her."

"Calm yourself, ma'am. Where did you lose her?" Jess said.

"In an alley down the street a ways. Something frightened her and she jumped out of my arms and ran down the alley. It was so dark I couldn't find her." The old lady burst into tears. "If I can't find my Lucy-Lu I don't know what I'll do."

Jess rose from his desk and patted the woman on the shoulder. "I'll help you find her." He grabbed a hurricane lantern from the shelf and said, "Now show me where you lost her."

The old lady led him to an alley just half a dozen storefronts from his office. Separating Bell's bakery and the New York Hat Shop, the alley was only about ten feet wide and completely dark.

"Lucy-Lu," the old woman yelled. "Lucy-Lu!" She listened and said, "Was that a bark I heard, Sheriff?"

"Could have been," Jess said. "I'll go look. You stay right here, ma'am."

"Oh, be careful, Sheriff," the woman said. "It's so dark."

Jess stepped into the alley, orange lantern light bobbing along the walls. The ground was treacherous underfoot, littered with empty bottles and other debris Jess didn't want to put a name to.

"Lucy-Lu," he said in the most dog-friendly voice he could muster. "Where are you, little girl?"

From ahead of him he thought he heard a whimper. "Lucy-Lu, are you there?" He raised the lantern above his head. "Lucy-Lu! Are you there?"

From behind him, faintly, he heard the old lady say, "Oh, do be careful, Sheriff . . ."

Jess moved deeper into the alley. "Lucy-Lu . . . Lucy-Lu . . ." There! He heard it just ahead of him and to his left, the whimper of a scared dog. "Lucy-Lu . . ."

A furry bundle jumped up from where she had been lying and promptly bit Jess on the ankle. "Lucy-Lu?" He laid the lantern aside and bent to pick up the dog. The little Pekingese growled and bit his hand, growled again and bit his other hand.

"Sheriff," the old lady said, "you're not hurting my precious, are you?"

"No, ma'am," Jess said, trying to shake the savage animal off his hand. "She seems quite excited."

"Hold her, Sheriff," the woman said. "I'll come. You've scared her."

Jess picked up the growling, snapping Peke and he was pretty sure Lucy-Lu was doing her best to tear his throat out. To his relief the old woman appeared at his elbow, lamplight casting most of her face in shadow. She grabbed the dog and it calmed down immediately.

"There, there, precious," she said. "Did the bad man scare you?"

"She bit me," Jess said. He showed her the blood running from a gash on the back of his hand. "The little . . . little . . ."

"Come, Lucy-Lu," the old woman said. "I won't let the nasty sheriff scare you again."

She turned and toddled back down the alley. The Pekingese had its head on her shoulder and it glared at Jess with glittering eyes.

"You're very welcome, ma'am," Jess called out.

But the little old lady kept on toddling and didn't turn around.

Jess bent to pick up the lantern and saw the place where the Pekingese had been lying. It was a pile of clothes, thrown haphazardly against a wall of the alley. He leaned closer and smelled the faint odor of incense.

They were Lillian Burke's clothes.

CHAPTER FORTY-FIVE

Dr. Sun had thrown the clothes away. He'd had no intention of examining them. But why pretend that he would? Sleepless, Jess lay in his cot and stared at the ceiling. What was he missing here?

Could Dr. Sun be the one who murdered Lillian Burke? The incense on her clothing indicated that she'd been in a Chinese opium den—or the physician's home. And why was Dr. Sun so anxious to get him out of the Acre, even to the point of buying him a spread?

No, it was impossible, Jess decided. The little physician had stood by him and had used his sword to defend him at the Alamo. It was hardly the act of someone who wanted him dead.

You and No Other.

Harry Stout was not the kind of man to compose such a sentiment. By all accounts he was a whoremaster and a buffoon. But Dr. Sun, a physician and a sophisticated man of the world, could. And he knew the properties of opium. Had he discovered a potent derivative of opium that could make him rich?

If that was the case, Kurt Koenig stood in Dr. Sun's way and he was marked for death. Jess wondered if Luke Short could have been wrong and the assassin's bullet was really intended for Kurt Koenig, not for him. His mind racing, Jess rolled off the bed and built a cigarette. Wilson Tucker had failed to kill him that morning, but he knew he was very much a secondary target after Kurt Koenig. Could that be why Dr. Sun decided to give him an easy out and had thrown in a ranch to sweeten the pot?

It was time to find answers. Jess drew smoke deep into his lungs and made his decision. He was going to toss the dice. By this hour tomorrow night the moon might rise and look for Jess Casey and he wouldn't be there.

No matter. It was time to do what had to be done.

Next morning Nate Levy met Jess at the door of the sheriff's office.

"You shouldn't be out of bed, Nate," Jess said.

"Damned Panther City Boys were holding a shindig in the next room," Nate said. "Kept me awake the whole night, them and their gals. I decided it was high time I got up and around."

"What can I do for you, Nate?" Jess said. "I'm headed for the White Elephant, Luke Short's place."

"Then I'll walk with you for a ways."

After a while Nate said, "You look tired, Jess."

Jess smiled. "Yeah, and I feel tired."

"I'm here if you need any help. Look." Nate took a Remington derringer from his pocket. "I bought this at a gun store and a box of ammunition for it. If you want to make a play, I'll back you up."

"You keep the belly gun in your pocket, Nate," Jess said. "What I have to do is no concern of yours."

"Zeus wasn't a concern of mine?"

"Sorry, Nate. Yes, I know he was," Jess said.

"Jess, your enemy isn't Luke Short. I hope you know that."

"He isn't my friend, that's for sure."

"How well do you know that Dr. Sun feller?" Nate said.

Suddenly Jess was guarded. "Not real well, I guess."

"There's something strange about him, but I can't put my finger on what it is, if you know what I mean."

"Well, he's Chinese for a start," Jess said. "White folks can never figure out the Chinese. They do and say things we don't."

"I don't trust him," Nate said. "And neither should you."

"I've got to the stage in this town where I don't trust anybody," Jess said.

"Do you trust me?"

"Yeah, Nate, I'd say I do."

"They say eyes are the window of the soul, Jess. You ever hear that?"

"No, but I guess it makes sense."

"When he was treating me, I looked into Dr. Sun's eyes and couldn't see anything. Only blackness that went on forever and ever, deeper and deeper. I saw nothing, no soul." Nate smiled. "Ah, listen to me. What I don't see with my eyes I must not invent with my mouth. Maybe I'm mistaken."

"Have you ever been mistaken about a man before?" Jess said.

"Not that I can remember. And here I must leave you. I'm tired now."

"Thanks for the company," Jess said. "And keep that gun close, Nate."

"And you take good care of yourself, Jess. Remember that worries go down better with soup than without."

Like all sporting gentlemen Luke Short was not an easy man to rouse in the morning. But Jess Casey roused him anyway, even in the face of Luke's threat to gun him right where he stood.

"You're calling in your favor," Luke said when he finally laid aside his gun and sat up in bed and allowed hope to gleam in his eyes.

Jess studied the opulent bedroom and said, "You do yourself well, Luke."

"The damned White Elephant was built around my bedroom," Luke said. "Now what do you want? And I warn you, I'm still considering whether or not to shoot you."

"Can I shade Wilson Tucker on the draw and shoot?" Jess said.

Luke blinked a time or two then said. "This is it. Here's the favor I owe you. I'll escort you back to the jail and put you to bed with a sedative."

"Can I shade Wilson Tucker?" Jess said.

"Listen up," Luke said. "You ain't got a hope in hell. You ain't got a prayer. You drawing down on Wilson Tucker is as hopeless as whipping a dead horse . . . as trying to put out a barn fire with a shot glass full of water . . . as arguing with the angel of death. Catch my drift? Now for God's sake go sleep it off and leave me the hell alone."

Luke slid farther into the bed and pulled the covers over his head.

"Where can I find him?" Jess said.

"Where he's always been, the Alamo," Luke said, his voice muffled. "He's got a fancy woman there."

"I can call in the favor and ask you to go with me to the Alamo," Jess said.

Luke threw the covers off his face. "And go up against Wilson? Are you crazy, cowboy? You don't call out a man like Wilson Tucker if you don't have to."

"He tried to kill me yesterday, remember?"

"Yeah, I know, but he missed, so no harm done."

"Luke, I'm calling in the favor you owe me. I want you to go with me to the Alamo and then stay at my side today until I say you've returned the favor."

Luke groaned. "Damn it, as soon as I saw you

storm through my bedroom door I said to myself, 'Luke, it's time to shoot the cowboy.' Why didn't I listen to myself?"

"Get dressed, Luke," Jess said. "We have a long day ahead of us."

CHAPTER FORTY-SIX

"Sheriff, it seems like you never learn," Larry Kemp said. "You ain't closing down my place again. It's under the personal protection of Mayor Stout and another party I can't mention."

Jess's nose wrinkled. "Kemp, don't you ever bathe?"

"You didn't come here to smell the landlord," Kemp said. "What the hell do you want, and why do you have a killer with you?"

"Thanks for the compliment, Kemp," Luke said. "I won't soon forget it."

"Mr. Short is no part of why I'm here," Jess said. "My business is with Wilson Tucker."

"He's not here," Kemp said.

"Get him up and tell him I await his convenience in the bar," Jess said.

"You damned fool, he'll kill you," Kemp said.

"The cretin is right," Luke said. "You can't handle Wilson."

"Tell him, Kemp," Jess said.

Kemp said, "Your funeral, lawman."

After Kemp left, Luke said, "I'll see you buried decent, cowboy. It's the last favor I'll do for you."

"There's one thing more you can do, Luke," Jess said.

"Put a name to it."

"If Wilson Tucker kills me—"

"You mean when he kills you."

"—put a bullet in him."

"Sure. If he's got his back turned to me at the time."

"You're true-blue, Luke," Jess said.

"No, I ain't," Luke said.

Jess smiled. "You're right. You ain't."

A narrow hallway that smelled of piss and boiled cabbage led to the bar, an unassuming room with some tables and chairs and an area left clear for dancing. A battered, bullet-pocked piano stood in one corner and on the wall a cheap print of the Alamo was draped in the Texas flag. The bar was made of rough pine, repaired here and there with slats from Arbuckle coffee crates. Like the hallway, the place smelled of piss and boiled cabbage.

His spurs chiming, Jess stepped to the wall and studied the Alamo print. He turned when he heard someone enter the saloon.

It was Wilson J. Tucker, dressed in black pants, elastic-sided boots and a white shirt opened at the neck. Tucker wore two Colts and he held a steaming coffee cup in his left hand.

"You wanted to see me, Sheriff," he said.

Jess nodded. "I'm here to arrest you for the murder of a woman known to this city only as Dixie and for the attempted murder of an officer of the law, namely myself."

"The old woman talked too much and her death was a small thing. But you were lucky yesterday, cowboy. If Luke Short hadn't showed up when he did . . . well, I'd have gunned you." He smiled. "Man's got to be careful around Luke. On his good days he can be a handful."

"Who paid you to kill me, Tucker?" Jess said.

The gunman laid his cup on a table. "I want to get this over with before my coffee cools," he said. "By the way, Sheriff, your gun is too high. Man, it's almost under your armpit. You won't be fast on the draw and shoot with that. Lower it some."

"Who paid you to kill me?" Jess said.

"All right, I'll answer your question since you're already a dead man. But once my talking is done, I'll gun you. Savvy?"

Jess said nothing and Tucker said, "My client says you're not very smart, cowboy. In the beginning he tried to kill you a couple of times because he didn't want a new lawman around. But then he realized that you'd be of more value as a cover for his activities so he befriended you."

Jess said, "He wants to sell a new opium drug."

"Yeah, especially now when he can finally guarantee a steady supply," Tucker said. His guns had fancy stag-horn handles. "He's pushing things now, calling in a promising young feller named Tom

Horn who's in the same business as me. But before he gets here I've been ordered to tie up loose ends. First I'll kill you, cowboy, then Kurt Koenig, Luke Short and a few others. After that my client will control all of the drug trade in Fort Worth." Tucker grinned. "We're talking millions here, a fortune."

A thought cartwheeled through Jess's mind. How fast was Tucker? He answered his own question: probably as sudden as a lightning strike. Damn it, keep him talking.

"And your client murdered Zeus, the prizefighter, and then Lillian Burke?"

Tucker tested his coffee. "Not much longer, cowboy. It's getting cooler." He directed his attention back to Jess. "That's more of a private matter with my client. He wanted the girl because he thought she was a virgin and he set store by that. He courted her, bought her nice things, put her up in his home and then one night she gets sky-high on morphine and tells him she once slept with a black man. A bad mistake."

"And that man was Zeus."

"Yeah, of course. The black got blamed for robbery and the killing of a shop girl and my client hired some Acre toughs to lynch him. Then, when Lillian Burke heard of the black man's death she tried to run away. Understandably, my client was annoyed and his thugs went after her. She was brought back, whipped, strangled and nailed to a cross. Which brings us full circle to yesterday."

"One last question: Is your client that fat pig Harry Stout?"

"The mayor?" Tucker said. "What are you talking about?"

"It's simple, Tucker. Is your client Harry Stout?"

"No. Are you crazy? My client is your good friend Dr. Sun. He plans to get rich with his new drug and then go back to China a wealthy, important man. He wanted to take a beautiful virgin bride with him, but that didn't pan out."

Tucker grinned. "Now, if you'll excuse me, I must get another cup of coffee." The grin faded and Tucker's mouth tightened thin and hard. "Grab the iron cowboy," he said.

CHAPTER FORTY-SEVEN

A clumsy scullery maid named Mabel Ball saved Jess Casey's life.

The girl was carrying a stack of cheap tin trays from the kitchen to the bar when she tripped on the uneven wood floor and fell. The trays made a tremendous racket as they clattered all over the floor.

Wilson Tucker, his back to the hallway, jumped in surprise and quickly swung his head to his left. It was an instinctive movement that took only a split second but it was all the time Jess needed.

He drew and fired.

At a range of just five feet, Jess's bullet slammed into Tucker's chest dead center and did terrible damage to the gunman's heart and lungs. But Wilson Tucker was a man with bark on him. He took a step forward and raised his Colt. But the bullet that crashed into the left side of his head dropped him and put his lights out forever.

Luke Short stood at the entrance to the bar, a smoking Colt in his hand. "Sheriff, you just called in your favor," he said. Then, angrily, "Why the hell didn't you hit him again?"

"Dud round," Jess said, his face pale. "All I heard was a click."

Luke holstered his gun. "Let me see that piece," he said. He saw the wary look on Jess's face and said, "I'm not going to shoot you, cowboy. At least not today."

Jess passed the Colt to Luke and the little gunman opened the loading gate and rotated the cylinder. Three unfired rounds and two empty shell casings fell into the palm of his hand.

"You didn't reload after yesterday?" he said.

Jess shook his head. "I guess I forgot."

"If I hadn't been here your forgetfulness would have got you killed."

Luke shook his head, then hauled back and slapped Jess hard across the face. Too stunned to react Jess stood there for a moment. Then he said, "Why the hell did you do that?"

"So you'll never forget what I'm about to tell you. Always, and I mean *always*, reload your weapon after a shooting scrape." Jess opened his mouth to speak, but Luke held up his hand. "No ifs, buts or maybes . . . always reload. Have you got that, pilgrim?"

Jess rubbed his cheek. "Don't ever do that again, Luke."

"And don't you ever go into a gunfight with an empty Colt."

"I'm not likely to forget," Jess said. "Am I?"

Luke said, "Damn, Casey, if you survive a year in the Acre it will be a miracle."

Nate Levy had heard rumors.

The whispers came from the black community in Fort Worth, which numbered around seven thousand and lived in the south end of town. Zeus had been their hero and many were angry at the manner of his death.

Moses Johnson was a washed-up, bare-knuckle tent fighter who'd taken too many blows to the head, but he was smart enough to know that Nate was always good for a grubstake.

He sat upright in a chair in Nate's hotel room, his battered hat at his feet. His huge hands, corded with veins, lay on the top of his thighs and when he breathed his flattened nose made a faint whistling sound.

"I hear bad t'ings, Mr. Levy," he said. "T'ings about a black boy." Johnson's chocolate-colored eyes were webbed with red veins. "Black folks say Mayor Stout didn't do much to save him when the lynch mob came."

"Moses, you're talking about Zeus, huh?" Nate Levy said.

"Zeus was a good man, did right by folks. Did right by me. He never done bad, no."

"He was sure a good man," Nate said.

"Then why did the white peoples kill him?" Moses said.

"Because he was a black man, I guess."

"I'm not in the fight business no more."

"I know you're not, Moses. You were good, very good."

The black man scratched his head. "I got real trouble remembering t'ings, me."

"You were talking about Mayor Stout," Nate said.

"Mayor Stout, yes. Nobody notice black folks who work at City Hall, but black folks hear t'ings. They say Mayor Stout went home early day Zeus was killed. He lef' a poor ol' white man in charge. Poor ol' white man couldn't stop them vigilantes, no."

"Why would Mayor Stout do that, Moses?"

"'Cause he was paid. That's what black folks say."

Moses Johnson picked up his battered hat and got to his feet. "I fergit why I came here, Mr. Levy."

Nate smiled. "Perhaps you need a loan, Moses."

"Yeah, I t'ink that's what it was, me."

Nate gave the man ten dollars and said, "Until your next payday."

"I don't know when that be, Mr. Levy," Moses said.

"Oh, I'm sure it will be soon," Nate said.

Moses shuffled to the door then said, "I was class one time, wasn't I, Mr. Levy?"

"One of the best, Moses. You had fast feet and a killer right hand."

Moses lifted a huge fist and grinned. "Yeah, now I remember."

When Nate Levy pulled the handle of a brass pulley contraption it rang a jangling bell inside the mayor's house. A couple of minutes passed before the door opened and the vast figure of Harry Stout stood in the doorway. Behind the man Nate caught a fleeting glimpse of a young woman wrapped in a sheet running from one room to another.

Horny Harry beamed. "Well, well, Mr. Levy isn't it? My door is always open to Children of the Book and I wish others would do the same. Unfortunately I'm rather busy with city business at the moment, so come back later, tomorrow maybe, or the next day."

"Do you always conduct business in a dressing gown?" Nate said.

"Best to be comfortable, I always say. Now, if you will excuse me." Stout made to shut the door, but Nate put his thin shoulder against it. "Were you paid to throw my boy Zeus to the wolves, Stout?" he said.

The mayor's jowly face fell. "What in the world gave you that idea?"

"You left City Hall early the day Zeus was dragged out and murdered," Nate said. "You left an old watchman in charge." His hand dropped to the pocket of his coat and he came up with the Remington derringer. "Who paid you?"

Stout stuck his head outside the door and looked around. Then he said, "You'd better come in."

Stout, the muzzle of the belly gun sticking into his back, led the way to a room off the main foyer. "This is my parlor," he said, waving Nate inside. "I think you'll find it quite comfortable."

In the background a woman's voice called out, "Harry . . . I'm waiting."

"I'll be with you shortly, ah, Miss Jones," Stout said. He smiled at Nate. "The pressures of business never cease."

Nate Levy sat in a chair but he kept the derringer leveled on Stout.

"I did not betray Zeus," he said. "The day in question I had to hurry home because I had a . . . business meeting with Miss Jones. I had no idea he'd be abducted from City Hall. It was an outrage."

"Why did you leave one old man to guard him?" Nate said.

"Because such a terrible thing had never happened before, so why would I take extreme steps to keep Zeus safe? I consider the portals of City Hall to be sacred, and up until Zeus was taken they were."

"Did you help frame Zeus for the jewelry store murder?" Nate said.

"No, I did not. I was as surprised as everybody else when he was accused. The testimony of the shop girl was damning."

Stout's replies had a ring of truth and Nate put the derringer away and got to his feet. "Stout, I think you're a damned scoundrel," Nate said. "You were derelict in your duty to Zeus and that was why he was murdered. You're a disgrace to yourself and this city."

Stout retreated into bluster but Nate ignored him and walked out of the room. As he opened the front door the woman's voice sang out, "Horny, honey, I'm getting lonely . . ."

"And you're welcome to him," Nate yelled before he slammed the door shut.

CHAPTER FORTY-EIGHT

Jess Casey was about to commit murder and the whiskey helped ease the pain of what he had to do.

"Nate, I have to do this myself," he said, lowering his glass. "You can have no part in it."

"You'll have to live with it afterward," Nate said. "A cold-blooded killing lies heavily on a man."

"You were planning to kill Harry Stout," Jess said.

"That urge passed quickly. He's a buffoon."

"For a long time he was my prime suspect," Jess said.

"He doesn't have the brains God gave a goose," Nate said.

Jess smiled. "Maybe you should have shot him anyway, out of spite."

"Did Luke Short hear what Wilson Tucker told you?"

"No. He didn't." Jess drank more whiskey and said, "My case against Dr. Sun will not hold up in court; his lawyers would dance rings around me."

"Afterward, what will you do, Jess?"

"Leave Fort Worth and find a cowboying job somewhere. I can still fork a bronc." He smiled. "Even though I no longer have a bronc."

Nate glanced at the clock. "Why midnight?"

"It seems like a fitting time to murder a man, end an evil. You know, when ghosts prowl and witches fly and all that stuff they have in the picture books."

"Did you take Luke Short's advice?" Nate said.

"Concerning what?"

"About loading your gun."

Jess rubbed his cheek and grinned. "I'll never forget it."

"Twenty-five minutes to midnight," Nate said.

"I know. I'm watching the clock. I liked him, you know. I thought Dr. Sun was a fine man."

"It's easy to be wrong about people. I was wrong about Harry Stout."

"Yeah, me, too," Jess said. "I was way wrong."

With an air of finality, Jess placed his empty glass on the desk.

"Nate," he said, "I may swing for what I'm about to do. If that happens, I've left an address in the top drawer here, my sister in El Paso. Sell my traps and see that she gets whatever money they bring. Tell her . . . no, don't tell her anything. Just make sure she gets the money."

"Count on it, Jess," Nate Levy said.

"I'm beholden to you, Nate."

Jess got to his feet, let out a couple of notches in his cartridge belt and lowered his holster. "Wilson Tucker said I wear my gun too high," he said.

"I guess he was the expert," Nate said. "Only now he's dead."

Nate Levy followed Jess out of the office and onto the boardwalk. There was a halo around the moon and coyotes yipped in the brush country. Somewhere close a woman cried out in her sleep and an alarmed dog barked then fell silent.

Nate watched Jess Casey walk away from him, the sheriff's big-roweled Texas spurs ringing. "Hey, Jess," he said, "you step out like a puncher."

Jess walked on.

"Did you know that?" Nate said, louder this time as the distance between them grew. Again Jess made no answer, and Nate whispered, "Good luck, cowboy. Good luck to both of us."

Lamps burned in the home of Dr. Sun and when Jess Casey stood at the door he smelled the fragrance of burning incense from within. He tried the handle but the door was locked. Jess rapped hard three times, imagining that it must sound like the official knock of a lawman.

After a few moments the door opened a crack and Mei-Xing said, "Too late. Come back tomorrow."

Jess ignored that and pushed his way inside. The hallway was lit by lanterns that cast a dull red glow. Then Dr. Sun's voice, low, unhurried, came from an open door to Jess's right.

"Good evening, Jess," he said, a smile in his voice. "I wondered when you'd come. Please, enter my parlor, as the spider said to the fly."

Wary of a trap, Jess drew his Colt and walked to the open door.

"Come in, come in, Jess," Dr. Sun said. "Old friends like us need not stand on ceremony."

The physician wore a dark blue robe embroidered with stars, moons and other celestial objects. His sword lay on a table nearby.

"I'll get right to the point," Jess said. "I want you to sign a confession that you murdered Lillian Burke. That's just one of your crimes, Doctor, but it's enough to hang you."

"Is that all, Jess? My, you set your sights low."

"Will you sign a confession?"

"Of course not," Dr. Sun said. "Me hang for killing a slut? I don't think so. Besides, how can you even prove such a thing?"

Jess nodded, his face grim. "I can't. That's why I will execute you tonight, Doctor, save the hangman a task."

Dr. Sun spread his robed arms. "I have no gun, Jess. You are contemplating cold-blooded murder indeed. And for what? I planned to give the woman you mention the world, the entire world. I would have taken her back to China, where she would have been a great lady with a fine house, servants, carriages, expensive clothes, all the things a woman craves. But then, one night after we had a minor quarrel, the slattern became angry and told me she'd slept with many men, one of them a black man. A black man! After that, how could I let her live?"

Jess said nothing, the Colt steady in his hand.

"Are you deaf as well as stupid? Answer me. How could I let her live?"

"You nailed Lillian to a cross," Jess said. "That was obscene."

"Whimsy, dear boy. I had it done in a moment of whimsy, that's all. It was a moment of self-indulgence that I rather regret now. It was far too theatrical, but no more than she deserved."

Dr. Sun poured himself wine from a decanter and stood with the glass in his hand. "Yes, Jess, I tried to have you killed several times, because I thought you might interfere with my plans. But recently I've come to appreciate your finer qualities. With you beside me and Wilson Tucker's gun we can rule this town and grow rich in the process."

"Tucker is dead," Jess said.

For the first time that night Dr. Sun seemed shaken. "You killed him?"

"Me and Luke Short. It was a joint effort. I had empty chambers in my gun."

"How remiss of you. Well, no matter, we can hire other gunmen. But first we must get rid of Koenig and Short and take over their share of the opium business. Then I will introduce the wonderful new drug. Do you know what dope fiends will pay for their . . . what do they call it? . . . 'ticket to heaven'? A fortune! We'll be rich, Jess, you and me."

"Did you murder Addie Brennan in her bed to keep her quiet about who really shot her?"

"Ah, you wish to speak more trivia. No. I'm not that crude, Jess. I hired Norman Arendale for that. He's a former actor, a murderer of some repute. And you don't have to worry about Dorothy Mills, the shop girl I bribed." Dr. Sun smiled. "This will make you laugh. Arendale took the same train as she did. I rather fancy that dear Miss Mills's dream of fame in the theater came to an abrupt halt somewhere between here and the locomotive's first wood-and-water stop. We will use the talented Mr. Arendale again, of course, you and I."

"Sign the confession, Dr. Sun," Jess said. "Don't make me kill you."

"You won't kill me, Jess. I can see in your eyes that you don't have the belly for it. Stick with me, become rich, travel with me to China if you wish and become a great lord. The life path ahead of you is paved with gold, Jess. And women! Do you know you can buy a beautiful girl in China for the price of a cow?"

"Sign the confession," Jess said.

"Then I was right the first time. You're an idiot, Jess. You're worse than the slut Lillian Burke. I have destroyed many people, young and old, in this benighted city and now, alas, I must destroy you."

Jess felt the knife plunge into his back between his shoulder blades and at first there was no pain; only moments later did it begin to throb. He felt his knees go weak and for a moment he thought surely he'd fall. Dr. Sun, his sword raised, advanced on him, the glittering blade held high for a killing stroke. Jess shoved his Colt out in front of him and fired. A second report sounded at the same time. Someone else was firing. Dr. Sun staggered back and the sword dropped from his hand.

"No more, Jess!" he said. "I can give you the whole world."

"This is for Lillian Burke and an old lady called Dixie," Jess said. Pain and shock drove him to his knees, but he worked his gun. He pumped bullet after bullet into Dr. Sun, firing after the man was dead. Reload, Luke had said. Well Dr. Sun had taken six shots to the chest and belly and now he bled out on the floor like a felled hog.

"He's done, Jess. Let him be."

A hand dropped on Jess's shoulder. He turned his head and saw Nate Levy, a Remington derringer in his hand. "The girl stabbed you and I done for her." Then, tears in his eyes, Nate said, "I think you're gonna die, Jess."

"The hell I am," Jess Casey said before darkness descended on him.

CHAPTER FORTY-NINE

Jess Casey woke to sunlight.

He opened his eyes and saw the radiant face of a beautiful woman staring down at him. "I guess I beat the odds and made it to heaven, huh?" he whispered.

"No, you didn't, General Custer, you're in hell, at least a half acre of it," Destiny Durand said.

"Are they going to hang me?" Jess said. "I shot a man, emptied my gun into him."

"Hang you? You're a hero, cowboy. You're the man who killed Dr. Sun, the Demon Doctor of Doom Street."

"There is no Doom Street in the Acre," Jess said, puzzled.

"Well, there sure as hell is now," Destiny said. "Joe D'Arcy, the newspaper editor, got Mayor Stout to name an alley near Sun's house Doom Street. D'Arcy said he needed it for his front-page headline. Here, let me help you to sit up. You lost a lot of blood."

Once Jess was settled, Destiny said, "You've been out for three days. Kurt and Luke Short came to visit and Luke said he won't even think about killing you until you get better."

"Nice of him," Jess said.

"Luke brought you black grapes but Nate Levy ate them, him being an invalid and all."

"Nate shot the girl . . ."

"Mei-Xing? Yes, I know he shot her. She was the one who stabbed you. Nate just winged her. To save her own neck she spilled her guts about Sun strangling Lillian Burke and all the other people he had murdered."

"I went to his house to murder him," Jess said. "I knew I couldn't prove anything against him, so I went there to kill him."

"A lawman with a knife in his back killing another man coming at him with a sword is hardly murder. In the Acre they call that self-defense. In the Acre they call most killings self-defense."

Destiny rose and walked to the hotel room table. In the fashion of the time her bustle was huge and her dress rustled. She brought a basket back to the bed and said, "Cheese, soda crackers and a bottle of wine. Kurt said you'd be hungry when you woke up."

"He's right about that," Jess said.

"Then I'll leave you to eat," Destiny said. "Do you need a chamber pot?"

"Ask me that after I drink the wine," Jess said.

"By the way, Custer, your doctor was young Dr.

Alan Barclay. Kurt says he's brilliant and an expert on knife wounds."

"Then I'll thank him later," Jess said.

"You won't, not when you see his bill," Destiny said.

Jess had just finished eating when Kurt Koenig stepped into the room. "How are you feeling, Sheriff?" he said.

"All right, I guess," Jess said. "I was stabbed in the back."

"I know. The little Chinese gal almost done for you." Koenig laid a paper sack on the table beside the bed. "I brought you some black grapes," he said. "They're good for invalids, or so they say."

"Where is Luke Short?" Jess said. "He brought me grapes but Nate Levy ate them."

"He won't visit you again. Luke's hypocrisy only goes so far."

"Kurt, don't reopen the Green Buddha," Jess said.

Koenig smiled. "Even on your deathbed you're still on the job. To set your mind at rest I won't. I'm tearing it down. Too many ghosts of dead people in there thanks to Sun, one of his more bloody attempts to put me out of business, the scurvy swab. But the good news is that I plan to rebuild and keep the original name."

"What will it be?" Jess said, brightening.

"An opium den, of course. The Green Buddha lives again."

"Kurt, I'm warning you, I plan to end the opium

trade in Fort Worth, starting with the Acre," Jess said. "Nothing has changed."

"I thought you'd had a bellyful of the peacekeeping business and planned to quit," Koenig said. "That's what Nate Levy told me."

"That was true, but lying here thinking about it, I plan to stick, make the Acre a decent place for people to live. Until the opium trade is gone that's not going to happen."

"Then we're destined to butt heads, Jess, because I ain't about to lose a big chunk of my income and neither is Luke."

"Can we agree to be enemies?" Jess said.

"If that's the way you want to play it."

"My mind is made up on that. I have to take a set against you and Luke," Jess said. "There's no other way."

"The Acre isn't big enough for the three of us, huh?"

"That's the way the pickle squirts."

"You know I want to make you a partner," Koenig said. "And I mean a full partner in all my businesses, opium and morphine included."

"So did Dr. Sun."

Koenig smiled. "Then it's war to the hilt, I guess," Koenig said. "Once you're on your feet again, of course. I can't shoot a gentleman who is lying abed sick as a poisoned pup."

"Sorry it has to be this way, Kurt," Jess said.

"Don't be sorry. A man does what his conscience tells him to do. That's how it works for you and it's how it works for me. And for Luke Short, come to that. He has a conscience of sorts."

Koenig stepped to the door. "One thing you can be sure of, Jess, we won't stab you in the back. Now shooting you in the belly, well, that's a whole different matter."

CHAPTER FIFTY

Jess Casey thought something was afoot when Nate Levy insisted that he shave and trim his mustache. His suspicions grew when Nate produced a ditto suit in the loud check the little man favored but Jess certainly did not. Along with this came a plug hat, shirt and tie.

"I bought the suit from Aaron Goldberg's used clothing store," Nate said. "I gave him an idea of your size and he said this fine garment will fit you like a glove."

"Hell, Nate, I'm not wearing that," Jess said. "What's the big idea?"

"You'll wear it today, General," Destiny Durand said. "And after that you need never wear it again, just your usual rags."

"It's for your own good, boy," Nate said. "You have to make a good impression. Now let's get you dressed."

"A good impression for who?" Jess said.

"For whom," Destiny said. "You'll find out shortly. Now put on that suit and I'll turn my back until you get the pants on. I've never seen a naked man before."

"If I didn't feel so damned weak . . ." Jess said.

"Do it, Sheriff, or I will look at you with your pants off," Destiny said.

The suit fit where it hit and when Jess tried on the hat it promptly fell down over his eyes. Nate solved that problem by stuffing newspaper into the sweatband and then he stepped back to admire his creation.

"You look like a young royal prince," Nate said.

"You look adorable," Destiny said, smiling, her joined hands pressed to her cheek.

"I look like an idiot," Jess said. "What's all that noise?" He made to step to the window, but Destiny stopped him. "No, don't look out there. You'll spoil the surprise," she said.

Jess said, "What kind of surprise. Am I getting my picture made?"

"Something like that," Nate said.

Kurt Koenig opened the door and stuck his head inside. "The adoring populace awaits their hero," he said.

"Then let's go," Nate said.

The street outside was crowded, the focal point a lanky sorrel horse wearing Jess's saddle. Mayor Harry Stout, beaming, held the animal's reins. As soon as the City of Fort Worth Brass Band caught sight of Jess, a clash of cymbals preceded an enthusiastic if ragged rendition of "For He's a Jolly Good Fellow" and the crowd joined in, singing the words.

The mayor handed the reins of the sorrel to a minion, advanced on Jess and hugged him ferociously, much to the sheriff's embarrassment. "How good it is to hug a real hero," he said. "I'm quite beside myself with joy."

Stout then launched into a politician's speech, praising himself for his efforts to raise the necessary funds to buy a fine new horse for the hero Sheriff Jess Casey.

He said, "I could say, 'Here stands the killer,' but nay, I will not. I will say, 'Here stands the avenging angel who smote down the nefarious Demon Doctor of Doom Street in his vile lair.'"

This brought a cheer and Patrick Burke the brewer held a great handkerchief to his face and sobbed uncontrollably. People patted Jess on the back, forgetting he'd been stabbed there, and caused him considerable pain.

After speaking darkly of Chinese demons and the Yellow Peril and the vulnerability of American maidenhood—"As if he'd know," Destiny whispered—Stout produced a flat, black jewelry box and presented it to Jess with a flourish.

"Made at great expense to this fair city, I am here today, Sheriff Casey, to present to you this fine badge"—he hesitated, then—"made of gold-plated silver!" Again Stout waited for the cheer that duly followed. "I give it to you as a token of our esteem and admiration, a replacement for the emblem that bears the scars of your valor."

As the band struck up a spirited rendition of "Bessie in the Barn," Jess opened the box and saw a fine sheriff's badge reclining on a bed of red velvet. He showed the badge to the crowd, which roared its approval. Unfortunately the sorrel, alarmed by the noise, reared and bolted and a posse of small boys was immediately dispatched to fetch it back.

"Fear not, the errant beast will be returned," the mayor yelled. Then, in a loud aside, "It seems that horses harbor no honor for heroes."

That last drew a cheer and Stout rounded on Jess and said, "Well, my boy, this is your day . . . and mine."

"Thank you, Horny Harry," Jess said.

And the crowd cheered again.

J. A. Johnstone on William W. Johnstone
"Print the Legend"

William W. Johnstone was born in southern Missouri, the youngest of four children. He was raised with strong moral and family values by his minister father, and tutored by his schoolteacher mother. Despite this, he quit school at age fifteen.

"I have the highest respect for education," he says, "but such is the folly of youth, and wanting to see the world beyond the four walls and the blackboard."

True to this vow, Bill attempted to enlist in the French Foreign Legion ("I saw Gary Cooper in *Beau Geste* when I was a kid and I thought the French Foreign Legion would be fun") but was rejected, thankfully, for being underage. Instead, he joined a traveling carnival and did all kinds of odd jobs. It was listening to the veteran carny folk, some of whom had been on the circuit since the late 1800s, telling amazing tales about their experiences, that planted the storytelling seed in Bill's imagination.

"They were mostly honest people, despite the bad reputation traveling carny shows had back then,"

Bill remembers. "Of course, there were exceptions. There was one guy named Picky, who got that name because he was a master pickpocket. He could steal a man's socks right off his feet without him knowing. Believe me, Picky got us chased out of more than a few towns."

After a few months of this grueling existence, Bill returned home and finished high school. Next came stints as a deputy sheriff in the Tallulah, Louisiana, Sheriff's Department, followed by a hitch in the U.S. Army. Then he began a career in radio broadcasting at KTLD in Tallulah, which would last sixteen years. It was there that he fine-tuned his storytelling skills. He turned to writing in 1970, but it wouldn't be until 1979 that his first novel, *The Devil's Kiss*, was published. Thus began the full-time writing career of William W. Johnstone. He wrote horror (*The Uninvited*), thrillers (*The Last of the Dog Team*), even a romance novel or two. Then, in February 1983, *Out of the Ashes* was published. Searching for his missing family in a postapocalyptic America, rebel mercenary and patriot Ben Raines is united with the civilians of the Resistance forces and moves to the forefront of a revolution for the nation's future.

Out of the Ashes was a smash. The series would continue for the next twenty years, winning Bill three generations of fans all over the world. The series was often imitated but never duplicated. "We all tried to copy the Ashes series," said one publishing executive, "but Bill's uncanny ability, both then and now, to predict in which direction the political winds were blowing brought a certain immediacy to the table no one else could capture." The Ashes series would end its run with more than thirty-four books and twenty million copies in print, making it one of the most successful men's action series in American book publishing. (The Ashes series also, Bill notes with a touch of pride, got him on the FBI's Watch List for its less than flattering portrayal of spineless politicians and the growing power of big government over our lives, among other things. In that respect, I often find myself saying, "Bill was years ahead of his time.")

Always steps ahead of the political curve, Bill's recent thrillers, written with myself, include *Vengeance Is Mine, Invasion USA, Border War, Jackknife, Remember the Alamo, Home Invasion, Phoenix Rising, The Blood of Patriots, The Bleeding Edge*, and the upcoming *Suicide Mission.*

It is with the western, though, that Bill found his greatest success. His westerns propelled him onto both the *USA Today* and the *New York Times* best-seller lists.

Bill's western series include *Matt Jensen, the Last Mountain Man, Preacher, the First Mountain Man, The Family Jensen, Luke Jensen, Bounty Hunter, Eagles, MacCallister* (an Eagles spin-off), *Sidewinders, The Brothers O'Brien, Sixkiller, Blood Bond, The Last Gunfighter*, and the new series *Flintlock* and *The Trail West*. May 2013 saw the hardcover western *Butch Cassidy: The Lost Years.*

"The Western," Bill says, "is one of the few true art forms that is one hundred percent American. I liken the Western as America's version of England's Arthurian legends, like the Knights of the Round Table, or Robin Hood and his Merry Men. Starting with the 1902 publication of *The Virginian* by Owen Wister, and followed by the greats like Zane Grey, Max Brand, Ernest Haycox, and of course Louis L'Amour, the Western has helped to shape the cultural landscape of America.

"I'm no goggle-eyed college academic, so when my fans ask me why the Western is as popular now as it was a century ago, I don't offer a 200-page thesis. Instead, I can only offer this: The Western is honest. In this great country, which is suffering under the yoke of political correctness, the Western harks back to an era when justice was sure and swift. Steal a man's horse, rustle his cattle, rob a bank, a stagecoach, or a train, you were hunted down and fitted with a hangman's noose. One size fit all.

"Sure, we westerners are prone to a little embellishment and exaggeration and, I admit it, occasionally play a little fast and loose with the facts. But we do so for a very good reason—to enhance the enjoyment of readers.

"It was Owen Wister, in *The Virginian*, who first coined the phrase '*When you call me that, smile.*' Legend has it that Wister actually heard those words spoken by a deputy sheriff in Medicine Bow, Wyoming, when another poker player called him a son of a bitch.

"Did it really happen, or is it one of those myths that have passed down from one generation to the next? I honestly don't know. But there's a line in one of my favorite Westerns of all time, *The Man Who Shot Liberty Valance*, where the newspaper editor tells the young reporter, 'When the truth becomes legend, print the legend.'

"These are the words I live by."

Keep reading for a special preview of the next epic
from national bestselling authors
WILLIAM W. JOHNSTONE and J. A. JOHNSTONE.

THE TRAIL WEST:
MONAHAN'S MASSACRE

The accidental gunslinger Dooley Monahan
has quit wandering and settled down to a
farmer's life. But when the itch for adventure
gets too strong, he packs up and rides west.
Along with his horse, General Grant, and Blue,
a dog who's too smart for his own good,
Dooley rides for the Black Hills to strike it rich
in the goldfields. But fate has other ideas.

When the trigger-happy Dobbs–Handley gang
holds up the Omaha bank, Dooley is mistaken for
one of the robbers and a price is plastered on his
head. With every lawman in the territory hot on
his trail, Dooley has no choice but to join up with
the murderous outlaws. If the hangman doesn't
get him, his new friends will, but Dooley won't
turn back. With Blue and General Grant at his
side, Dooley will make his fortune—come hell,
high water, and everything in between.

Coming this March.

PROLOGUE

Naturally, Dooley Monahan had never cared a whit for Nebraska. After all, when a man is born in Iowa, he frowns upon that great state due west that lay just across the Missouri River. Come to think on it, Dooley never liked Illinois much, either, over to the east. And especially not Missouri, what with its bushwhackers and outlaws such as the James boys and the Younger brothers and that crazy governor named Boggs the state south of Dooley's home state had once had elected. Had he ever really given Wisconsin or Minnesota much thought, Dooley might have decided that he didn't care much for those places, either.

But Nebraska had always been something of a rival of Iowa, at least from what Dooley had been reading in the *Council Bluffs Journal* that he had found accidentally put in with his mail at the general store in Des Moines. Well, actually, it wasn't so much all of Nebraska that the editor, one Jonas

Houston, waxed most violently against with his poisoned pen. Just Omaha, which lay just across the wide Missouri River from Council Bluffs, Iowa.

When Dooley crossed the ferry and landed in Omaha, he didn't see what all the ballyhoo was about. Nebraska, and Omaha, looked fine—maybe even, Dooley had to reluctantly admit—a sight better than rickety, ramshackle, and rank-smelling Council Bluffs. But not Iowa, overall, with its rolling hills and verdant pastures and corn and mud and everything that Dooley had grudgingly grown to like over the past two years back on his farm.

Omaha, Nebraska, was all right, Dooley had decided as he loaded up his supplies into the saddlebags, gave his blue dog a bite of biscuit, and swung into the saddle on his bay gelding.

A minute or two later, Omaha and Nebraska— and Dooley Monahan's life in general—went straight to hell.

CHAPTER ONE

As he rode west down the wide, muddy street, Dooley Monahan felt content. He had a belly full of coffee and biscuits and gravy, a newspaper article—torn out from page three of the *Council Bluffs Journal*—and enough supplies, or so the merchant at the general store had told him, that would get him to the Black Hills of Dakota Territory, where Dooley had decided he would make his fortune at that gold strike up yonder. And a fellow he had met at the Riverfront Saloon had sold him a map that would take him to the Black Hills and avoid any Sioux warrior who might be after a scalp or two. Two blocks back, he had even tipped his hat to a plump blonde who had not only smiled at him, but also even offered him a "Good morning, sir."

"Yes, sir, ol' Blue," Dooley told the blue-eyed dog walking alongside his good horse, "it sure is shaping up to be a mighty good day."

That's when a bullet tore through the crown of his brown hat.

A couple of years had passed since, as best as Dooley could remember, somebody had taken a shot at him—but Dooley had not been farming for so long that he forgot how to survive in the West. Ducking low in the saddle, he craned his head back down Front Street where the shot had come from while his right hand reached for and gripped the Colt .45 Peacemaker he wore in a well-used holster slickened with bacon grease.

On one side of the street, that plump blonde girl dived behind a water trough. On the south board-walk, a man in a silk top hat pitched his broom onto the warped planks, slammed one shutter closed, and dived back inside the open door of his tonsorial parlor.

What looked to be a whole danged regiment of cavalry charged toward him, the hooves of wild-eyed horses churning up mud like a farmer breaking sod—but only if that farmer had Thoroughbreds instead of mules, and a multidisced plow that could rip through the ground at breakneck speed.

"The James boys!" came a shout.

"It's the danged Youngers!" roared another.

"The Reno Gang!" yelled someone.

"We're the Dobbs and Handley boys, you stupid square-heads!" shouted a man with a walrus mustache. He rode one of those wild-eyed horses that were coming straight for Dooley Monahan; his dog, Blue; and his gelding, General Grant.

"Bank robbery!"

"Murder!"

"St. Albans!"

Dooley had read about St. Albans—not in the *Council Bluffs Journal,* but some other newspaper, maybe one in Des Moines back when he was living with his mother and father and long before he got the urge to ride west and find gold and had made a name for himself as a gunman who had killed a few outlaws. St. Albans was a town in Vermont or New Hampshire or Maine or maybe even Minnesota—but not Iowa or Nebraska—where Confederates had pulled a daytime robbery of a bank during the Civil War. So whenever the James-Younger boys or the Dobbs-Handley Gang or some other bunch of cutthroats or guerillas robbed a bank in daylight hours, folks still cried out . . .

"St. Albans! St. Albans! Foul murder! Robbery!"

Or:

"Get your guns, men, and let's kill these thievin' scum."

The men of Omaha, Nebraska, had taken up arms by now. Bullets whined, roared, and ricocheted from barbershops and rooftops, from behind trash bins or water troughs. Panes of glass shattered. The riders thundering their mounts right at Dooley Monahan answered in kind.

General Grant did two quick jumps and a stutter

step, which caused Dooley to release the grip on his walnut-handled Colt. His left hand held the reins. His right hand gripped the horn. And seeing his dog bolt down the street, leap onto the north-side boardwalk, and move faster than that dog had ever run gave Dooley an idea.

He raked General Grant's sides with his spurs and felt that great horse of his start churning up the mud of Front Street himself.

Later, when Dooley Monahan had time to think everything through, when he came to realize everything that he might have done—*should* have done—Dooley would realize that perhaps his best move would have been to dive out of the saddle and over the hitching rail and fall onto his hands and knees on the boardwalk. Then, he imagined, he would have crawled rapidly east—toward Iowa—until he reached the water trough, where he gallantly would have dived and covered the body of the plump blonde, shielding her with his own body, earning much praise for his heroics and chivalry from the editor of the *Council Bluffs Journal* and maybe even Omaha's *Weekly, World, Herald, Register, Call,* and *Mormon Prophet.* General Grant, most likely, would have galloped off after Blue, found shelter down an alley, and Dooley Monahan would have avoided confusion and near death. A parson would have found his horse and dog and led them back to the saloon on Front Street where Dooley would have been talking to the plump blonde. She would have kissed Dooley full on the lips for saving her life, Dooley would have been given a couple of cigars and a bottle of whiskey, and he would have continued on to the gold mines of the Black Hills— if there were mines, or maybe he would just have filed a claim on some creek. Either way, he would have been well on his way to a fortune, and not running for his life.

Yes, that is what Dooley should have done.

But when a man is mounted on a fast-running horse and facing a charging horde of rough-looking men, with bullets slicing dangerously close, even an experienced farmer turned cowboy turned gunman turned gold seeker turned amnesiac turned recovered amnesiac turned farmer turned fortune hunter does not always elect to do the smart or proper thing.

Instead, Dooley did what came to him first. He spurred his horse, and General Grant led him westward down Front Street. He leaned low in the saddle, and almost not low enough, for one bullet grazed the skin tight across his left shoulder blade.

The frame, sod, and bricked buildings of busy Omaha seemed blurry as Dooley glanced north and south. He saw the flashes of guns from a few windows or doorways, but none of the bullets came that close. Still, he managed to yell, "Don't shoot at me, you fool Nebraskans! I'm just trying to save my own hide!"

They couldn't hear him, of course. Not with all

the musketry and the pounding of hooves and, perhaps, even Dooley's own heartbeat.

General Grant had always been a reliable horse, and as fast as many racehorses. But Omaha's streets had become a thick bog after a bunch of spring rains, and the fine bay horse had spent the past couple of years on an old farm a few miles outside of Des Moines—so he wasn't quite up to his old form. Before he knew it, Dooley felt riders on both sides of him. He wanted to slow down, but even as he eased off his spurs, General Grant kept running as hard as his four legs could carry him. And Dooley understood that the bay gelding really had no choice. Too many horses were right behind him. Even if the horse or Dooley could have stopped, they would have been trampled by outlaws and bank robbers trying to get out of Omaha as fast as they could. Dooley could not go to the left, because a bearded man on a buckskin mare blocked that way. Dooley could not veer off to the north side, either, because a tobacco-chewing man wearing a deerskin shirt and riding a black stallion held Dooley and General Grant in check. There wasn't much Dooley could do except ride along with the flow of the outlaws and pray that he didn't get killed.

Of course, later, Dooley thought that maybe, had he drawn his pistol and shot one of the bad men riding along either side of him, he might have been able to leap General Grant over the dead man and save his own hide.

Which never would have worked in a million years.

On the other hand, had Dooley possessed the sense of mind to draw his hogleg and put a bullet through his own brain, that might have been the easy, if a coward's, way out.

The man with the deerskin shirt pulled ahead of Dooley, but a rider in striped britches on a pinto mustang quickly filled the opening. The man in the deerskin put his black mount right in front of Dooley and General Grant.

That, Dooley decided, wasn't such a bad thing to happen. No fool Nebraskan would now be able to shoot Dooley dead, mistaking him for one of the bank robbers. At least these men of the Dobbs-Handley Gang were protecting Dooley's life.

By now, Dooley was sweating. His lungs burned from breathing so hard. His butt and thighs ached from bounding around in the saddle. Mud plastered his face from the black stallion galloping ahead of him. Mud splattered against his denim trousers and stovepipe boots. He glanced to the south and saw the bearded man riding the buckskin mare stare at him. Dooley tried to smile. The man turned away, raised the Remington .44 in his right hand, and snapped another shot toward some citizen and defender of Omaha, Nebraska.

Then the outlaws, with Dooley right among them, turned north.

More gunfire. More curses. More mud and shouts.

Dooley glanced up at a three-story hotel. A man on the rooftop stood up, did a macabre dance as bullets peppered his body. The Winchester rifle—or maybe it was a Henry—pitched over the hotel's façade, and the protector of Omaha—for Dooley glimpsed sunlight reflecting off a tin badge on the lapel of the man's striped vest—followed the repeating rifle and crashed through the awning and onto the boardwalk in front of the hotel.

That caused Dooley's stomach to rumble. He thought he might turn to his side and lose the whiskey he had downed at the Riverfront Saloon and the biscuits and gravy and coffee from Nancy's Diner. But he did not vomit, and he thought that power might have saved his life. For surely had he sprayed the man on his right, the man in the deerskin shirt on the black stallion would have shot him dead.

And that man was a mighty fine shot, for he was the one who had killed the lawman on the rooftop of the hotel.

The horses kept running, though by now the gunfire was dying down. And the buildings weren't so close together anymore. Before long, the

Dobbs-Handley Gang had put Omaha, Nebraska, behind them.

They kept their horses at a gallop.

And Dooley Monahan had no choice but to keep galloping with them.

CHAPTER TWO

Eventually, the lead rider's horse began to tire—as did the mounts ridden by the other outlaws—and the pace slackened, but did not stop. Dooley wanted to say something, but, on the other hand, he really didn't want to get killed. He swallowed any words he thought of, especially when the men to his side began shucking the empty shells from their revolvers and reloading. They filled every cylinder with a fresh load—most men, including Dooley, usually kept the chamber empty under the hammer to make it less likely to blow off a toe, foot, or kneecap. When they had their six-shooters loaded, they began filling their rifles or shotguns, too.

They did this while their horses kept at a hard trot.

Which took some doing.

Dooley kept both hands on his reins. He didn't even look at the Colt in its holster. At least, Dooley thought he still carried the revolver. For all he knew, it might have been joggled loose during that hard run and was buried in Omaha's mud or the tall grass they now pushed through.

They turned south, swung a wide loop to avoid any trails, farms, travelers, or lawmen, and kept their horses at that bone-jarring, spine-pounding trot. Dooley felt, more than heard or saw, a couple of the riders in the rear pull back. Most likely, he expected, to watch their back trail and let them know if any posse took off after them. From Dooley's experience, posses could be slow in forming—especially when that posse of well-meaning but not well-shooting citizens knew it would be going up against the likes of Hubert Dobbs and Frank Handley and the murdering terrors who rode with them.

South they traveled without talking. General Grant, though, kept tossing his head back, hard eyes trying to lock on Dooley, and probably cursing him in horse-talk for running him this hard for no apparent purpose. Dooley wondered what had happened to that blue-eyed dog of his. Well, Blue wasn't actually Dooley's. The dog didn't belong to anyone, as far as Dooley knew, but he had more or less adopted the dog some years back. Fed him. Befriended him. He sure hoped he hadn't lost him again. Good dogs—any dogs—were hard to come by.

Of course, when the outlaws finally stopped

running, Dooley would be able to go back to Omaha and maybe find old Blue and—

When they stop, most likely, they'll kill me.

The thought almost caused Dooley Monahan to pull back on the reins, but he quickly stopped an action that would have caused quite the horse wreck. And if spilling members of the Dobbs-Handley Gang, maybe laming a mount or two, and busting collarbones and wrists and arms of outlaws, didn't incite murder among those owlhoots . . .

Ahead, he saw the river, and now all of the horses slowed down. Oh, no one stopped. The leader jumped off what passed for a bank, and Dooley and the men riding on either side followed.

The water felt good as it splashed over Dooley's wind-burned, mud-blasted, sweaty face. General Grant's hooves found solid bottom, and the gelding pushed through the water toward the shore.

This, if Dooley had his bearings straight, would be the Platte River. Wide, but not that deep, even after all those thunderstorms and being fairly close to where the river flowed into the Missouri. It was wet, though, and Dooley took a moment to scoop up some with his right hand. He splashed it across his face, repeated that process, then found another handful and brought it to his mouth. There wasn't that much to swallow, but what did go down his throat felt good, replenishing, but most of the wetness just soothed his dried, chapped lips.

The two riders on his left and right pulled ahead

of him, but Dooley knew better than to try to escape now. He tried to think up various options, but no matter what idea came to him, the end result most likely would lead to Dooley Monahan's quick and merciful death. Unless Handley or Dobbs decided to stake him out on an ant bed, cut off his eyelids so the sun would burn his eyeballs out before the ants started eating him alive. Then that death wouldn't be anything close to quick or merciful, but it would most certainly be eternal death.

Those three riders had reached the banks about twenty yards ahead of Dooley now. He heard horses snorting, and men grunting behind him.

Water cascaded off the horses as they climbed up the bank. The riders—that bearded man on the buckskin mare, the man in the deerskin shirt, with a cheekful of chewing tobacco, on the powerful black stallion, and the puny gent in the striped britches, who rode a brown and white pinto mustang—turned around, drew their revolvers, cocked them, and waited.

The Platte began to get even shallower, and soon General Grant was carrying Dooley out of the wide patch of wetness. Behind him came the other riders, who grunted or cursed or farted. Dooley let his bay horse pick its own path up the bank until he reined in in front of the three men. He stared down the barrels of a Smith & Wesson, a Colt, and a Remington. Behind him he heard another noise.

You never forget what a rattlesnake sounds like. Maybe you think you know how it sounds—or how it makes you feel—but once you hear that rattle, you know exactly what it sounds like and you know it will practically make you wet your britches.

Quite similar to the whirl of a rattler is the cocking of a single-action revolver . . . the thumbing back of two hammers on a double-barreled shotgun, and the levering of a fresh cartridge into a Winchester or Henry rifle or carbine. Those were the sounds coming from behind Dooley Monahan.

Not the rattlesnake, of course. Not that sound. Though right then, Dooley would have preferred it to those metallic clicks.

Dooley eased the reins down, letting them drop in front of the horn. The horn he gripped with both hands, and leaning forward, he nodded his head at the men in front of him.

"Who the hell be you?"

That came from the man in the deerskin shirt. He wore a wide-brimmed dirty hat that might once have been white but had been dirtied up and sweated through over some years. Or it could have been gray, but had been faded from so much alkali dust and the blistering sun of the Great Plains. Dooley didn't think the hat had ever been black.

Brown juice came out of the man's mouth like he had opened a spigot, and he wiped the tobacco juice off his lips with a gloved left hand. The right held that cannon of a pistol, a Smith & Wesson that looked just a tad smaller than a cannon. He was the biggest of the men, which explained why he rode that giant black stallion. Dooley couldn't quite guess, but he had to figure the man stood six-foot-four in his boot heels, and had to weigh around two hundred and forty pounds. Maybe more.

"Name's Dooley," Dooley said. "Dooley Monahan."

The bearded man on the buckskin mare pursed his lips as if in deep thought. Thinking did not mean the man took the .45 caliber Colt away from Dooley's chest. He just thought.

He appeared to be more medium size, maybe not even as tall as Dooley, but tougher than a railroad tie and maybe twice as solid. Muscles strained through his muslin shirt, and Dooley couldn't quite remember when he had ever seen a beard that long on any man. There had been that woman back at that circus in Davenport that time, but you expected that when you paid two bits to see the bearded lady at a circus in Davenport. Her beard didn't seem real, though. This gent's certainly wasn't glued on.

"We ain't got no one goin' by Dooley in this gang, does we?" the man on the massive black mount finally asked.

"Ain't got nobody usin' the handle Monahans, neither."

That sentence came from the third cuss, the one

with the striped britches. He was puny. A spring wind might have carried him off like the furs on whatever those weeds with the furlike tops were called. Puny, and pale, with the coldest blue eyes Dooley had ever seen, sunk way back in his head. His blond hair, soaked by sweat and some Platte River water, hung like greasy rawhide strings. He was even uglier than that bearded lady back at that circus eighteen months back in Davenport, Iowa.

The man seemed so sickly, the big Smith & Wesson never steadied in his pasty white hand, but neither did it ever exactly not aim at one of Dooley's vital organs.

"Monahan," Dooley corrected. "No s. Just Monahan. Dooley Monahan."

He thought if he kept talking, they might not kill him.

"Shut up," barked the man on the black horse.

"Kill him, and let's ride," said the one on the buckskin mare. "Posse'll be chasin' us directly."

"How did you come to be ridin' with us?" asked the sickly one on the pinto. "Dooley *Monahans*." He stressed the last name and especially the *s* on the end of it, even though it wasn't Dooley's name.

Dooley shrugged, but kept gripping that saddle horn. If he let go, those men would think he was going for his Colt, and he'd be plugged before he could explain by a .45, .38, and .44 bullet—and no telling what calibers or gauges from the men behind him.

"Came to Omaha to stock up," Dooley said honestly. "Was riding out down that main street when you boys started whooping and hollering and riding."

"And shooting," said someone behind him.

"And shooting," Dooley added.

The men behind Dooley chuckled. The ones in front of him did not even blink or crack a smile.

"Y'all kind of swept me up," Dooley went on. "Wasn't anything I could do but keep riding. If I stopped, you would have run over me. That would've caused quite the spill. Probably got one of you boys caught, if not killed."

"We're obliged to you for that," said another voice behind him.

"Do you know who we are?" asked the tobacco-chewing man on the big black.

Dooley's mouth went dry. He could only shake is head.

"Hubert," came the first voice behind him. "My horse's gone lame."

"Now do you know who we are?" The man spit out more tobacco juice and shifted the quid to the opposite cheek.

Dooley just swallowed, but what he swallowed was mostly air. His mouth felt dried out like his skin did when he was farming. And his muscles did not respond when he tried to shake his head.

"C'mon, boy," said the man with the long beard.

"How many bank robbers you ever heard called Hubert?"

"Shut the hell up, Frank," barked the tobacco chewer. "Hubert ain't no name to be ashamed of. Belonged to my grandpappy on my ma's side, and his grandpappy's long before that."

The bearded man grinned. "And now you know my name, Dooley Monahan." At least he pronounced Dooley's name correctly. "Frank Handley."

"Which," said the big man on the big black, "makes me Hubert Dobbs."

"Which makes us," said the thin man on the pinto mustang, "the Dobbs-Handley Gang."

"A pleasure," Dooley managed to say.

"Step down off that horse," said the man who had not introduced himself.

"But first," added Frank Handley, "pull that hogleg from your holster . . ."

"Real careful," warned Hubert Dobbs.

"Real careful," coached the second voice behind Dooley.

"And," said Handley, "drop it to the ground."

Dooley Monahan obeyed.

"Let go of the reins and step away from the horse. Kinda in my direction." The tobacco chewer spit again. "That way. That's good. Two more steps. Now one more. Now don't move. Good. You take directions real good."

"Thank you," Dooley said.

The puny man leaned over in his saddle, and now managed to steady the .38 caliber Smith & Wesson. "Do I kill him now, Hubert?"

"No, Doc," Hubert Dobbs said. "Gunshot would draw a posse."

Which meant the sickly-looking man on the rangy pinto would be Doc Watson, the coldest and most vicious killer to ride with the Dobbs-Handley Gang.

"I can slit his throat," came a new voice behind Dooley Monahan.

"You could," Frank Handley said, "but Dooley Monahan rode with us. Maybe by accident. And maybe for just a few miles. But he rode with us. And we don't murder men who rode with us. It ain't in the code of the outlaw."

Dooley's heart skipped a beat. His mouth started to open to thank, to praise, Frank Handley.

Then everything went black.

CHAPTER THREE

Somewhere in the depths of dreams, delirium, or death, everything struck Dooley Monahan with perfect clarity. But that was the way things had been the past couple of years. When he was sleeping—and being clubbed over the head with a shotgun stock and left unconscious, not to mention for dead, on the far side of the Platte River, which was a form of sleeping—Dooley Monahan could think clearly and remember clearly. Awake, even after four cups of coffee, Dooley's mind tended to fog over.

"Thinkin'," the circuit-riding Methodist minister who rode and preached on the Des Moines–Corydon–Accord–Lamoni–New Virginia–Old Albany City loop had often told Dooley, "ain't your strong suit, son."

But he was asleep now—technically, unconscious—and he could remember. Everything.

"I should have told Hubert Dobbs that I once

rode with Monty's Raiders," he muttered in words that would have been unintelligible had anyone other than a jackrabbit been around to hear him.

Riding with Monty's Raiders, of course, had been by accident, too.

Way back in 1850, when Dooley was but twenty years old, his pa, the now dearly departed David Monahan, had sent Dooley south to fetch a cow. The cow he had procured, but afterward he met some boys who seemed friendly enough but turned out to be part of Monty's Raiders. Of course, by then, Monty McHugh, who had formed the raiders, had given up robbing pig farmers and corn farmers in Iowa and had made a fortune selling soap to miners in Hangtown, California. But the new members of the gang, liking how Monty's Raiders sounded so gaily on one's tongue, had kept that handle.

The new Monty's Raiders put up with Dooley for a while, then knocked him senseless and left him for dead—much as the Dobbs-Handley boys had just done—and Dooley became a drifter, turned cowboy, and wound up playing poker in a bunkhouse in the Dakotas when he had gotten into an argument with Bob Smith.

Well, whiskey, and not blows to his noggin, fogged much of what happened, but the long and short of things said that Dooley Monahan put one bullet through the heart of Bob Smith, who, the law soon learned, was not Bob Smith but one Jason

Baylor, who had posters on him planted inside every lawman's office between Missouri and Montana.

Then, in 1872, three years after Dooley had plugged Bob Smith né Jason Baylor, Dooley had drifted into the Arizona Territory, where he had found a newspaper article that told him he ought to be heading north. California? Or was it Alaska? Someplace like that. Dooley still had trouble remembering everything. Although he did remember why he was drifting. Jason Baylor had some family, and that family did not like having one of its own killed by a cowboy who nine times out of ten could not hit a barn door six feet away with no wind, no noise, and a fence post to rest his gun on. Between 1869 and 1872, Dooley had been carrying around the voucher the lawman had given him after Dooley had plugged Jason Baylor. All Dooley had to do was turn in the voucher at an accredited bank and he would be presented $500 in cash money. Enough for Dooley Monahan to make it to a booming gold town and strike a fortune. Dooley had been heading to that gold strike, as soon as he found a bank to cash in on his reward, and that's where he was going to when he camped one night in the Mogollon Rim—he could still smell those pines in that mountainous country—when he had first found that blue-eyed dog.

"Where are you, Blue?" Dooley muttered as he rolled over on the Nebraska plains. The rabbit did not hear him this time as the rabbit was desperately trying to avoid becoming a hawk's supper. The hawk did not hear Dooley, either.

The dog was one of those merle shepherds. No. No, merle was the color. That's right. Somewhere between blue and gray, with patches of black tossed about. White feet. White chest. And some copper spots on his legs, muzzle, and a couple of dots, also copper, over his eyes. An Arizona shepherd. Because Dooley had found the dog somewhere between Payson and Show Low. Had Dooley been in San Francisco, it would have been a California shepherd. Had he picked up Blue in Australia, it would have been an Australian shepherd. Had he been in Iowa, it wouldn't have been anything but a mutt, and, most likely, a mutt with the mange.

Blue had belonged to a family of settlers. Dooley remembered that. It caused a tear to run down his cheek as he rolled back over. Apaches had massacred the family. The blue dog was an orphan, so Dooley, after burying those awful bodies, had let the dog tag along with him. He was a good dog. Made Dooley feel like he really wasn't traveling alone.

So Dooley had been heading to Phoenix. Maybe Tucson. He didn't think it was Flagstaff, although it might have been Prescott. He ran into a sheriff named Carmichael who was traveling with a red-headed cowboy Dooley had worked with in Utah before he had even shot Smith/Baylor deader than dirt. Butch Sweeney was a kid, but a cowboy to ride the river with, and before Dooley really understood why, Butch Sweeney had been with him. So had a girl.

What the Sam Hill was her name?

It wasn't Sam Hill. Judith? No. Judas? Don't be silly. Jennifer. No. You were closer with Judith. Judy? Julie. That was it. Julie. No. No, it wasn't. Julia. Yes. Definitely. Julia. Julia Arizona, because he had met her in Arizona.

He laughed and rolled over, slid down the embankment closer to the Platte. Julia Arizona. That was a joke. She wasn't like some shepherd dog. In fact, now that things began clearing up a mite, he saw her face. She was a pretty girl. Maybe even beautiful or would be in a few years. Back then, Julia Cooperman—that was her name. Not Arizona. Julia Cooperman, thirteen years old. Sweet. Spunky. But tortured. Pained. But a good kid.

And they had taken care of those other Baylor boys, too. So Dooley's $500 reward had turned out to be worth $1,625. In gold.

Which would have staked Dooley and Julia and Sweeney to a trip to Alaska, where they would make even more money.

So they had ridden from Phoenix all the way to San Francisco, California, with plans to board a packet and sail north to Alaska.

Yet something happened. He remembered rubbing General Grant's neck, then felt as if someone had just taken an axe and split his head clean in half. Dooley fell into that dark, dark void, and when he finally woke, to a splitting headache but at least his head remained intact, he couldn't remember much of anything. Including his name. That much he learned from his wallet, and he also realized he had more than $1,000 in cash. Whoever had clubbed him good had not been intent on robbing him. He knew his bay gelding was General, but General what? And he had no idea what the Sam Hill he was doing in San Francisco. In fact, the only reason he knew he was in San Francisco was because of so many signs in that big city saying it was San Francisco.

SAN FRANCISCO MORNING CALL

CAFÉ SAN FRANCISCO

SAN FRANCISCO'S BEST LIVERY

SAN FRANCISCO'S LARGEST WAGON YARD

SAN FRANCISCO'S GAUDIEST WHOREHOUSE

The dog, which at that moment he figured to be a California shepherd, seemed to be his. So Dooley Monahan mounted his horse and took his wealth and his merle dog and rode out of the big city by the bay and decided to head to Virginia City.

Obviously, the memories came back to him, by and by.

In Virginia City, for instance, he started saddling the horse in Virginia City's Best Livery Stable when he just said as he reached under the gelding's belly for the cinch . . . "Grant."

He blinked, brought the strap up, and blinked some more.

"Grant. General Grant. That's your name."

The bay gelding snorted and even seemed to nod its head in agreement.

Which told Dooley Monahan something else.

"I must be a Yankee."

Southerners, he knew, would not likely name their horse after Ulysses S. Grant.

If, indeed, he had named the horse General Grant after the Union Civil War hero and president— that's right, Grant was now president of these United States. He remembered that even before he saw an article in the *Virginia City Enterprise* that had a few choice comments about President Grant's policies and choices for political offices.

He lost $233.76 of his more than $1,000 at roulette and blackjack in Virginia City, so decided to take his shrinking fortune and his blue-eyed shepherd dog and bay gelding named after a Union war hero (and disaster of a president) toward Montana.

Somehow, he wound up in Cheyenne, Wyoming, instead.

By then he had begun to call the dog Blue, and the dog wagged his tail and the bay gelding nodded its head in agreement.

In Cheyenne, he heard a couple of cowboys brag in a saloon that they had lynched a damned old sodbuster. Dooley dropped his beer—half-full or half-empty, depending on your point of view—and said out loud, "Iowa."

At Fort Bridger, Wyoming, he had paid four dollars and thirty-five cents to a doctor, who had treated Dooley, given him a tincture of some medicine that tasted most foul but caused Dooley to sleep like a baby and gave him some of the wildest dreams. The doctor said that this amnesia—which was the word he used to describe Dooley's loss of memory—could end, could be permanent, and even could cause Dooley to die an early death of a stroke or aneurysm or suicide.

"But it doesn't appear to be that bad of a case," Dr. Smoker had said, and he smoked like the 2-4-0 locomotive on the railroad tracks nearby. "You remembered the dog's name. You remembered your horse's name. You assumed you are Dooley Monahan and that is likely correct."

"Assumed?" Dooley had asked.

"You could have stolen the wallet from the real Dooley Monahan."

"Nah." Dooley shook his head. "I think I'm Dooley Monahan."

"Why's that?"

"Who the hell would call himself Dooley Monahan if that wasn't his name?"

Dr. Smoker, between coughs, went on to say that various things would cause Dooley to regain most of his memory. And that's what happened.

In Cheyenne, he understood that he hailed from

Iowa. The word *sodbuster* jogged that memory back into place, and Dooley remembered he was a farmer. So he rode back.

Other memories would come back to him—but some of those he didn't care to remember. Besides, he was sleeping right now—unconscious—and wondered if he would remember anything when he woke up. Right now, though, he didn't care if he ever woke up because he was having a might fine dream. And he had used up the last of that opium or whatever the sawbones had called it years ago.

It was the plump girl from Omaha. And Dooley had saved her life. And now she was showing proper respect by kissing him all over, and Dooley's hands were going to some places on her body that were plump where they should be plump and felt might fine. But then the plump blonde started licking his face. And she kept right on licking. Wet, sloppy licks from a tongue that felt like coarse leather. And Dooley had no choice but to open his eyes and say . . .